I Give It to You

I GIVE IT TO YOU

A NOVEL

Valerie Martin

NAN A. TALESE | DOUBLEDAY

NEW YORK

www.doubleday.com

DOUBLEDAY is a registered trademark of Penguin Random House LLC. Nan A. Talese and the colophon are trademarks of Penguin Random House LLC.

Jacket images: painting by Giuseppe Pelizza da Volpedo, courtesy of 11 [HellHeaven] Art Gallery; paper © autsawin uttisin/Shutterstock Jacket design by Emily Mahon

LIBRARY OF CONGRESS CATALOGING-IN-PUBLICATION DATA
Names: Martin, Valerie, 1948– author.
Title: I give it to you : a novel / by Valerie Martin.
Description: First edition. | New York : Nan A. Talese, [2020]
Identifiers: LCCN 2019046739 (print) | LCCN 2019046740 (ebook) |
ISBN 9780385546393 (hardcover) | ISBN 9780385546409 (ebook)
Classification: LCC PS3563.A7295 I25 2020 (print) |
LCC PS3563.A7295 (ebook) | DDC 813/.54—dc23
LC record available at https://lccn.loc.gov/2019046739
LC ebook record available at https://lccn.loc.gov/2019046740

MANUFACTURED IN THE UNITED STATES OF AMERICA

1 3 5 7 9 10 8 6 4 2

First Edition

For John

A friend is, as it were, a second self.

—CICERO

PART 1

Villa Chiara

Villa Chiara is protected from the world outside by a high stone wall and an ancient gate with the initial S swirled in iron on each wing. The dusty, sunstruck road, scarcely wide enough for two small cars to pass each other without knocking their mirrors, cleaves to the wall for half a mile. On the far side, ranks of iconic sunflowers stand at attention like stolid soldiers, indifferent to the elements, awaiting their orders.

When you turn in to the gates, what strikes you is that, though very near the road, the sparse yard that serves as a parking area feels private and cool. This gravel and packed-dirt patch is closed on four sides. On two, gardens of roses and herbs, backed by plum and apricot trees, disperse gentle fragrances into the hot afternoon air. Parallel to the gate, the charming *limonaia* stands with its back to the wall. Glass and verdigris copper doors glint beneath the shelter of the rafters, which extend over a small stone terrace. Artfully placed hip-high pots of rosemary and lemon trees create a cool and semiprivate sitting area.

On the fourth side, the imposing pale pink facade of the villa closes in the drive. A graceful triangular double staircase rises from two directions to a wide landing before the arched manorial door. The villa has three floors. The lowest, behind the staircase, is the *cantina,* an unfinished space used to store farm equipment as well as wine and olive oil, both products of the property. The two upper levels are lined with tall shuttered windows looking out over the drive. The house isn't grand but rather grandly substantial, and because of the perimeter wall it is impossible to view it from any distance. The Villa Chiara thus creates for itself an encapsulated space, peaceful, retired, without views.

༺ⴰⵣ༻

I arrived at Villa Chiara a week before I met its owner, Signora Beatrice Salviati Bartolo Doyle. I knew only a few facts about her. She was employed as a professor of Italian at a small college in upstate New York. When she wasn't in America, she lived in the villa with her aged mother. Obviously she had, at some point, married a man of Irish ancestry. She had a grown son, David, who resided in Munich with his German wife and their baby son. She had spent some years in Los Angeles when her son was a child. She rented out a small apartment at the villa, but only to tenants recommended by friends. I was fortunate enough to know one of these, Ruggiero Vignorelli, who was a colleague at my own college in Pennsylvania.

The apartment, created from the limonaia, an outbuilding designed to shelter citrus trees in the winter, comprised a kitchen and sitting room on the first floor, a large airy bedroom and minimalist bath—the shower was an open tiled area with a drain and a showerhead—on the second. Signora Doyle had renovated it for her son and his wife so that they might have more privacy when they drove down from Munich to visit. It was the first of many decisions about her property that suggested a lack of foresight. In a few years the couple would have two children and the space would be too small.

On my first visit, in the summer of 1983, I had written instructions from Signora Doyle directing me to the far end of the villa, beyond the imposing staircase, where I was to knock at the door I would find beneath a wisteria arbor and ask for Signora Mimma, Signora Doyle's cousin, who lived there and would give me the key to the apartment. I had very little Italian, but I hoped it would be sufficient to see me through this simple task. I parked my rental car in the drive facing the villa and easily spotted the wisteria bower and the door. There was no bell, so I rapped sharply three times on the dark wood, waited until I had counted to fifty, and rapped again. I heard footsteps dimly, slowly approaching, and then the door slid open and a chubby white-haired crone peered out at me, squinting as if I gave off light. *"Buongiorno, signora,"* I said. *"Sono qui per prendere la chiave dell'appartamento di Signora Doyle."*

She gave me a pert perusal from head to toe, furrowing her brow and nodding slightly. I feared that, as often happened, she hadn't understood a word I said. At last, with a polite smile, she said, *"Qui non c'è nessun appartamento,"* and carefully, but firmly, closed the door in my face.

There is no apartment here? Then it occurred to me that I'd forgotten to ask for Signora Mimma. But if I knocked again, the crone would surely answer and tell me there was no apartment. I wandered back to my car, opened the door, sat on the seat, and looked up at the villa.

It was clearly a venerable building; I guessed seventeenth century, with a facelift along the way. The jutting inverted V of the staircase that led to the central door had a quality of being tacked on, though certainly not recently. The entrance to the cantina wasn't visible from the drive, as the stone stairs formed a deeply shaded archway that hid it from view.

The roofline of the villa took a step down at the far end and jutted out, making an L-shaped wing covered with the same pale pink plaster. The door I had been directed to, beneath the wisteria arbor, stood flush to the ground and opened into a stone-floored entryway. In the moment when I had seen it, this entrance appeared to me cool and inviting. The second floor had smaller windows and must have lower ceilings. Perhaps this wing was the original structure. In my observation, money often served to raise the rafters of a house. When families grow wealthy and powerful, they need more headroom.

The villa seemed to be of two minds, one noble, chilly, and serious, the other homely and cozy.

Nothing moved, nothing breathed. And then a bird streaked out from one of the three cypresses that guarded the gate and disappeared beneath the rafters of the limonaia. I got out and followed the bird to the glass door. Should I try it? I stepped into the cool shade. I could see through the doors to the sitting room. Terracotta floors, solid-looking furniture, a good table and two chairs, a few steps at one end leading to the upper floor. I allowed my hand to stray to the door handle, pressing it down tentatively. It was locked. I backed out into the drive and looked up at the ovoid windows of the second floor. My Tuscan apartment.

I heard the crack of a door opening, and then a pleasant female voice called out, *"Signora, signora."* I turned to find a robust, handsome woman with an abundance of dark hair tied up in a knot on her head, wearing what my mother used to call a housecoat. She held out one hand as she approached me eagerly. *"La chiave,"* she said cheerfully. *"La chiave."*

"The key," I called back to her. *"Bene. Grazie. Mille grazie."* We met halfway across the drive and she pressed the key into my hand. *"Lei è Signora Mimma?"* I said.

"Mi chiamo Anna," she said.

So the other one was Signora Mimma, the cousin of Signora Doyle.

Later I learned Anna's full name, Anna Falco. She lived with her husband, Sergio, in a stone house across the road from the villa, and her family had been in service to the Salviatis for generations. She was housekeeper, cook, and caretaker of the villa. Sergio kept the gardens, served as an all-around handyman, and supervised the hiring of locals for the yearly harvests of grapes and olives. They had one grown son, Leonardo, who was a bank clerk in the nearby spa town of Rapolano Terme. He had never married and still lived with his parents.

Anna led me back under the eaves of the limonaia and watched as I turned the key in the latch and yanked at the handle. *"La tira su, signora,"* she said, pushing up at the air with her palm. I pulled the handle up and the door opened.

Inside she showed me the small kitchen, demonstrated how to turn on the gas stove, opened the refrigerator to reveal an unlabeled bottle of wine and a triangle of hard cheese wrapped in a towel. She gestured to a loaf of bread covered with a cloth on a sideboard. I repeated the word *grazie* with several degrees of sincerity, delight, appreciation, and helplessness. Each time she nodded and replied softly, indulgently, *"Prego."* Then she brushed her palms together, as if at the completion of a job well done, nodded at me with an expression of finality, and slipped out the door. I followed, taking the key from the lock and closing the door behind her. I stood watching as she crossed the drive and briskly disappeared under the arbor. I was on my own.

I had signed a month's lease with Signora Doyle and paid the last installment before I left the States. In her final letter, which included directions to the villa and instructions about the key, she had advised me that she would be arriving on the second week of my stay. She knew I was a professor at a small college and that I had published a few mildly successful works of historical fiction. She concluded her message lightly: "I look forward to meeting you and reading your work. If you are looking for old stories, of course, you know you are coming to the right place."

❧

In my first week at the Villa Chiara, I spent the mornings in the apartment, drinking tea, eating fruit and bread, reading simple Italian stories, and struggling with grammar exercises in an Italian text until noon. Then I drove out to the various hill towns for long meals on the terraces of restaurants with views that lifted my spirits like angels' wings. After this I toured the local museums, churches, and—those favorite haunts of the historical novelist—graveyards. Some of these included discreet monuments in fenced areas listing the names of those who had died on the battlefield in the last war. In a general way, I knew the story.

Italy didn't enter World War II until June 10, 1940, when Mussolini stepped out on his balcony at the Palazzo Venezia and declared hostilities against "the reactionary democracies of the West." By that time, France, Belgium, Luxembourg, the Netherlands, and Norway had surrendered to Hitler's armies and were occupied by German forces. The next day Britain responded by bombing Turin, Genoa, Naples, Milan, and Taranto, all centers of industry and transportation. Francisco Franco sent Mussolini a congratulatory message from Spain. Mussolini believed the war would be over in a few months.

By this time many Italian antifascists had fled to the hills, often to avoid conscription into the army. They lived in forests and caves, scavenging for food from local farmers. These were the partisans, comrades who lived and fought by stealth, much admired by the local villagers for their courage and their fraternal spirit. As is often the case in wars, when the fighting was over, a majority of survivors claimed to have secretly supported the winners. Once it was clear that the Germans would be defeated and Mussolini's fascist government would fall, minor functionaries all over the country changed their stripes and their allegiance and joined the partisan forces. Italian soldiers abandoned their units; they too sought refuge with the partisans.

Mussolini's fall from power was swift and then slow. After twenty years of calling all the shots, he was removed by a vote of the council he had himself created and arrested by the king, who appointed a new prime minister. This new government spirited the Duce away to an alpine resort-prison and immediately surrendered to the Allied forces already swarming up the peninsula from Sicily. Overnight these invaders were transformed from enemies into liberators. Italian troops were disbanded. Whole units were taken prisoner by the occupying German forces and sent to "work camps" in Germany. Those who escaped joined the antifascists in the hills, where they resolved to do whatever they could to make the German retreat from the south difficult and, if possible, fatal.

Hitler wasn't ready to give up on Mussolini, his friend and mentor in the maniacal business of total despotism. He rescued the Duce from the mountaintop and installed him in luxurious lodgings on Lago di Garda, creating a protofascist state called the Republic of Salò, where diehard Italian fascists now flocked to support their obviously lost cause. Italy had effectively no government or two governments, depending on how you looked at it. The country devolved into a state of civil war. Major cities—Rome, Florence, Milan—were occupied by Germans intent on a scorched-earth policy as they retreated from the Allies. Everyone on every side knew what the end would be, and that it would be brutal.

Nowhere was the moral confusion attendant upon the defeat of the Axis powers as thoroughgoing as it was in Italy. In the final days of that horrific war, few could call themselves heroes, but all were called upon to muster whatever courage they could find just to stay alive.

The end had plunged the country into despair. Was that why I found so few memorials to the glorious fallen in Tuscan graveyards? Italy hadn't just surrendered; she changed sides entirely. These days no one talks about it, but those who can remember know perfectly well that the American forces landing in Sicily weren't charged with liberating innocent citizens of a besieged democracy. They were coming to kill Italian fascists.

✿

One evening in the second week of my stay, as I turned in at the gate in my rented Fiat Panda, a reliable machine I had come to think of as a friend and which I addressed as Signor Panda, I discovered a battered Fiat Cinquecento parked close to the staircase of the villa. My landlady had arrived. Doubtless she had just made a long transatlantic journey and being, as she must be, a woman in her fifties, she surely looked forward to a quiet evening and an early bedtime. The sun was setting; it stayed light until well past the dinner hour, and I had my own plan in place: a dish of pasta, a bottle of local red wine, and a notebook in which each evening I organized impressions, facts, and details of the day's excursion. I also looked forward to an activity now sadly lost to the civilized world, writing a long letter to a friend. From the table where I worked I could see the villa staircase, and as I finished my meal I watched Anna Falco come out of the cousin's door carrying her big basket. She held the handles close to her chest in the crook of her arm and ascended the staircase, letting herself in at the door, which was evidently unlocked. Dinner for the *padrona,* no doubt. How pleasant it must be to return to your villa and have a fine meal delivered to you, your bed already made and the sheets turned back, the palatial rooms clean and welcoming, all comfort and quiet in your sweet world of privilege.

But then it occurred to me that Signora Doyle wasn't alone; she lived with her mother. Her ancient mother, as my colleague Ruggiero had described her. I had spotted this wizened lady a few times in the past week, dressed all in black, carefully descending the stone steps, one hand gripping the rail, the other wrapped around the curved handle of a black cane with a rubber tip. With slow but surprisingly sure steps, she crossed the drive and went in under the arbor. Presumably she dined with the cousin. But now that her daughter was home, dinner came to them. The reunion of mother and daughter must be an occasion much anticipated by both.

Later, as I was on the third page of my letter and the last third of my bottle of wine, lights went on in the villa. Dim lights, to be sure, scarcely enough to read by. And then, dissolving in the night as a cube of sugar does upon the tongue, with irresistible sweetness, there came ethereal music. I recognized it at once. Beethoven, String Quartet No. 14 in C-sharp minor. A night bird tweeted a soft triplet from the garden. I smiled as I took up my pen. The bird was in the right key.

All around me German music harmonized the still Italian air, charming the birds right out of the trees on a mild summer night in Tuscany.

⋅⋆⋅

I was up early in the morning, and the air was so fragrant and fresh that it seemed perfectly natural to open the door of the limonaia and pull a chair out to the wooden table on the covered terrace. There I sat with my book and my cup of tea, waiting to be found by my hostess. The fact that I had not done this before, though the weather had been felicitous for several days, could be explained by my shyness about my inadequate Italian and my unwillingness to reencounter either the inhospitable cousin or the earnest servant. My chair was so positioned that Signora Doyle couldn't fail to see me should she descend the staircase to her car. I was cravenly eager to speak English.

I had read only a few pages when I heard the door open and then the sharp machine-gun *rat-a-tat* of a woman in high heels. In the next moment, Signora Doyle—it must be her, I thought— appeared on the drive, looking directly at me. I had been expecting the American academic style, practical shoes and long tunic over longer skirt, curling gray hair haphazardly cut, casual, comfortable, and neat. This professor was as stylish as a runway model, tall and slender, nor did she look anywhere near her age. Her hair was black, sleek, cut at an angle so that it swept down across her cheek-bones to graze her clavicles. Her skin was like burnished gold, the gift of the gods to their darling Italians, and her sharp eyes under thick, straight brows were nearly black. Her features were more arresting than pleasing, her nose too sharp, her lips too thin for her to be called a beauty. She wore a gray silk blouse under a short canary-yellow linen jacket, a black pencil skirt, and most wonderful and painful-looking high-heeled sandals with a network of golden straps from ankle to toes. As she approached the limonaia, she appeared harried and completely collected at the same time. "Good morning," she called out to me, and I replied, "Good morning, Signora Doyle."

"So you are here, comfortably having your tea. I hope you've settled in with no problems."

"Everything is perfect," I said. "I've been having a wonderful time."

"And working hard, I'm sure. Ruggiero told me you are working on an important project."

I blessed my colleague, who knew, I felt sure, nothing about my work. "I've made some notes," I said. "But mostly I'm afraid I've been researching Tuscan cuisine."

"No, I'm sure you are up to something exciting," she said. It was the first volley of the constant play of contradiction she would offer me; I came to understand this as part of a rhetorical style, not uncommon in Italian conversation.

"Well," I said.

"I am just going to the bar for my *cornetto* and *caffè*. Will you come with me? It is very near."

I closed my book and took up my cup. "I'd love to do that," I said. "Let me grab my purse."

English, I thought. Beautiful English. And now I would find the right bar and be in company with the *padrona* of Villa Chiara. I put my cup in the sink and lifted my purse from the hook, then stepped outside, pulling the door behind me. Signora Doyle had gone to her car and stood bending into the open door, clearing something from the passenger seat. I came up behind her and she turned, smiling. "You must call me Beatrice," she said, pronouncing it in the Italian way, *Bay-ah-trree-chay,* and thereby summoning the ghost of Dante, who lingers still in these hills and groves.

In the car Beatrice drove very fast and talked at high volume about America, treating me as an equal on that subject as we were both employed at small colleges. At her college, she explained, the students were very good, but the administration was nothing but buffoons who thought only of cutting their budgets, and when they tried to think of where to cut they could think only of Italian. This was true at my own college; foreign-language departments, and for some reason always Italian first, were endangered. "Why," she exclaimed, "would anyone in their narrow little world ever need to speak Italian!"

"I need to learn Italian," I said. "And fast."

Beatrice parked in the half-empty lot of an Italian version of a strip mall: a collection of colorful storefronts, a hair salon, a pizza restaurant, an *alimentari* with ambrosial fruits and vegetables piled on an outdoor display rack. The bar, with the name Ciferri in blue script on white tile above the door, occupied the end of the row. Inside we found the usual industrial espresso machine, the electric juicer, baskets of oranges and grapefruit, the glass case of sandwiches and pastries, including two neat stacks of cornetti, the Italian version of the croissant, and the long marble counter behind which a young man who could have been a movie star rattled his cups and tended his machines. He hailed Signora Doyle as she opened the door, and two men in suits knocking back their little cups of espresso at the counter turned to appraise us. The barista repeated his greeting, inquiring, I understood, after the signora's mother.

Ah yes, I thought. The ancient mother. I had never spoken to her. When I returned from my adventures the house was usually dark, and I assumed the old woman went to bed when the sun set, as old people do in the country. It was my turn to order and I requested my *espresso macchiato,* my *cornetto semplice.* Beatrice said, "You speak perfectly well."

"I can do food," I said.

As we devoured our breakfast, the barista put a cornetto in a bag and set it and a scrap of paper on the bar. "For my mother," Signora Doyle said to me. I made a feeble attempt to take up the check. "Please," she said, pushing my hand away. "I invited you. Don't insult me."

"Thank you," I said.

"Prego," she replied.

Back in the car she spoke of American politics. "It is a country with no past," she explained. "So all Americans think about is the future. They have never been invaded by foreigners, and so they imagine only spaceships and aliens can harm them. This Reagan and his 'star wars.' He's impossible. He's not even a good actor."

There was much to agree with in this spasm of generalizations, but I didn't bother. I said, "It must have been brutal here during the war."

"Brutal," she repeated. "Yes. It was chaos. A living nightmare. No one was safe, no one could be trusted. The planes drilled down farmers with machine guns. They bombed schools full of children."

"The Germans," I said.

"The Germans, the Allies, the partisans. Italy was a battleground, all of it. People stopped taking sides and just tried to survive. My mother's brother, a poor madman who could barely speak, was shot in a skirmish in our driveway."

This stunned me. That banal patch of dirt and gravel inside the gates of the villa? Whenever I turned my rental car off the road and in at the gate, an impression of peaceful solitude soothed me.

I tried to imagine the mad uncle running there, pursued, the crack of gunfire, his falling, perhaps near the limonaia, blood spattering across the terrace, his dying agony there beneath the rafters. There would have been lemon trees then, in their russet clay pots: the scent of citrus mixed with the iron smell of blood.

"Were you in the villa?" I asked.

"The night he was killed? No," she said. "I had gone back to Firenze for school. I was fourteen. My mother was here. She saw it all."

⌇⌇⌇

At the villa we parted, and I spent an hour reading a guidebook to the hill towns of Tuscany and another hour failing to understand the proper use of Italian indefinite pronouns. Then I drove out to Montalcino to visit yet another museum, another church. I returned at nightfall, fatigued from my excursion in the fierce sun that still scorched the dry grass at the edge of the drive. Signora Doyle's car was gone. *She's dining with old friends,* I thought, *or relatives.* I pictured a grand villa with a terrace, aristocrats sipping prosecco, gazing out at the magnificent view as they discussed the political gossip of the day, while servants attended a side table laden with platters of tantalizing food. I'd seen a movie with a scene like that. The sun setting over the terraced hills, the long ranks of pale grapevines stretched over their wire supports, the gray cloud of the olive grove below, steadily darkening as the moon rose in the heavens. I let myself into my little slice of this paradise and switched on the inadequate light. It was so hot I left the door ajar and went straight to the refrigerator, which contained a cold bottle of white wine. As I stepped back to the kitchen table, I heard the crunch of tires and then the car lights swept across the drive. Beatrice Doyle switched off the engine but left the lights on for several moments. I could see her clearly; she appeared to be looking for something on the floor, then on the seat, then in the pigmy glove compartment.

At length she switched off the lights and sat a few moments longer in the darkness. I slid my glass onto the table, turned on the ceiling fan, pulled out my chair. At last she pushed the car door open, climbed out of the uncomfortable, surely sweltering seat (there was no air conditioning in the Cinquecento), and made straight for my door.

"Hello," I called out, pulling the door open wider. "Will you join me for a glass of wine?"

"It would be better if we go to my house; it is much cooler there," she said. "This little place traps the heat and doesn't let go."

I declined to comment on this statement of fact. I felt curiously defensive about the limonaia. It struck me that as lemons thrive on heat, its being hot wasn't a fault in the design of the building but rather of the use she had put it to. "I'd like that," I said.

"Have you had your dinner?" she asked. "Americans eat very early."

"No," I said. "I have something here. I'll eat later."

"It's too hot to eat," she observed. "I have a cold supper. There's plenty for us both."

"What can I bring?" I said. "I have some nice peaches."

She smiled at me indulgently. I had the impression she thought I was foolish. "Very well," she said. "Bring your peaches."

Dinner at the villa, I thought as I set my glass in the kitchen sink and took up the paper parcel of ripe peaches I'd bought in the town. My curiosity was so strong it inflated like a bubble in my chest. Would it be palatial or shabby genteel? Family portraits or valuable landscapes? My brain busied itself so arduously in speculation it amused me. I was like a child sitting before a theater curtain, waiting breathlessly for the heavy, dark folds to slide apart, opening upon a fabulous scene of mystery and intrigue in which a thrilling story would now commence.

⸻❧⸻

Paradoxically, the most notable feature of the Villa Chiara—which means "Bright Villa"—was gloom. The big door at the top of the stairs opened into a marble vestibule, cool and useless, the walls clotted with heavily framed paintings hung too high to see, the line of shutters firmly closed against any intrusion of light. Beatrice switched on a lamp as we entered the dining room and beyond that the kitchen, where she flipped a wall switch that illuminated a double strip of grim fluorescent tubes attached to the ceiling. I followed her, my eyes darting about to mark various details. The dining table: long, heavy, and covered in a patchwork of differently patterned tablecloths; the chairs: heavy and oversized, chairs for big people. There were framed paintings of outdoor scenes that looked old and interesting; one was a long narrow view of a seashore with mountains coming right down to the sand. An enormous sideboard the size of a van stood against one wall, its shelves crammed with all manner of plates, glasses, cups, its surface cluttered with silver service pieces, a dark wooden flatware box, and stacks of linen napkins. In the kitchen Beatrice made straight for an antique refrigerator with the freezer compartment inside at the top, a remnant of the fifties. She yanked open the door and commenced pulling out plates and containers, which she set one by one on the large marble-topped table that occupied the center of the plain little room. The stove, I noted, was gas with a pipe stuck through the wall, equally antique, and the sink was farm-style, with a wooden counter and deep porcelain bowl, big enough, I thought pointlessly, to wash a thirty-pound Thanksgiving turkey.

"Can I help?" I asked, clutching my bag of fruit in the doorway.

"You can take these plates to the table," she said. I took up a platter of prosciutto and a small plate of ricotta cheese and ferried them to the table. Beatrice followed me with a bowl of white beans dressed in oil and parsley and another of slippery artichoke hearts. She pointed to the box on the sideboard. "Knives and forks are in there," she said, turning back to the kitchen. I opened the box and took out a few pieces of the heavy flatware, arranged them at one end of the table, then drifted back to the kitchen. Beatrice was cutting open a cantaloupe, piling the slices onto a plate. She lifted her chin, indicating a basket next to a cutting board on the counter behind me. "Cut some slices of bread," she said. "And bring the basket to the table." I did as I was told. A few more passes from kitchen to table, the plates, the glasses, the napkins from the sideboard, the bottle of red wine opened, the water pitcher alongside, more dishes, thin slices of salami and hard cheese, and at the end two bowls of colorful minestrone served at room temperature directly from a big pot on the stove. We carried these to our places, she at the end of the table, I next to her, and she poured out the wine and water. When we were seated, she lifted her glass to mine and we tapped the edges together. *"Cin-cin,"* she said. She took a small sip from the glass and set it on the table.

"I know another toast you might like," she added.

"What is it?"

"A noi, e alla faccia di tutti quelli che ci vogliono male," she said. "To us, and in the face of all those who wish us ill."

"That's great," I said.

"It's a very Tuscan sentiment," she said. "Now tell me what else you'd like to know about the Italians."

"I'd like to know the story of this house," I said.

"That's a very long story," she said.

"And I'd like to hear the story about your uncle," I added.

"My uncle?" She looked mystified.

"The one who was shot in the driveway," I said. "During the war."

She took up her spoon and swallowed a mouthful of soup, looking at me closely. "You're a good listener," she said.

"You said he was mad."

"They made him mad," she said. "Poor fellow. His name was San-

18

dro." She paused, took up her wineglass, and sipped thoughtfully. I did the same, unwilling to interrupt what I took to be a mental reassessment of a memory soiled and faded by age and neglect.

"Not so long ago, we were a large family," she explained. "My *nonno,* my grandfather, Giacomo Salviati, an avaricious man who wanted always to be modern, had five children and they all lived in a grand palazzo in Firenze. There were three girls and two boys. He had other properties and factories and this villa and the vineyards and olive groves, which have been in the family since the seventeenth century. My two aunts never married, and at some point they moved to this house. My poor uncle Sandro went mad before I was born and was committed to an asylum for many years. I saw him only near the end of his life, when my mother brought him home."

"She brought him here," I said.

"Yes. She left one night and drove to Milano, and when she came back he was with her. She was afraid the Germans would raid the asylum, but they never did."

"And your other uncle?"

"That was Marco. He was a fascist, a real Blackshirt. He adored Mussolini until the end, and even then he didn't blame the Duce, he blamed the communists and the king. My mother was never certain Sandro was shot by Germans; it could have been partisans, looking for Marco."

"But you think it was Germans."

"No one knows. It didn't matter. He was dead. He could have been killed in crossfire. There was a lot of that."

"So what happened to Marco?"

"Oh, Marco came through just fine. He married a wealthy Lucchese."

"And he was no longer a fascist?"

"He took off the black shirt," Beatrice agreed. "He was a lawyer.

He and his wife, her name was Grazia, had two children, a boy and a girl, my cousins Luca and Mimma, who live"—she lifted her chin to the far end of the villa—"in the other half of this house."

"Is Marco still alive?"

"No. He became a bitter old man. My mother despised him. One day he had a stroke walking down the street in Firenze; he and his family were living in Nonno Giacomo's palazzo then. It turned out he'd made some very bad business decisions and the palazzo had to be sold. By that time, all that was left of the family was my mother, my two maiden aunts, who died in the sixties just a few months apart, and the cousins, Luca and Mimma. In the seventies there was a big division of the Salviati property. There are a few apartments in Firenze—my mother and the cousins each have one and the others are rented. There's land here and there; we had a factory near Bergamo that lost money until it closed a few years ago. The biggest part is this estate. Two-thirds of the land went to my cousins, one-third to my mother, but it was agreed that we would divide the villa, half to Luca and Mimma and the other to my mother, and ultimately to me.

"So it wasn't always two houses," I said.

"It still isn't," she said. "The connecting doors were simply closed. We don't open them. And of course Luca had to put a kitchen in over there. It's much nicer than the one here."

"Are you on good terms with them?"

"I get along with them well enough. My mother can't bear Mimma. She says she talks like a baby and has no sense. They're an odd couple, brother and sister—neither ever married. He's a psychiatrist and she's a lunatic, so they're perfect for each other."

I laughed, then gave my attention to the soup for a few moments, considering the complex relationships she had just described. "What was Sandro like when you saw him?"

Beatrice considered this question, casting back to an event that had taken her by surprise. "He was strange," she said. "Very confused, and he had difficulty walking and eating. But my mother maintains he was never mad. He wanted to marry a poor girl, and my grandfather wouldn't allow it. So he was put away."

"And Marco became the heir."

Beatrice nodded, pushing out her lower lip and opening her hand in a gesture that said, *This is obvious.*

"Wow," I said. "That's quite a story."

"Do you like it?" she said. "I give it to you."

⟡

Do you like it? I give it to you. Total strangers, acquaintances, close friends, even relatives have all offered me stories before—there's something about talking to a writer that makes people so uncomfortable they babble stories in self-defense. They seem to imagine that novelists go about sniffing drains and peeking behind curtains in search of clues, that they are constantly in need of characters or plots and their whole interest in other people is impersonal and professional, like those doctors who go to parties in hopes of being presented with interesting symptoms. Americans in particular are swift to point out that they have in their mental safekeeping the material of a great novel which they don't have time to write. *Have I got a story for you!*

It's an occupational hazard, and I don't mind it. The stories seldom engage me, as they are either plot-heavy or concerned with characters who don't interest me, such as people who climb mountains or women who triumph over adversity and become successful in some male-dominated field like architecture or physics.

But Beatrice's story, narrated so simply in straightforward responses to direct questions, intrigued me. That night, back in the limonaia, I sketched out a genealogy of the family, assigning names to her grandmother, to her father, to the two characters Beatrice had described only as "the maiden aunts," and to her uncle Marco's wife, a rich woman from Lucca.

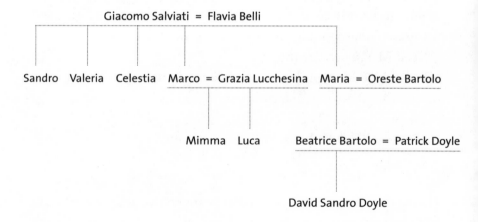

Giacomo Salviati = Flavia Belli

Sandro   Valeria   Celestia   Marco = Grazia Lucchesina   Maria = Oreste Bartolo

Mimma   Luca   Beatrice Bartolo = Patrick Doyle

David Sandro Doyle

Obviously, within just two generations, the depletion of the aristocratic line was nearly complete, and the sole heir to the villa would be Beatrice's half Irish-American son, David, who with his German wife would put the property back together again and presumably pass it on to their half German, one quarter American, and one quarter Italian children. Somewhere during the evening Beatrice had told me that her son's middle name was Sandro after her uncle, the original heir, who had died in the driveway after a lifetime of incarceration because his father was determined not to have a peasant in the family line.

The night Beatrice told me the story of her uncle Sandro, we stayed up talking until very late, and she appeared to find me agreeable company. She told me she was going to Firenze for the weekend, and when I got up the next morning, my head bleary from the two bottles of wine we had finished off, her little car was already gone. It was another in a series of perfect days, sunny and hot, and I made my tea and sat out on the terrace with my notebook, reconstructing the details of our conversation. I heard the door of the cousins' apartment open, and then from under the arbor a small, foppish man appeared, patting at the pockets of his jacket to find, I presumed, his car keys. He had thin blond hair, which must have been a lifelong trial for an Italian, skillfully trimmed at the front to disguise his prominent domed forehead. His eyes were close-set, of a leaden hue. Like his cousin, he had a strong aquiline nose that started between his brows. A colorless mouth over a receding chin made the bottom half of his face seem to fade away. This must be Luca, the psychiatrist who had never married and lived with his sister. I rattled my cup in the saucer to catch his attention. He looked up and found me in the shadows. *"Buongiorno,"* I said boldly.

He smiled, a tight, patient smile designed to disarm. "Good morning," he said very correctly and clearly. He knew all about me, no doubt: that I was an American, a professor who didn't speak Italian. "How are you enjoying your visit?" He approached me hesitantly. If I was dismissive, he could still turn off toward his car.

I put down my pen. "I'm enjoying it very much," I said. "Thank you."

He took a few steps closer. "My name is Luca," he said. "I am Beatrice's cousin."

"My name is Jan," I offered.

"You are Beatrice's colleague, I believe." Now he was very close, and we both lowered our voices appropriately.

"Actually, I'm a colleague of a colleague," I said.

"And you teach English literature?"

"I teach creative writing," I said. Instantly and as always I wanted to bite back this incriminating factoid.

"Ah," he said. "I'm not sure I understand how that can be done."

"You're not alone," I said.

He smiled again, an odd, indulgent smile, recognizing this as a subject that pained me and undecided, as he must professionally be, whether to pursue it or allow me to drift off on my own. "I see," he said.

"Your English is very good," I said. "How did that happen?"

"I fear it is rusty from disuse," he demurred. "I studied in America many years ago. I was in Boston for two years. I have never been colder in my life."

"Boston is brutal," I agreed.

He nodded, allowing his gaze to wander over the table, the teapot, my notebook. "But you are working and I am disturbing you."

"Not at all," I said.

Again he said nothing. His facial muscles resolved into an expression of unruffled, undistracted listening. Listening for what I said next. His eyes suffused with interest. If we were in his office, he would doubtless say something like, *And what brings you here to talk to me today?* I looked down at my page—notes about Sandro Salviati—and it occurred to me that this Luca was Marco's son. And Marco, according to Beatrice, was a fascist.

I raised my eyes, determined to say nothing.

"Is this your first visit to Italy?" he asked.

"No," I said. "I came just after college, a long time ago. I was with a couple of friends and we went to cities mostly. Rome, Florence, Milan, Venice. Over the years I've made trips to Rome to visit a colleague I have there. This is my first time in Tuscany. I've always wanted to see the hill towns."

"Yes," he said. "The hill towns are fascinating to tourists."

As he spoke, I heard a rustle beneath the wisteria and I glanced past his shoulder to see the crouching crone, his sister, Mimma, peering out from the edge of the arbor. "Luca," she commanded in a high-pitched screech. *"Vieni subito!"*

Come at once. I understood and so did he, but he didn't appear to be moved by her urgency. "My sister is a very anxious person," he observed. "And sometimes she becomes confused. I believe she gave you some difficulty about the key."

"It was my fault," I said. "Because my Italian is so poor."

"It is always somebody's fault," he observed cryptically.

I have a strong aversion to practitioners of the psychiatric profession, and not without reason. I know they can help desperate patients, particularly those who suffer from severe depression, and that there may be among them many individuals who sincerely want to ease the burden of helpless sufferers or who are themselves skeptical about their own practice. My brief against them is personal. Their reductive representation of human psychological complexity offends me as a writer. I abhor the trend among young writers who endow their characters with various syndromes or complexes they've discovered in the *Diagnostic and Statistical Manual of Mental Disorders,* a diabolical tool for assessing psychopathy which is updated every few years with reappraisals and refinements of symptoms ad absurdum, created to provide drug companies with new mental disorders they can then manufacture a drug to treat.

As a teacher, I blame both parents and psychiatrists for the many students who arrive in my writing classes paralyzed by dependence on psychotropic drugs. Not long ago I passed an otherwise satisfying fall semester watching a lively, talkative, nervous young writer whose prose style zinged with energy transform into a trembling zombie, hardly able to carry on a conversation, much less write a coherent sentence. By the end of the spring semester, when she dropped out of college, she had lost twenty pounds. Hers was not an unusual case. Late-night emails lamenting that a paper wouldn't be submitted by the deadline, or that attendance at class was unlikely, often cited "difficulty adjusting to a new medication" as the cause.

And finally, I hold the psychiatric profession responsible for the American reader's fierce determination to understand character, in fiction and in real life, as necessarily the result of victimization. For such readers, character development is a free-will-free zone, and people turn out the way they do because of what has been done to them. Confronted with complex characters, my students invariably search for the abuse that excuses willful malice or just mindless self-destruction. Emma Bovary fails to arouse their sympathy—

everyone was always nice to her, and her husband adored her. Why can't she be happy with the choices she makes? She should be on medication.

So when Luca Salviati discouraged me from taking on responsibility, while his sister, more and more desperate for his attention, beckoned under the arbor, I closed the subject. "It was a misunderstanding," I said. "No one is at fault."

"Obviously," he repeated.

I looked past his shoulder. Mimma's voice ascended half an octave as she repeated her cry. "Luca, *vieni, vieni.*"

"Your sister is calling you," I said.

His mouth stretched thin and turned up at the corners in a simulacrum of a smile. "Yes," he said. "Doubtless she fears you are seducing me."

This remark was so inappropriate it made me snort. "Please assure her, nothing could be further from my mind," I said.

"I hope you will enjoy your stay with us," he said. And with that he turned away and walked back at a leisurely pace to calm the fears of his cantankerous sibling.

⚜

On Monday afternoon, when Beatrice's gasping Cinquecento made the final leap into the driveway, I was ensconced at my table, leafing through a biography of Mussolini I had found in an English bookstore in Siena. The car jolted to a halt and for a few moments, as was her wont, she appeared to search the seat, the floor, the glove compartment for something she couldn't find. Perhaps it was something small and she did find it, but I couldn't see that. Then she threw open the door and swung her long legs out, rapping the ground with the narrow heels and rising up in one smooth motion, her spine straight, her chin lifted, to her full height. It had turned cooler overnight and she had pulled a light lime-green cashmere cardigan over her patterned blouse. She was wearing close-fitting but not tight black pants of some shiny, stretchy fabric. *She really knows how to dress,* I thought. She saw me there and raised her hand in greeting.

"How was Firenze?" I called out.

She hesitated, uncertain whether to engage or not. She could say it was fine, or hot, and go her way—no more was required. But as I watched her, curiosity got the better of her and she approached my outpost. "It was lovely," she said. "I am always happy when I am in Firenze. I walk the streets and eat a gelato. I am a child again there."

"You grew up there."

She was close now and stood looking down at me. "I did," she said. "I went to school there. What are you reading?"

I closed my book and showed her the cover.

"Ah," she said. "Mussolini. That villain."

"I didn't know he started as a socialist."

"He pretended to be whatever was necessary to consolidate his power."

"Did you ever see him?"

"No," she said. "I often saw his picture. It was everywhere. And I read the writing on the wall. Literally. *'Il Duce ha sempre ragione.'*"

"The leader is always right," I translated.

"Very good," she said.

"This was graffiti?" I asked.

She grimaced. "This was propaganda. The printing was of the highest quality. Another one was *'Noi sogniamo l'Italia Romana.'*"

I considered this. "We dream of a Roman Italy?"

"Close enough," she said. "You make a good little fascist."

I chuckled. "But I don't get it. Why a Roman Italy?"

"The empire," she said. "Mussolini thought he was Caesar Augustus. That's why we had to invade Ethiopia. To have an empire."

"Yes," I said, indicating my book. The cover featured a photograph of Il Duce, just his head and shoulders against a background of red and yellow, the colors of the fascist flag. His domed forehead and fierce eyes gazed coldly at the camera. Oddly, he was wearing what looked like a tuxedo jacket and black bow tie. "He writes about that," I said.

She laid her manicured fingers across the book, covering the image of the Duce. "Why are you interested in this sad business?" she asked. "It's over now. No one wants to talk about it."

"It wasn't so long ago," I said.

"That's true," she agreed. "I grew up knowing nothing else. I thought it was normal. I thought it was the world."

"You were a good little fascist," I teased.

She nodded. "We children all were, more or less. There were youth groups, like what Americans call Scouts; we all had to join. The school day started with singing 'Giovinezza,' a song about how Italians have been remade by Mussolini. We recited an oath of allegiance. Everyone had to do his bit for the Duce. But as I got older, I saw there were those who found ways to resist. And once the war came to us, the whole cloth came unwoven pretty quickly."

"And how did they resist, the resisters?"

"In little ways. And sometimes in big ways. It was dangerous; everyone knew that. Even I knew that." She paused. Her expression grew thoughtful, and I said nothing. I turned my book facedown and pushed it aside so that Mussolini couldn't hear us. Beatrice appeared to approve this action, for as I raised my eyes to hers, she nodded slightly, her lips pursed. "I'm thinking of a story I could tell you," she said. "It might be of interest to you."

At once I rose from my seat, turning toward the apartment. "Let me grab a chair from the kitchen," I said. "Will you have a glass of wine?"

"Yes," she said. "And some water, please." She watched me bustle about in her amused, aloof way. I brought out the chair, then went back for the wine and the glasses, then again for the water bottle. "I have a nice piece of Asiago," I said, gazing into my refrigerator.

"Please," she said, "no cheese. I've been eating gelato."

I closed the fridge and joined her at the table.

"Enough with the dairy," she said.

I laughed, pouring out the glasses. "Is this a story about your family?" I asked.

"In a way," she said. "It's a story I remember from the war, when I was a teenager in Firenze. I thought I was very important, but it turned out I was wrong about that."

A Rooftop in Firenze

AUGUST 1944

At fourteen, Beatrice Salviati Bartolo was a volatile bundle of hormones, surging and shorting out like an electric grid in a hurricane. Overconfident, argumentative, and smart, she confronted the world head-on, without guile or anxiety. Her schoolmates deferred to her; the girls imitated her style, and the boys, torn between her physical attraction and the danger of her explosive temper, teased her from a safe distance.

Beatrice lived in a war zone. Though once all Italy had been at war with the Allies, now there were two governments. One was officially at war with the Germans, but diehard Italian fascists were still at war with the Allies, and the partisans were at war with the fascists. Firenze, Beatrice's beloved city, was occupied by Germans and administered by fascists. Civilians tried to live around the Germans. But the local fascist officials, at last in their element, used their power to take revenge on their enemies and to silence all opposition. There were food shortages, arrests in the night, buildings no one wanted to pass because the cries of tortured prisoners reached the street, and occasional machine-gun fire or the sound of a distant explosion. One day a brace of Blackshirts arrived at Beatrice's school and pulled a number of girls from her class, marching them

30

off they knew not where. The teacher explained that the girls were foreigners and didn't belong in the city. "But Rachele and Giuditta were born here," one of Beatrice's classmates complained. Later her mother told her the poor girls were Jews and would doubtless be sent to die in Germany.

All this frightened Beatrice; how could it not? But there was another war that consumed her attention, and that was her never-ending battle with her mother. In the lofty, graceful rooms of the palazzo, Maria Salviati Bartolo waged a battle on two fronts. She had married late—she was thirty when Beatrice was born—and her husband, Oreste Bartolo, had died in a flu epidemic when his daughter was only three. Maria was strong-minded and determined to control her diminished family. Her struggle to dominate her daughter was a skirmish compared to the protracted, full-out campaign she waged against her brother Marco. This was a war of equals, to the death.

Marco modeled his conduct on that of his hero, Benito Mussolini, and he demanded from his family everything that the Duce required of his followers: fear, respect, adulation, and affection. The patriarch, Giacomo, had died some years earlier from complications following an accident he'd suffered while inspecting a threshing machine near Villa Chiara. Maria maintained that it was a blessing their father had passed on, as the disgraceful behavior of his son would have shamed him and driven him to despair. Marco had full rein of the family, as he had seen to it that his older brother, Sandro, was declared incompetent and locked away from his patrimony. Marco ruled his female kingdom, his mother and his three sisters, with callous indifference. His friends were thugs who were allowed to treat the palazzo as a fascist club. His mother told herself that it was the influence of base acquaintances that made her son so ruthless and discourteous, but Maria observed that in his gang, his *fascio,* Marco was clearly the dominant member. He bore down on the women at every meal on the subject of the sacred *patria,* the

31

rightful place of Italy in the world, the spoils of war that would fall to them once the Allies were defeated and the Duce and Adolf Hitler sat down at the table in Berlin and parceled out the world.

When Mussolini was arrested and the Germans came pouring into the Piazza della Signoria on their powerful motorcycles, followed by a stream of trucks, machine guns at the ready, and finally two lumbering tanks, all jolting to a halt under the sullen gaze of Jupiter, Marco breathed a sigh of relief. The Americans would be stopped before they got to Rome, and he would be in line for promotion in his fascist squad. He was in thrall to the Gestapo and joked with them on the street in his halting German about the laziness and faithlessness of the Italians, as if he were not one of them.

The Americans were in Naples, and then for a long time they were stalled at the Cassino line. Maria stalked the halls of the palazzo, wringing her hands. When would they come? Every day more young men, and some old, slipped away into the hills, where it was said they hoarded arms, sniped at Germans, and lived like wild beasts. It wasn't safe to leave the city, especially for the likes of Marco.

Maria's friend Alice Bosco had a radio and could listen to British reports, but it was hard to know what to believe. The newspapers, it was understood, hadn't printed anything but propaganda, carefully controlled by the Duce, for twenty years. School let out, the summer dragged on; the heat made a furnace of the narrow streets, and people leaned out from their upstairs windows at night, trying to catch a breath of air. The city was a tinderbox, and the match could be heard pulling up a line of phosphorous sparks against the strike plate, slowly, so slowly; the suspense was agony. The Allies were in Anzio, marching distance from Rome, but they couldn't break the German line.

Beatrice was in love. He was a brooding, mercurial, emaciated boy of seventeen, and he hated the fascists, the antifascists, the Germans, the partisans, the whole lot. In fact, in his view the Italians were getting what they deserved, and he wanted none of it. When the war was over and the Italians were defeated, defeated, defeated, he would escape; he would walk, if he had to, over the Brenner Pass into Switzerland and after that on to Paris, if Paris was still standing. But for now he had time to meet Beatrice before supper and walk along the Arno, across the Ponte Vecchio, and up to the Boboli Gardens, where it was cooler and they could clutch each other in the shade of the ancient oaks on the Viottolone. She came home to her furious mother with bitten lips, disheveled hair, and no appetite at all for the chickpea soup and dry bread that was as ubiquitous as the heat.

One night she arrived late and slipped into her place next to her aunt Celestia, willing herself to be invisible. The conversation around the table was tense, and the soup tasted of tears. The Germans had picked up Alfonso, the cook's husband, as he was strolling after dark in the Oltrarno, which, as Marco pointed out, everyone knew was thick with partisans. What was Alfonso up to there—where was he coming from? Was he part of some radical cell, sniping at the police from alleys?

"His brother lives there," Maria replied flatly. She had endured a long, weepy encounter with the cook. "He went to bring him bread."

"Exactly," said Marco. "A loaf with a pistol baked inside. They stop at nothing."

"Where did they take him?" Beatrice asked, laying her spoon on the plate beneath the bowl.

Maria and Marco exchanged looks charged with animus. The maiden sisters, Celestia and Valeria, had not spoken a word, both wide-eyed over their bowls.

"The house in Via Bologna," Maria said coldly.

Valeria nodded. "They call it Villa Triste," she said.

Marco slurped in three spoonfuls of soup, his eyes still locked with his sister's. He dropped the spoon in the bowl and reached for the flatbread, which he tore apart angrily. He stuffed a corner in his mouth and chewed for several moments, working his jaws until they popped. When he had swallowed he reached for his wineglass. "I'll go over after supper," he said. "And see what I can do for him."

And to Beatrice's astonishment, her mother nodded, lowering her eyes to the napkin spread across her thighs. "Thank you," she said.

⌇⌇

As the days grew longer and hotter, everyone followed the daily account of the slow retreat of the Germans before the steady advance of the Allies. It was no longer would they come, but when. Marco and his friends faced the ruin of their prospects. No one doubted that when the Allies arrived and the partisans came down from the hills to join them, they would show no mercy to their fascist counterparts. Many of them had been waiting for twenty years to take revenge. The Allies were in Orvieto and then in Terni. All through July, with curfews and arrests, the Germans struggled to control the restive citizens of Firenze. One dark night on an angry street of Oltrarno, they sparked a riot by shooting a four-year-old boy as he ran for the door of his parents' house. After that antifascist snipers were without fear, firing pistols from balconies and darting out from street corners, taking revenge for dead or tortured relatives, for betrayals and lies, and most of all for making their country what everyone knew they now must be, the losers in a worldwide battle for the future of Europe.

Luigi Bosco, husband of Maria's friend Alice, owner of the coveted radio and an adviser to Marco in his dealings with city officials, had been a fascist from the early days, when Mussolini broke from the socialist party and established his journal, *Il Popolo d'Italia*. Luigi had risen to local power on the wave of anti-Russian, pro-military sentiment that fueled the fascist takeover of the state. Maria disliked Luigi, but he was useful to the family, especially during food shortages and for travel documents. Shortly after the German occupation, when the local fascists at last had the power to take vengeance on anyone who had ever offended them, Luigi Bosco had made a quick trip to Rome and returned with a young woman named Silvia Gracchi, whom he described as a paying tenant. A brilliant painter, he claimed, a niece of yet another cousin, Silvia had come to Firenze to study art. She moved in with the Bosco family, Luigi, Alice, and their two teenage daughters, close friends of Beatrice. Silvia declared herself relieved to be out of Rome. Romans were starving, everyone knew that; bread on the black market cost ten times what it used to, and meat was unheard of unless you kept a pig or a goat in your courtyard, the resort of some poorer families on the outskirts, so the presence of this tenant-relative was unsurprising. She was eighteen years old, slender, elegant, with dark hair and shiny brown eyes that were gold in a certain light, like coins. Her manner was mild, interior; she often paused before speaking, as if waiting to hear what she was about to say. She spoke several languages, including German. Beatrice was fascinated by her. She seemed mature beyond her years, quietly confident. She never argued or raised her voice. Of course, Beatrice thought, that was because she was really a paying guest in her relatives' house, and also because she was a Roman and had a more cosmopolitan view of the world.

Silvia and Alice Bosco had dined at the Salviati palazzo that hot night when Marco came in red-faced and sweating with the news that the Germans had evacuated everyone who lived within a mile of the Arno. Upward of 10,000 citizens were wandering the streets, and many had barged into the cool marble rooms of the Palazzo Pitti, where the museum director agreed they could lay down cots amid the treasures and glowering statues, as well as beneath the portico and in the *cortile,* which faced away from the Arno. "What does it mean?" Beatrice cried. Marco hung his head, wiped his brow.

"They're going to blow up the bridges," Maria said. "To keep the Americans from following them." She sneered at her brother. "What will your lot do when your German masters aren't here to protect you?"

"My teacher lives near Ponte Santa Trinita," Beatrice said. The sound of men shouting drifted in from the street, coming closer and closer, and then there was the thudding of the heavy knocker on the door.

"It's Luigi," Marco said, going out hurriedly. "I told him to meet us here. We can see what's happening from the roof."

The women stood silent, gazing at one another. Celestia burst into tears, and Valeria passed her arm around her sister's waist. "Let's go to our room," she counseled. "And close the shutters."

⌒❧⌒

"So that night," Beatrice told me, "we all went up to the roof and watched the Nazis blow up the bridges. Luigi Bosco was as pale as a statue; somehow he'd told himself Firenze would be spared. Marco was pretending it all made perfect sense; the Germans had no choice, they must protect their rear as they advanced to the Gothic Line. There they would be joined by reinforcements loyal to the Duce, who was hiding out in his phony kingdom on Lago di Garda. Everyone knew it was a perfect rout, most of all the Germans, who were methodical as machines. They'd spent the day laying charges all along the Arno, looting stores, and stealing petrol to fuel their vehicles. We climbed up the narrow steps to the roof. I always loved to be up there—we hung our clothes to dry there, the one chore I ever volunteered for—because of the view. We could see the city laid out before us like a picture book, with the towers of the Duomo and the Palazzo Vecchio looming over the rooftops. There was a blackout, the streets were dark, the sky was black overhead, and it was so hot the air pressed like damp velvet against the skin. We gathered near the ledge and looked southwest, toward the river. Buildings blocked our view, but when the first explosion went off with a boom and a bright cloud swirling with white dust rose above the rooftops to the west of us, we all knew what it was. 'It's the Ponte Vittoria,' Luigi said. Marco looked at his watch and said, 'It's ten to ten.' I wondered then how long it would take, how the explosions and the bright columns of smoke might change as they moved closer to us.

"It took all night. With each explosion, one of us called out the familiar name. 'They have blown up the Ponte Carraia,' my mother announced. 'That's the Ponte Vespucci,' Marco said. 'They're not going west to east.' Then Alice Bosco turned toward a loud boom coming from east of us. 'It's San Niccolò,' she said. There were long pauses, hours, in between, while we stood stunned, patiently waiting for the next explosion. Suddenly two deep booms sounded to the north, far from the river, and we all turned to see more sparks and smoke surging heavenward. Silvia Gracchi clutched her head between her hands, crying out with great feeling, 'Oh no. Oh God, they have destroyed the synagogue.'

"Our eyes turned upon her like a pack of dogs simultaneously scenting a rabbit. We all fell quiet as she stood there, sobbing into her palms. Then my mother turned to Luigi and laughed. 'So this explains your tenant,' she said. 'I should have known.'"

Here Beatrice paused and took a swallow of wine while the import of her story sank into my brain.

"She was Jewish," I said.

"She was a Jew," she agreed. "Hiding out in the local fascist official's house. Luigi had gone to Rome when the Germans started arresting Jews. I don't know why he agreed to do it, but he had some papers forged for her and brought her out. Gracchi wasn't her real name."

"Was she really a relative?"

Beatrice shrugged. "Perhaps," she said. "I never knew."

"What happened to her?"

"The Germans never found her. Her family was sent to Germany in the roundup in Rome and none of them came back. After the war I think she went to America."

It was my turn to be silent, and I took the opportunity, sipping from my wineglass, to imagine the little group of family and neighbors and the mysterious young tenant from Rome all gathered on a rooftop to watch their ancient city being systematically destroyed.

"I haven't thought of that night in years," Beatrice said. "A few days later the New Zealanders and the South Africans poured in, waving and handing out chocolate from their tanks and trucks. Some of them were Maori warriors with tattooed faces; it was too bizarre. But we stood on the street and hung out the windows waving back at them. For us, the war was over."

⌒⁂⌒

As Beatrice told me stories about her family, I found myself thinking of them as characters in a complex narrative. She made me privy to a world I might never have noticed, just below the surface of the present. I'd visited Florence and marveled at the Duomo and the Piazza della Signoria, barged about the Bargello, and remained upright for many hours in the Uffizi, until I felt my brain overcharged and saturated with applied color and images from various mythologies; it was overwhelming, exhausting. I was fascinated by the medieval period and the Renaissance, as who is not, but everything between then and the present was a blur. Now when I thought of Florence, I imagined the girlish Beatrice trotting across the Ponte Vecchio with a gelato in one hand and a bookbag in the other. As our time together went on, I added to these the war stories, the family and friends gathered on the roof to watch the bombing of the bridges, the snipers picking off fascists from balconies, and the fascists arresting partisans and hauling them through the narrow streets and alleys to the notorious house of torture on Via Bologna. When I drove out in Signor Panda along the winding roads, ever upward to yet another hilltop town, flanked by the ranks of vineyards, fields of sunflowers, groves of olives, the prodigious cultivation of this ancient soil, the postcard prospect dissolved and I saw hellish scenes of low-flying planes, machine-gun fire, men and women diving for cover amid the thick trellised vines beneath the flowering trees, explosions collapsing stone houses onto their residents, and the continuous passage down the potholed roads of convoys, long lines of trucks and tanks packed with soldiers, armed and serious, or armed and laughing, or their heads drooping on their chests from lack of sleep, men on a mission to kill whoever they thought needed killing. It was as if the heart-stopping beauty and serenity of the scene before me was a scrim, and a change in the light might reveal a very different world, one of dark terror, brooding, cruelty, and suffering.

Beatrice had grown up in a fascist regime; it was all she knew. When she was a teenager, that world began to unravel. She had stood on a rooftop and watched as her city went up in flames and smoke, and she knew that her country was on the losing side of a worldwide conflict, and for the worst reasons—or for no reason but the blind trust her fellow citizens had invested in a leader who held them, ultimately, in contempt. She shrugged at her youthful self now, at her innocence and willingness to welcome a new order. Surely she was sickened by the aftermath: the fury of the retreating Germans—once allies, now enemies—the depravity and horror of the scene in Piazzale Loreto in Milan, when the crowd, maddened by the humiliation and death their leader had visited upon them, discovered the corpses of the Duce and his mistress Claretta Petacci summarily dumped in a public square and fell upon him in fury, beating, kicking, pissing on, stabbing, even shooting his dead body until he was scarcely recognizable as human. At last, satiated and vindicated, they strung him up by his feet from the roof of a gas station, and those who had cameras took photos to preserve the gruesome moment, while the crowd jeered and howled with joy.

Was Beatrice ashamed of her country? Was that why, as soon as she came of age, she made up her mind to leave it, to turn her back on the impossible moral conundrum presented by the postwar order, and set off on her own to discover America?

PART 2

Beatrice in America

I t was unusual for women to take advanced degrees in the 1950s, though perhaps less so in Italy than in the United States. The Italian education system doesn't separate college from high school as definitively as we do in America, and women have not been historically excluded. Harvard didn't admit women to graduate study until 1920, and Yale held out until 1969. By contrast, the university at Bologna hired a young scientist named Laura Bassi to teach in the physics department in 1732.

Beatrice had studied English in her high school and at twenty-two completed her *laurea* degree, the equivalent of a BA in literature, at Bologna. She had discovered and was enthralled by American writers, particularly Faulkner, Hemingway, and Steinbeck. She devoured mysteries by Raymond Chandler and joined the throngs of her fellow students who adored American films. She had seen her countryman Vincente Minnelli's bizarre Hollywood drama *The Bad and the Beautiful,* and the moving, terrifying *In a Lonely Place,* but the cinematic vision of Los Angeles that most appealed to her imagination, with its palm trees and lavish swimming pools, was *Sunset Boulevard*.

Once she graduated, Beatrice resisted her family's expectation that she marry a rich Italian and produce heirs to manage and enrich the family's interests. Her father had died when she was three, and her mother was her only adviser. As far as Maria was concerned, Beatrice was as educated as she would ever need to be. It was time to find a husband.

But Beatrice was an avid student, apt at languages and a voracious reader of English, German, and French novels. She was also adept at writing insightful exegeses of texts and conversant with the critical vocabulary of the day. She made up her mind to go to America and continue her studies.

She was encouraged in this ambition by Professor Ziti, an elderly Venetian gentleman who had spent the war years in Boston and New York. At his recommendation, she applied to the master's program in American studies at Boston College, a reputable institution that her mother could not object to, as it was founded and run by the Jesuits. Her acceptance letter included the promise of a fellowship and information about the college residential halls. Professor Ziti congratulated her with a paternal hug and a copy of Henry James's *The Bostonians,* which he claimed was as good an introduction to Boston society as she would ever find.

At home, as Beatrice expected, there was a scene, a furious, raging battle that went on for two days, scorching the earth through every meal and in various rooms, often before the nervous, drawn faces of her maiden aunts, who represented to her the fate she was willing to risk all to avoid. When the screaming was over, she packed her suitcases and went out to the taxi waiting on the street. As she made her way through the ponderous, voluminous silence of the Palazzo Salviati, the very walls accused her, and her shoe soles, rapping against the stone floors, fired gunshots into an entire continent of disapproval. Her mother did not deign to say goodbye.

꒰⚜꒱

Beatrice arrived in Boston in early September. The city basked in
its most tender light and wore its most colorful costume, designed
by nature to enchant the visitor and distract the jaded citizens
before they were all herded together onto a chute that led directly
to a meat freezer. Beatrice had a brief tour in the taxi from South
Station to Chestnut Hill. The number and complexity of construction sites blocking or invading long, shaded streets of nineteenth-
century row houses surprised her. The city reminded her of photos
she had seen of London. A lot of brick, she thought. She had imagined houses made of wood.

She was expected at the college residence, a dour brownstone
edifice with long windows and an impressive staircase at the front,
where Mrs. Porter, a matron in a gray flannel suit and shoes like
small leather coffins, greeted her officially. "You have come such a
long way to join us," she said. "How was your crossing?"

Beatrice tugged her suitcases from the sidewalk up the stairs. "It
was wonderful," she said. "I slept every night like a lamb."

"That's good to hear," said Mrs. Porter. "But I'm sure you'd like
to go straight to your room and freshen up." She held the door
open wide as Beatrice passed into the dim foyer of the building.
Deeply Victorian. Lots of carpet, lots of very dark wood, a built-in
bench with hooks for coats and an umbrella stand attached at one
end. Mrs. Porter passed ahead of her, leading the way.

Her room was up a flight of carpeted stairs and down a hall, at
the back of the house. To her relief there was a pretty arched window with a view of a thick sycamore tree trunk. The furnishings
were sparse: a single bed made up with starched white sheets and a
brown wool blanket, a desk with drawers, a solid mahogany wardrobe, and two chairs, one for the desk and one, with a cushioned
seat and curved Queen Anne arms, for reading. The bath, Mrs.
Porter informed her, was down the hall, the dining room in the
basement. Tea was served at four and her fellow students would be

pleased to meet her there. But perhaps, after her long journey, she would prefer to rest.

Beatrice confessed that she was tired, but a cup of tea wouldn't be amiss, and as it was only three, she could freshen up and find her way to the dining room at the appointed hour.

"Excellent," said Mrs. Porter. "We will see you then. Just keep going down the stairs until you can't go anymore. The door is on your right, but you'll hear us before you see us. Tea is always a lively gathering."

Off went Mrs. Porter, leaving Beatrice alone with her two suitcases and her view of a tree trunk. It dawned on her that she would never see the sun from that window. She slipped off her shoes; the bare wooden floor was cool and smooth against her stocking feet. She lay on her back on the bed, crossing her arms over her chest. The ceiling was high, white, with a bronze and white glass light fixture hanging from the center by a brass chain. Distantly she heard the sound of water running through pipes in the walls.

"*Mi sento come se fossi in un romanzo,*" she said. Then she smiled, thinking of the English: I feel like I'm in a novel.

⚜

Beatrice's first weeks in America were packed tight with impressions, both physical and mental. Her expectations stood confounded at every turn. The routine of seminars and lectures was surprisingly restrictive, her fellow students largely passive, lacking ambition and curiosity, two conditions she had imagined to be quintessentially American. But they were also welcoming to her, and she soon fell in with a group who met at the graduate student lounge, where there was always a large percolating pot of bad coffee and a box of the bland cider doughnuts they all appeared to crave. The best surprise was that her English was adequate—everyone understood her, and, even more reassuring, she understood them all. The amusing Boston accent was in good supply, but the graduate students came from far afield—California, Illinois, Washington State, Washington DC, South Dakota, and there was even one poor sickly young man from Mississippi, who, driven by his passion for Emerson and Thoreau, had found his way to Boston. There were a few Europeans—a Frenchman from Alsace who spoke Italian with her, always on the subject of mountain climbing, a red-haired Irishman from Dublin who never stopped baiting the lively, small, and thoroughly dapper Englishman from Bristol. Most were men, all were Catholics, only a few ever actually went to Mass. Of the three women, two were from New England and one from Chicago. With these three Beatrice naturally formed defensive bonds, though they actually had little in common. New England women, in her view, were curiously masculine, uninterested in style, assertive, even combative, independent, and largely humorless. The young woman from Chicago was an art lover and had studied abroad in Paris and Rome. She liked to talk with Beatrice about Caravaggio.

The classes were small, and though there were no tutorials in the British sense, the professors, routinely excellent and entirely male, met individually with their students and guided their thinking, suggesting critical texts with special emphasis on their topics. Her research seminar professor, a serious polyglot whose office shelves were lined with fiction in four languages, wanted to talk about Italian writers, especially Moravia, Pavese, and Vittorini. He had been in Italy during the war and recalled the liberation of Rome.

It was all infinitely calming to Beatrice. She lived like a nun in her little cell, she ate very bad food whenever she felt like eating, she spent long hours in her library carrel, piling books higher and higher even as she narrowed her topic. She missed Italy, the beauty of her city, the sound of her language, the intensity of the sun, but she didn't miss her family. Her American life was exactly what she had hoped it would be: all her own.

The break at the end of the fall semester was a long one and the campus was largely closed for several weeks. Her mother had arranged for her return passage before she left; it was one of the things they had argued about, as Beatrice had the idea that she would take the time to visit Los Angeles, the city of her American dreams. As it turned out, this would have been an impossible trip. Los Angeles, she now knew, was as far away as Italy and required a train journey that took nearly as long as the ship would take to cross the Atlantic.

She had enjoyed her first crossing, and when the time came again she looked forward to shipboard life, the lively, lighthearted engagement among the passengers, the safety of a tiny stateroom, the strolls along the deck after dinner with the moon, the water, and nothing else beyond the rail; all this appealed to her spirit of adventure. She wanted her life to be an adventure; that was the revelation of her first crossing. She would be in her life, if possible, always going off, always heading into the unknown.

But of course this wasn't practical, and in Boston she had discovered what she had only suspected, that she was also called to a life in which the greatest adventures took place between the covers of a book. The academic routine of study, discussion, writing, and more study appealed to her and soothed her naturally rebellious spirit. This was a conflict.

A final check to her fantasy of Beatrice the intrepid explorer came on the last day of her return voyage. The weather had been tempestuous, the sea turbulent, and there were whole days when the passengers were restricted to their rooms as the decks rolled and the sea heaved great sheets of water over the rails, pulling anything and anyone who wasn't lashed down out into the roiling depths. The captain skirted one storm only to barrel right into another. All night she clung to her bed, silenced by a roar like a train in a tunnel. Toward dawn the awful sway gradually leveled out, the scream of the wind lost its edge, faded; she could hear only the low hum of the engine below and then the sound of the heavy doors opening and closing, human voices, laughter. Her fellow passengers were uniformly pale and cheerful at breakfast. The ocean had turned from black and white to sparkling sea-green. Beatrice had scarcely eaten for two days and ordered the full American, amusing herself with the discovery that the bacon she had shunned for four months was quite tasty. She spent the morning packing up in her narrow room and then joined the others in a long, slow pacing of the deck. At length the most farsighted among them called out and all found their places along the rail to watch a dark dot in the distance slowly begin to spread. The sea appeared to fall away from it, as if it had been submerged. The sun, near its zenith, lacquered the edges in green and gold. Gradually the expanding blob became a coast, a rocky promontory, and then a city emerged, nestled into the pale gray hills like a jumble of precious jewels offered to the indifferent sky in the palm of an ancient hand. "Italia," Beatrice said softly, leaning against the rail. To her surprise and terror, her nose itched, her vision blurred, and her heart tugged forward against her ribs. She had gone away, she would again, she did not doubt it, but now, as she dashed the unwelcome tears from her eyes with the backs of her hands, she admitted that for better or worse, this would always be where she would be going when she said she was going home.

At the Salviati palazzo, Beatrice found the family in such an uproar that her arrival only contributed to the confusion. Unbeknown to her as she clung to the rail of the bed in the cabin of the storm-battered ship, her uncle Marco had concluded a meeting with his banker, walked across the sunny Piazza della Signoria, and turned in to the Via Porta Rosa, where he collapsed on the doorstep of a jeweler's shop. By the time the ambulance arrived, he was dead.

The maiden aunts had been ensconced at Villa Chiara and were now expected to arrive on the afternoon train to Siena; the funeral would take place the following day. Maria had been out all morning arranging the details, at the church, at the funeral establishment, at Marco's office, and at the bank. Now she was shouting into the telephone in the hall. Beatrice set her bags down and wandered into the dining room, where she found Grazia, Marco's widow, seated at the table, her hands clasped against her chest, breathing laboriously while her children, Luca and Mimma, milled about in the shadows, muttering to each other. It was Luca who informed Beatrice of the unhappy event.

"Why didn't someone send me a telegram on the ship?" she complained.

"What difference would that have made?" Luca replied coolly. It occurred to Beatrice that Luca was now the lone surviving male in the family.

"It's just such a shock," she said.

"Naturally we were all shocked," he said. "But your mother has everything under control. She has been much occupied."

They could hear Maria in the next room concluding her phone conversation. *"Sì, sì, no, sì, certo, certo, ciao."* She hung up the phone and came to the dining room door, where she stood, unsmiling, regarding her daughter. "Good," she said. "You are here. You must go and meet your aunts at the station."

Welcome home, Beatrice thought.

⁕

The next few days comprised a series of shocks to the children and grandchildren of Giacomo Salviati. When his father died, Marco had taken over the management of a fortune much diminished by the vicissitudes of war. A bank the family was heavily invested in failed, a factory in Torino was bombed, and the agricultural sector all over the country was in ruins.

Marco backed the wrong side in the war and was not a popular man. In his business dealings he combined bombast with a near total ignorance of the dangers of taking on debt. He lived lavishly, drove expensive fast cars, wore expensive designer clothes, kept more servants than the family needed. He owned a small plane, just like the Duce, and lost another fortune acquiring racehorses. When he had run through his own family's money, he raided his wife's considerable dowry. He had used the palazzo as collateral on two large loans he had no way of repaying. The morning he died, the bank officers had made it clear that the family holdings were in a dire condition. His creditors were many, and they were impatient.

"He was an idiot," Maria concluded. The aunts had arrived; the family was assembled around the dining table. Maria had been in a meeting with bank officials for hours and had come away in a fury. "He was lucky to drop dead in the street," she said, "so that I don't have to murder him. And I am lucky because now I don't have to meet him in hell for murdering him."

Beatrice exchanged a charged look with Luca, acknowledging their shared experience of the hostility between his father and her mother. Luca and Mimma had always appeared lifeless to Beatrice, as if their combative and profligate father somehow drained the color out of them. Mimma had a simpering manner and an unstable disposition. She often burst into tears for no apparent reason. Now, when they all had cause for tears, she sat dry-eyed, nervously crumpling and flattening a napkin in her lap, her gaze fixed on her brother.

Like Beatrice, Luca had come home for winter break. He was spending a year in Germany studying neuroscience at the same institute attended by his idols, Alois Alzheimer and Ugo Cerletti. Soon he would have a practice of his own. There had always been something fixed and unfeeling about him, Beatrice thought. As a child he had refused to let his sister keep a little dog she'd brought home from her school, and later he made sure that she was not allowed to study dance, which briefly interested her. He wasn't a brute, like his father, but he had a will to power, which he exercised with guile, cunning, and deceit. Now he was heir to a ruined fortune.

"Will we have to sell this house?" he asked his aunt.

"It's possible," Maria said. "Lawyers will study the matter and take advantage of our stupidity and weakness."

Grazia clapped her palm over her mouth and emitted a deep-throated groan. Her father was a prominent socialist and had opposed her marriage to the iniquitous Marco. Maria acknowledged her sister-in-law's suffering with a candid nod. "You should cry," Maria said. "You'll be going home to your father with an empty purse."

Beatrice experienced an unusual sensation, which she recognized as a twinge of sympathy for her mother. Maria was clearly the only competent member of the family, and all the hair-raising, sorry business of rescuing what could be rescued from the outstretched hands of her hated brother's creditors would fall to her. Whenever the subject of money came up, Luca's standard reply was "I know nothing about such things." There he sat, gazing with that clinical interest at his distraught mother, just as he might consider a bug struggling to stay afloat in a whirlpool.

On an impulse, Beatrice said to her mother, "Can I do something to help?" Maria shifted her attention from Grazia, now sobbing into her napkin, to her daughter. "You," she said. "The best thing you can do is go back to America."

⁂

Patrick Doyle entered Beatrice's life in January, two days after the fifth big snowstorm of the year, when the temperature had dropped to 10 degrees and the shoveled sidewalks of Boston College were coated with a smooth thin sheet of invisible ice. The sun was low and blinding but it gave no warmth, and there was a biting breeze that penetrated the outer layers of anything alive, searching out the warmth of a beating heart. Beatrice was wearing a leather coat, a silk scarf, a woolen beret, a long flannel skirt over silk stockings, and soft leather boots with medium heels, a stylish outfit that offered so little by way of protection she might as well have come out in a cotton frock and sandals. Her book satchel was full and heavy, dragging down one arm as she clung with her free hand to the central stair rail of the residence. She achieved the sidewalk, turned in the direction of her class building, took four steps, and found herself lying flat on her back on a sheet of ice. As she went down, she heard her head crack against the pavement, and for several moments her state of confusion was complete. She flailed her arms like a beetle overturned upon its carapace, and a weak cry of fear escaped her lips.

From somewhere above her a voice inquired, "Did you hit your head?" And there he was, bending to her, an angel's pale face surrounded by a halo of wolfish fur, smiling benignly in that way an angel must smile, curious and invincible, just down for a visit, amused by the opportunity to perform yet another service to a helpless, damned human in distress.

"I did," she replied, reaching up with her gloved fingers to grasp his thickly padded forearm. He pulled her to a sitting position and remained leaning over her, his face hidden by the bristling fur lining his coat's hood. She drew her knees up, preparing to stand. He grasped her arms just above the elbows. "Hold on to me," he said.

She did as he commanded, gripping hard around what must have been his biceps, though all she could feel was a thick down-feather cushion. He was more like a sofa than a man, she thought. She got to her feet, facing him, and he held her firmly, standing upright on ice. "You dropped your bag," he said, releasing her. As he stepped past her to retrieve the book satchel, she turned to watch him. Her boots skidded again and her arms jerked up, flapping desperately to regain her balance. This time he caught her from behind, catching her around the waist so that she backed into the warm embrace of his softly enveloping coat. "Where are you going?" he said.

"Gasson," she replied. "I have a class."

"I'll walk you there," he said. "Take my arm."

"That's very kind of you," she said.

He released her waist and slid his arm inside hers, so that they were side by side. "You have to pick up your feet," he said, urging her with a hand inside her elbow. She lifted one boot, put it down, then the other, holding tightly to his arm. "You're right," she said. Carefully they began to walk along the treacherous icy cement.

"You're not American," he observed.

"I am Italian," she said.

"Oh." He nodded. "EYE-talian."

"My name is Beatrice," she said, giving it all four syllables.

"That's quite a name," he said. "I don't know if I can even say it. I'll call you Bee."

They took a few more steps, reaching a section of crusty ice that had been salted and was easier to navigate. "I'm Patrick," he said.

"This is better here," she said, releasing her death grip on his arm. "I think I can go on by myself."

"Not in those boots," he said.

"They are perfectly good boots," she replied.

"Good in Rome, maybe," he said. "But this is Boston."

One of the boots in question discovered a slippery patch and straightaway slid out across it. Beatrice staggered against her rescuer, who braced her gently against his side. "Just hold on to me," he said. "And don't let go. I'm going to take you all the way there."

⌒☙⌒

Beatrice had never been seriously courted before. There had been boys she believed she was in love with who encouraged her with kisses and embraces, but she had resisted the ultimate submission they required and they had moved on. In college the indolent son of a wealthy Milanese family had trifled with her affections for a few months, then dropped her abruptly, as if he had reached the end of a mysterious contract she didn't know she'd signed. Though a few of her classmates were engaged or otherwise paired off, most social occasions at the university were group affairs. By the time she and her classmates donned their long gowns and pressed the laurel crowns into their hair in preparation for the commencement parade through the colonnaded streets of Bologna, Beatrice thought that their innocence distinguished them as much as their education.

Patrick Doyle's way of being in the world was new and baffling to her. She had no experience with a suitor who eschewed artifice, who was in his affection as honest and earnest as the day was long. He gave her something she had seldom received from anyone, except perhaps dear Professore Ziti, and that was his complete attention. It started that first day at the classroom building, where he insisted on knowing when she would be out of class so that he could walk her back to the residence. "I'm not a child," she said.

"That's obvious," he agreed. "But I won't sleep tonight if I'm wondering whether you're facedown in a snowbank with a broken ankle. Tomorrow we'll go out and get you some proper boots. Then you can be on your own."

In fact Beatrice had twisted her ankle painfully in the fall and could still feel the tender spot at the base of her skull. The walk back to her lodging was long, and by the time her class was out it would be dark, that profoundly deep, impenetrable, frozen, black New England dark that came down with a thump like a theater curtain. "You must have other things to do," she said.

"I don't," he assured her. "I'm through for the day. What time does the class end?"

"Five forty-five," she said.

"I'll be right here," he said. He pushed the furry hood of his coat back and his black curls frothed across his pale forehead merrily. His expression was as affable as a retriever's waiting for her to throw a ball. "Say your name again," he added.

"Bay-ah-trree-chay," she said.

He repeated it carefully. "Bay-ah-trree-chay. Have a good class."

"Well," she said. "You're very kind."

"It's my duty," he said. "I want you to love Boston. It's my city."

"That may not be an easy goal to achieve," she said.

"It's a great city," he insisted as she turned to join the thickening stream of students carefully shifting their bookbags from one side to the other, unbuttoning and unzipping and pulling off layer upon layer of coats, scarves, sweaters, hats, and gloves as they doggedly ascended the marble stairs to the realms of knowledge promised to them by their God, their parents, and the Jesuits.

The next morning Patrick met Beatrice at the residence and escorted her to the tram, her first excursion outside the confines of the college. They got off on a busy street lined with shops, walked a few blocks arm in arm, and stopped at one that featured, front and center in the window, a pair of the unlovely blue and brown lace-up boots Beatrice had observed on the feet of so many fellow students, both male and female.

"They're so ugly," she said.

"Just try a pair," Patrick urged her. "Sometimes beauty isn't so practical."

"Practical," she repeated gloomily.

Patrick flashed his mischievous, disarming smile. "It's going to be winter for a long time," he said.

They entered the shop. It was empty but for the salesman, who was moving boxes of shoes from one stack to another against the rear wall. He turned to them, greeting them cordially, and glanced at Beatrice's inadequate footwear with an expression of deep sympathy. "She's an Eye-talian," Patrick assured him. "This is her first winter."

"Have a seat," he said, gesturing to a row of padded chairs with neat little footstools lined before them. "I'll be right with you."

As it turned out, there were several styles of boots. Beatrice took up one that appealed to her: dark gray suede, lined in black fur that peeked out over the top, giving it a jaunty, cozy air. She turned it over and examined the striated sole. "Absolutely waterproof," said the proprietor. She tilted the box to look at the price. "They are not very expensive," she observed.

"Try them on," Patrick said.

When she removed her own boots, both Patrick and the salesman gasped at the transparent feet of her stockings. "Oh, for God's sake," said Patrick. "Don't you have any socks?" The salesman darted to the counter and returned with a pair of heavy black woolen socks, which he slipped over the offending stockings before Beatrice could protest. "I am being manhandled," she said agreeably. In fact she was enjoying the attention of the two Americans, who appeared to have bonded on a mission to make, at least of her feet, a product that could stand up to a Boston winter. As the salesman carefully laced the new boots she felt she was being equipped for a battle. "I've not worn anything this flat since I was a child," she said.

"Right," said Patrick. "The last time you were free."

Beatrice noted, as she had before, Patrick's equation of virtue with liberty. She took it as an American preoccupation, perhaps even one confined to Boston or New England. The phrase "Give me liberty or give me death" passed through her mind as she stood before her audience, her feet wrapped in wool, then fur, then leather, from toe to calf, safe, warm, and flat. She thought that in the case of the icy streets outside the door and the boots on her feet, the liberty-or-death option might actually be literal. She took a few steps across the carpeted store. She'd been amused by the way her classmates clomped about in their heavy, ugly boots, crossing their legs in class with one boot rocking like a heavy pendulum. They were so cheerful and indifferent to the inelegance of their footwear it confounded her, but now, as she plodded about the shop with Patrick and the salesman looking on, their eyes glued approvingly on her incarcerated feet, her spirits lifted.

"They look great," Patrick said. "How do you feel?"

She turned to him, standing, as she rarely did, with her feet planted flat and slightly apart. She bent her knees, as if she were skiing, or just falling, stood up straight again. He was right. The boots were liberating. "I feel like an American," she said, and they all laughed.

⌘

Patrick was only two years younger than Beatrice, but they occupied separate spheres at the college. They had no mutual friends and no classes together. It flattered his vanity to be seen with a graduate student, or so Beatrice concluded, as he never introduced her to anyone he knew without pointing out this fact. "She's a grad student," he said, as if this described a status so outré it must be intimidating. And then he invariably added, "And she's an EYE-talian."

If she was an exotic to him, he was an endearing child to her. She humored him and baited him and even corrected him, and he found her patronizing manner a refreshing difference from the mousy, clingy American girls he had known. His mission to make her love Boston required long tram rides. He took her to an old Italian market where Beatrice and the proprietor chatted in Italian, and he insisted on serving her the one thing she missed most of all the many things she missed about her homeland: a tiny cup of perfect espresso. They went to Copley Square, with its admirable library and Gothic Episcopal church, to Faneuil Hall, and across the river to Cambridge, where Patrick explained the exclusivity of Harvard with the dreamy humility of a commoner affirming the monarchy's unquestionable right to rule.

The winter wore on and her wardrobe expanded to include a fur hat with flaps and a pair of woolen gloves. They went to movies and once to a dancehall, though neither of them could dance the high-energy jitterbug that was in vogue, so they sat at a side table drinking beer, unable even to speak above the booming of the band.

Beatrice was entertained by these adventures. She called Patrick "my American education." But gradually, as the snowbanks blocking every corner began to melt, they went to fewer entertainments that took them far afield, and their outings narrowed to regular evenings at the one American institution Beatrice didn't particularly enjoy, the college bar.

There was nothing like it in Italy, she explained to Patrick. A bar in Italy served espresso first and foremost, though one could have wine and even whiskey, which Italians didn't drink very much. There was food, sandwiches and pastries, and one stood at the bar or sat outside at a table. In America a bar was a dreary, dark hole with nothing to eat and nothing to drink but beer or horrible mixed drinks that made young women vomit, and the patrons sat lounging over tables for hours with their beer frothing over on the coaster and those dreadful peanuts in little dishes, the shells littering the floor, and the bad music was very bad, the same vacuous songs over and over, so loud one could scarcely hear.

Patrick cupped his hand over his ear, laughing at her. "What?" he yelled. "I can't hear you."

"I am getting a headache in this place," she said.

He took a long draft from his beer glass and smacked his lips, looking cheerfully about at his fellow patrons, mostly students, mostly drunk. "I like it here," he said.

He lived with two roommates in a shabby apartment; her residence didn't allow visitors above the common rooms, so they had few occasions of privacy together. He held her hand on the street, put his arm around her chair, speaking close to her ear when they were sitting together in a bar or a movie. One night as they were walking back from a bleak Swedish film, which she had explained to him was allegorical, he raised his hand to her cheek and said, "I want to kiss you." He wanted to shut her up, she understood, but she didn't hold it against him. She looked around; they were near the residence, and there was a narrow space between the staircase and the steps to the basement area. Patrick saw it too and drew her into the darkness, down one step; then, resting one hand on her waist, he raised her chin with the other and gently brought his lips to hers. She felt it strongly, a deep erotic charge that parted her lips and brought her hands up in a circlet around his neck. He pressed her closer, holding her body against his with a steady pressure on her lower back. She opened her eyes and saw that his thickly lashed eyes were closed. She made no effort to pull away, and so, for many moments, they stood embracing in the darkness. At length a couple passed on the sidewalk and he released her. They stepped up out of the stairwell into the fog-shrouded glow of the streetlamp.

"My first American kiss," Beatrice said.

He laughed. "Don't you go doing any comparison shopping," he chided. Joking, she thought, but not entirely in jest.

"No," she said. "I won't."

After that night, whenever they were together, they both consciously sought secluded places where they could embrace without being observed. They found an unfrequented carrel in the basement of the library—this was the first time they were able to shed their coats and get some sense of each other's flesh. These sessions were both intoxicating and frustrating. Beatrice observed that Patrick was restless afterward, truculent and quick to take offense. They didn't talk about what they were doing, what it might mean for their future. That winter was for Beatrice a kind of continually astounding present; she was always on edge, alert to the contrariness and the contingencies of the now.

She didn't concern herself with the family she had left behind. Her mother's battlefront had shifted, and she no longer required a daughter to satisfy her need for dominance. Beatrice was free to enjoy her American life. She particularly liked her classes and her professors, as well as the hours spent talking about books, reading books, writing about books. She was catching up on the writers her American classmates appeared to grasp on a cellular level: Hawthorne, Melville, and then Crane, James, and Wharton. She was intensely excited by Crane's *Maggie: A Girl of the Streets*. "For the first time," she announced during the class discussion, "I understand how fatalism and the passion for reinvention are inextricably bound in the American identity." The other students chuckled at her enthusiasm, and the professor said, "That's putting it rather well, I think."

The graduate students had various events, discussion groups, visiting speakers, and meetings they called "smokers" where everyone smoked cigarettes and consumed bowls of potato chips, events from which Patrick was naturally excluded. He had periods of exams, study groups, and sporting events he attended on his own. He was passionate about baseball, which bored Beatrice. Some afternoons they met for coffee at a bright, cheap diner near the campus. Beatrice quickly gave up on the thin, acidic beverage Americans called coffee and ordered large pots of tea. On one such meeting in mid-March, when Beatrice had been elated to discover a delicate swelling at the tips of the skeletal hydrangea outside the residence, she found Patrick at their usual table nervously perusing a thin sheaf of typed pages. Between sips from a heavy white mug of coffee, he carefully tapped the ash from a cigarette into a tin ashtray.

It was a story he'd written, he explained, and the thing was, he knew it was good but he wanted a "first reader" before he sent it off to a magazine. In their earliest conversations he had confessed to writerly ambitions, but for some time he'd said little on the subject. Now, as she ordered her tea and a slice of apple pie, the only American dessert she truly enjoyed, she could feel the intensity of his anxiety about this next step in their relationship.

"Of course I will read it," she said. "But I don't know how good a judge I'll be. I read mostly stories by dead Americans."

He blew smoke in a puff over his lower lip. "I just want to be sure there aren't any typos or punctuation errors," he said. "I'm not good at commas."

"Ah," she said. "In that case I can help you. I am very good at commas."

He stubbed out the cigarette and stacked the pages together carefully—lovingly, she thought. There were not so many pages after all. He reached for the packet of cigarettes.

"Since when are you smoking?" she asked.

He gave her a sly smile. "My roommate gave me a pack because he's trying to quit," he said. "And he knows I can't afford to buy them."

"So you will stop when you run out."

"Right," he said. "I would never waste money to buy them. Do you want one?"

"No," she said. "It's a disgusting habit. I'm glad you won't become addicted."

He pushed the packet away with one hand and held out the story to her with the other. "This is what I'm addicted to," he said.

The self-dramatization of this remark gave Beatrice pause, but she said nothing, taking the pages, folding them against the table, and sliding the sheaf into her bag as the waitress arrived with her tea and pie. "I'll read it tonight," she promised.

"Sure," he said.

She understood that he had wanted her to read it at once while he sat watching her, smoking cigarettes and drinking coffee as he followed the expressions of surprise and interest that would flicker across her face as she read. "I'll read it carefully," she said. "And we can meet here in the morning."

"Sure," he said again, looking past her at the waitress, who was talking with a couple at the table next to theirs.

"I'm very complimented that you would ask me to read it," she said.

"Flattered," he said.

She frowned. "That's right," she said. "I'm flattered."

⌖

The story was titled "The Truck Keys." It concerned two young men, one a "drifter," the other an innocent student, called by everyone, including the author, "College Boy," who is working on a fishing boat for the summer. College Boy meets the drifter in a waterside bar after a hard day of hauling nets and dumping fish into vast tanks, first in the boat and then on the shore. He smells, the drifter informs him, "like fish guts." The two agree to go to another bar; the drifter insists he knows someone who will stand them drinks there, but it's down the road a piece and he has no car. In the parking lot the two argue aimlessly about who should drive College Boy's truck. The drifter complains that the student is too drunk; also he knows where they're going. At length the student agrees, gives the drifter the keys, and off they go. At the bar, which is just like the previous bar, the drifter soon starts an argument with a stranger, which turns into an actual physical fight with a broken beer bottle as a weapon. The bartender calls the police, who take the drifter away, handcuffed and raging, in their squad car. The student finishes his drink, goes out to his truck, gets into the driver's seat, digs in his pocket for the keys. That's when he realizes the drifter has the keys and has taken them with him to jail. The end.

Why does no one have names in this story? Beatrice said to herself as she read the final sentence. She flipped back through the pages. She'd marked a few punctuation errors, three typos, two with the same reversal error, *dirfter* for *drifter,* and suggested two paragraph breaks. The story was mostly dialogue and tense dialogue at that; still, it ran only ten pages. The *p* on Patrick's typewriter needed cleaning; it was consistently smudgy. In fact, the quality of the print was too inky overall. She would bring him a bottle of the excellent cleaner she used on her own Olivetti.

In the morning, there he was in a booth, with his coffee in front of him. He looked, Beatrice noted, haggard, unshaven; dark crescents had bloomed under his eyes. The pack of cigarettes was on the table beside the cup, but mercifully he wasn't smoking. The waitress followed her to the table, pulling out her order pad. They always ordered the same things: Patrick had eggs over easy, toast, hash browns, and bacon, while Beatrice had two slices of toast with butter on the side.

"And your tea," said the waitress.

"Yes, thank you," said Beatrice.

"So what did you think?" Patrick asked as soon as the waitress left them.

"Good morning," she said. "How are you today?"

He smiled weakly, acknowledging his rudeness. "Right," he said. He sipped his coffee.

She laughed, opening her case to take out the story. "It is very good," she said. "Very amusing."

"Amusing," he repeated.

"Yes," she said. "The ending, of course."

"I thought it was a pretty dark story," he said.

Her tea arrived. "Why do they not put the bag in the water while it's still hot?" she said, tearing open the packet and dropping the bag, string and all, into the steaming water.

Patrick watched her, silent. Brooding, she thought. Mysteriously angry. Just like the drifter in his story.

"Yes, of course," she said. "It is very grim. And terse. It made me think of Hemingway."

This perked Patrick up. "I don't like a lot of adjectives," he said. "I like to keep it plain. Plain speech. Ordinary speech."

Beatrice resisted the observation that *plain* and *ordinary* were adjectives. "So it is," she said. "I have only made a few marks; I think they will be clear." She laid the story on the table between them, turning back to her case for the bottle of cleaning fluid. "And I brought you this. Your print is smudgy. Apply this to the type heads and blot them with a soft cloth. You'll be amazed at the difference."

⁊⚹⚬

The month of March was a new kind of trial. When it wasn't raining it was snowing; the temperature refused to rise above 40 degrees, descending some nights well below freezing. The wind was constant and gusty, as if imitating the eternally roiling ocean just off the shore. The campus turned to mud. There was a soggy brown puddle in the library entrance hall, piled with dripping umbrellas. Beatrice stuck with her fur-lined boots, which she had come to cherish, but Patrick switched to knee-high rubber fisherman's boots, the right footwear, he explained, for "mud season."

The spring break was too short to return to Italy; there was no question of going home. "I miss Italy," she told Patrick. "It's spring there and they're pruning the vines, the fruit trees are flowering."

His plan was to return to the Cape, hole up in his father's house, and work on his stories. "You should come with me," he said. "We could walk on the beach."

"Where would I stay?" she asked.

They were crouched together over a small table in the crowded college bar she disliked. Patrick was on his third beer, Beatrice still nursing her first. "We should get married," Patrick said.

Beatrice took another sip of her beer. She had been thinking of how fine it would be to enjoy a glass of good red wine, a proper cup of espresso. "Are you proposing to me?" she asked.

"Why not?" he said. "It would solve all our problems."

At just that moment, Patrick's roommate, a skeletal young man named Carl, who lived on cigarettes and coffee and fancied himself a poet, appeared at their table, clutching a small glass of dark beer in one hand and a half-smoked cigarette between the thumb and forefinger of the other. "Hey, lovebirds," he said. "Can I join you?"

⸙

Beatrice wasn't insulted by Patrick's unromantic proposal, nor did she have difficulty enumerating the problems being married would solve for them both. On the walk back to the residence he pressed his case. In a few months he would graduate with a degree that was largely useless, and she would have another year of graduate study on a visa with a fixed term. "I just want to get some kind of job that I can do at night and then spend my days working on the writing," he said.

It amused and faintly worried her that Patrick described his ambition as "the writing."

"If we were married," he continued, "we could get an apartment and be together, and you wouldn't have to stay in that shitty residence. We could cook our own food and save money."

"I didn't know you were so practical," she said.

"It wouldn't just be practical," he said. "Think about it. We would sleep in the same bed! No more pawing in the doorways and the library. Bee, I want to make love to you so much sometimes I can't think of anything else. It's killing me."

"At last," she said.

"At last what?" he said.

She patted his shoulder with her gloved hand, then ran her fingers under his jaw. "A good reason to get married," she said.

He laughed. "Right," he said.

"You have to let me think about it," she said.

"How long?"

"We should wait until you graduate."

"I don't see why."

"We should meet each other's parents."

"I don't see why. We don't need their permission. I'm twenty-one."

"Almost," she said. His birthday was in April.

"Let's get married on my birthday," he said.

They had arrived at the residence. "Unbutton your coat," he said. "I want to feel you against me." He unzipped his own and drew her into the shadows, pressing her close inside the shelter of their coats. His kisses were so eager and greedy that she raised one arm to brace her neck against her wrist. His hands swarmed over her, as if in search of something, something valuable, something he'd lost beneath the surface of her flesh. "Bee," he murmured, caressing her ear with his tongue. "Say yes. Just say yes."

An American Character

He's not an educated man," Patrick said. "He didn't have the opportunity. He's had a hard life, but he never complains."

They were leaning their heads together between two seats near the front of the Peter Pan bus they'd boarded at South Station. Outside the rain pelted the windows with a wintry mix that gathered on the lower edge in a scrim of ice. It made Beatrice sleepy and mildly depressed. She wasn't looking forward to meeting her fiancé's father, and she suspected he would have little interest in making her acquaintance. He might even be suspicious, as she was a foreigner and older than his son.

As she had made no comment, Patrick continued. "Since my mother died he's mostly working, and when he's not working, he drinks. She used to keep him more on the straight and narrow."

Patrick's mother had died of lung cancer when he was sixteen; Beatrice knew this. She had been a heavy smoker and had left a closet that smelled still, after five years, of tobacco. Near the end of her life, her family moved her to a nursing home, and there, in a dark little room with no view of the world she loved, she had breathed her difficult last breath. Patrick was a late-life baby; his mother was thirty-seven when he was born, the youngest of three children. His brother and sister were ten and twelve years older and now had families of their own.

His mother had been a teacher in the local high school. She had a teacher's college degree and a love of literature, which she fostered in her son. She taught *Moby-Dick* to high school juniors every year for twenty years. This was a detail Patrick offered as indicative of her determination and forbearance. Her students adored her. At her funeral they couldn't fit all the flowers in the same room with the coffin and the displays had overflowed into the hall.

Beatrice had once tried to read *Moby-Dick,* but Melville's high flights of rhetoric confused her, and his characters' hyperbolic rants tired her. Her English, she concluded, wasn't good enough. She wasn't confident that the world of the novel, which struck her as absurd, was not simply intended to be humorous. She gave up and tried *Billy Budd,* recognizably allegorical and hence easier going for the ambitious Americanist. When she tried to picture Patrick's father, she gave him the pale watery gaze, the jutting disputatious beard, the permanently down-drawn mouth of Herman Melville as he appeared in the engraving on the inside cover of her unread paperback copy of *Moby-Dick.*

Patrick leaned across her to rub his gloved hand against the glass. "We're almost to Hyannis," he said. "I want you to see the bridge." His expression, both eager and wary, informed her that it was important that she be impressed by the bridge. She peered through the glass at the passing landscape. The rain had stopped; the scene was flat and dull: tattered evergreens hovering behind scrubby leafless bushes coated with ashy grime from the constant flow of trucks, cars, and buses on the road. There was no sign of water. Then, as Patrick pressed close against her shoulder, the road curved gently and the massive steel girders framing a vista of heavy dark clouds came into view. The bus entered this frame, rising gently. "Look," Patrick said, though she was looking. Now she could see the wide shimmering gray skein of the channel, and as she did a sharp beam of sunlight slashed through the clouds, burnishing the steel girders to gold, the water from deep blue to violet with an emerald sheen. "It's lovely," she said, meaning it, relieved to be meaning it.

Patrick sighed, his lips near her ear. "When we get to the other side," he said, "I know I'm home."

⁓✿⁓

Patrick's father looked nothing like Herman Melville. He was a small, wiry man, coiled in on himself, bright-eyed, roughly shaven, his complexion weathered and leathery, his mouth bloodless but smiling. He wore an open waterproof coat, jeans, and knee-high, laced-up boots with thick rubber soles. A black watch cap pulled down over his forehead failed to contain the thick and curly gray mop of his hair. He stood back from the crowd gathering near the luggage hold of the bus, his hands thrust into the pockets of his jeans. Patrick pointed to him with a wave of his hand. "That's my dad," he said to Beatrice. He took her hand, leading her out of the crowd, and his father stepped forward to greet him. This was accomplished with a firm grasp of hands, their bodies drawing no closer than two strategically bent elbows allowed. Beatrice had noted the reluctance of American men to touch each other in public and wondered if the same reticence extended to family members. Evidently it did.

"This is Bee," Patrick said, and his father turned his attention, his full attention, upon her. "My father, Davey Doyle."

Davey Doyle closed Beatrice's hand in a grip she imagined crushing an oyster shell. "Welcome to Wellfleet," he said. "I hope you like seafood."

"I do," she said. "I've never eaten an American oyster."

"You'll be having them two ways tonight," he said, "if you're game."

"She's game," Patrick spoke for her. "Bee has a good appetite as long as the food is fresh."

Did she? Beatrice wondered to hear herself described in this way. She was constant in her protest against the dullness of Boston fare: the turgid hamburgers, the beans floating in sweet grease, the limp fried potatoes cut by a machine, and the lettuce leaf with a thin slice of anemic tomato tossed on top, brazenly served as a salad. Patrick ignored her complaints, but now she understood that he had been listening and had attributed her general repugnance to a marked preference for freshness.

"That's true," she said, nodding to Davey Doyle. He had an unnerving way of looking one right in the eyes, focused and amiable but challenging as well, the challenge being not to look away.

"Come along, then," he said, motioning her past him to the parking lot. "Do you mind riding in a truck?"

Patrick touched her shoulder. "I'll take your bag," he said, and she slipped the small rucksack that constituted her luggage from her shoulder.

The truck was not, as she feared, antiquated and pungent, but small, neat, bright green, and new. Patrick tossed their bags into the bed and pulled the passenger door open, urging Beatrice to slip in between him and his father. As she stepped up to the cab she thought she would prefer the window seat, but she said nothing, and in the next moment Patrick leaped in one side, his father slid in on the other, and she was trapped between Doyles. Unconsciously she straightened her spine. Davey started the engine and steered the truck out onto the road.

At last, she thought, wooden buildings. This was surely the America of her fantasies. They passed through the town center, lined with pretty shops, cedar-shingled or painted white with colored awnings, placards hung from poles attached to cheerful front porches. There was a nautical theme, decorative ship's rope, a dinghy used as a planter, a miniature lighthouse rising from the flat roof of a diner. "I see Harvey's closed," Patrick observed to his father.

"He moved up to Maine," Davey said. "His son's up there. Got a hardware store."

Silence bloomed inside the truck; outside the town slipped away. "Is Maine very far?" Beatrice asked chirpily.

⋅⊱✿⊰⋅

The house, a neat, square, unpainted shingled Cape with a dormer pushed out on the second floor and a deep porch across the front, rose from a concrete slab in a sandy yard. Someone had managed to grow two scraggly rhododendrons on either side of the painted wooden steps. A sturdy pitch pine shaded the west-facing wall. As Davey pulled the truck into the short drive, Beatrice noticed a bicycle leaning against a drainpipe near the front. "Here we are," Davey said, turning off the engine. Patrick threw his door open and jumped to the ground, looking back at Beatrice. She followed, sliding to the edge of the seat and stepping down gingerly. As her boots hit the soft earth, she felt her past and her future collide with a jolt. She gazed past Patrick at the darkened porch and forced herself to push back hard against a visceral foreboding, a warning that once she stepped into the house she would be at the mercy of two men she knew little about. Even as she scolded herself for this anxiety, she glanced back at Davey and noted that he tucked the truck key into his right coat pocket. Patrick went ahead, pausing at the porch steps as Beatrice approached. Then he smiled the sweet, unaccountably bashful smile that endeared him to her and said, holding his hand out to her, "You've come home with me. This is the happiest day of my life."

That night, in the narrow, sagging bed pushed up against the sloping wall of the fusty, overfurnished dormer room, Beatrice felt she'd entered an alternative universe. At least it was a warm one, she thought, burrowing a little deeper beneath the voluminous down comforter. The old house had radiators in every room and a wood-stove in what Davey called the front room that produced a solid wall of heat. There they had sat, the three of them, after a meal of raw oysters served on a bed of chopped ice, bowls of rich oyster stew, and plates of baked cod and potatoes, followed by an apple pie. It was plain food, Davey admitted, but fresh and nourishing. Beatrice gratified her host by taking second helpings of everything. There was only beer to drink, and she had finished two bottles. In the front room she took a rocking chair near the stove, confessing herself to be completely stuffed and tipsy. Davey went straight to a cabinet with family photos arranged across the top and took out a bottle of whiskey and two tumblers. Patrick, looking in at the kitchen door, smiled at his father's back. "She doesn't drink hard liquor, Dad," he said. "But I'll join you once I do up these dishes."

Beatrice glanced about the room. A red, napless carpet covered the floor, and the walls were paneled with pine planks. A lumpy couch defined a sitting area, with a brown leather reclining chair, the rocking chair, and a low table in the center. An old upright piano took up one corner, and two built-in floor-to-ceiling-bookcases crammed with books occupied the wall next to it. Beatrice focused on the books; they were close enough that she could read the titles. Patrick called from the kitchen, "What can I bring you, Bee? A cup of tea?"

"Yes, thank you," she said.

Davey took his seat in the reclining chair but leaned forward in it, holding his glass between his knees as if to defy the mechanics of relaxation. "I see you're perusing the library," he said.

"I am," Beatrice replied. "I see many of the novels I'm studying."

"My wife was a prodigious reader," he said. "She brought books into my life. She always read to the children and I listened in. Now that she's gone I've made it my project to read all these books she loved. It keeps me close to her. I don't understand them the way she did. She was an educated woman, a woman of lofty thoughts, high ideals. Sometimes she wrote comments in the margins, and when I find those it's as if I hear her living voice. She guides me, especially with the more difficult writers like Mr. Emerson and Mr. Adams and the James brothers. There's one book by Mr. William James that she particularly admired, all about religious experiences people have had all over the world. I'm just working my way through that one now, and I believe it is changing my thinking."

Patrick came in carrying a mug of tea and a saucer for the bag. "Here you are, love," he said, passing it to Beatrice.

"I've not read William James," said Beatrice.

"Have you not?" said Davey.

Patrick turned to the liquor cabinet and poured out half a glass of whiskey. "I haven't either, Dad," he said. "I think they don't teach him much these days."

"Really?" said Davey. "Well, that's a mistake. Do you suppose it's because he's not a Catholic?"

"No, Dad," Patrick said, amused at the idea. "They teach all kinds of literature at the college and a lot of it is plain immoral, I'm glad to say, but Bee and I mostly study fiction. Novels, you know, and stories, and poetry."

"Well, I know this William James isn't a novelist, but he's a fine storyteller and very observant of the ways of all sorts of human societies."

"I believe they teach his work in the psychology department," Patrick opined. "He's the father of psychology or something like that. And they like to call psychology a science."

"Well, I can see that; his book is very methodical, and the stories are true. He's gathered them up from his studies, but it surely don't read like a science book. Your mother recommended it as a study of human nature, if I remember correctly."

"I should look into it," said Patrick. "It can't be worse than his brother's deadly novels."

Davey chuckled. "You don't care for Henry, I take it," he said.

"Please," said Patrick. "Those awful sentences."

"I think Henry James has a beautiful, elegant style," Beatrice said. "But you must be patient. Have you read *The Portrait of a Lady*?"

"I've only read *The American,*" Patrick replied. "It's one hundred percent dated, an absolute snore."

Davey expelled a barking laugh. "That's right, that's right," he said, nodding approvingly at his son. "The new man must scoff at his elders and make his own way."

Beatrice sipped her tea. Her heart felt light in her chest and she breathed deeply, feeling a current of pleasure running along her veins all the way to her feet. She allowed her gaze to settle on Davey Doyle, leaning forward in his chair, his eyes fixed on his son with open affection, and then she looked past him at the piano, and at the fire in the woodstove busily consuming a log, and back to the bookcase, so crammed with books that some lay crosswise atop their companions. In this sad, cluttered little room, she thought, in this frozen, windswept corner of America, a man had loved his wife for her intelligence and her high ideals. Now that she was gone, he sat here before his stove, night after night, drinking whiskey and trying to raise his own intellect to the level of the woman he loved, to find her still alive in the books she had cherished. Beatrice closed her eyes. She was touched to her core.

They talked on, late into the night, and Davey persuaded Beatrice to let him prepare a hot toddy with whiskey, hot water, sugar, and a slice of orange peel, a potion guaranteed to aid digestion and induce sleep as well. When she had drunk it, she declared herself ready for bed. Patrick rose to lead her to her room. "Good night, Bee," Davey said, rising from his chair. "I'm pleased that Patrick brought you to see me. I may be gone when you wake; oystermen live by the tides. But I'll be back for lunch and perhaps we'll have a stroll on the beach."

"I'd like that," said Beatrice. On the stairwell Patrick put his arm around her waist and kissed her neck. "Your father is wonderful," she said.

"He's an old fool," Patrick said. "But he's got a good heart."

Upstairs, in the bed, Beatrice lay awake, listening to the murmuring talk that continued in the front room. She couldn't make out what they were saying, but now and then she heard Davey's barking laugh. They were in their cups, father and son, but their voices were calm, their exchanges sometimes quick, at others languid and congenial. Never a raised voice, never an obstreperous note, only a pause now and then to refill the glasses. She thought of her own family—what time was it in Firenze? They were just getting up, perhaps. When Marco had been alive, the quarreling had started before they got the first jolt of espresso. Now the family was scattered. Her mother had written that Luca and Mimma were moving to Villa Chiara and that she had taken over one of the apartments in the city. The aunts were undecided. They believed Maria would find a way to save the palazzo and refused to understand that this result was not in her power to deliver. The letter concluded with a concession Beatrice understood to have been wrenched from her mother by the exigency of her circumstances: "It is well that you are engaged in studies that may lead to employment in America."

Beatrice thought her mother exaggerated; surely a portion of the palazzo's furnishings, if sold, were worth a fortune. The family still possessed a productive farm and the attendant houses, outbuildings, and the Villa Chiara. Selling Marco's cars would bring in enough to buy a large flat in the city. No, she concluded, her family was a long way from indigence. Yet here she was in the poorest house she had ever entered, where the family survived literally on what they could prise from a cold and indifferent sea, and they passed the evening conversing agreeably about dead writers, literature, ideals, and ideas. She smiled at the recollection of Davey Doyle, moved by his son's ambition to make his name as a writer, nodding his shaggy head over his whiskey glass. "That's a noble course, and a difficult one," he said seriously. "You'll find much to discourage you, I don't doubt, but you must expect that and push on. Just push on, son," he said. "That's the best way."

⤞⤝

When she woke, the sun had transformed the dingy tan shade on the window to a rectangle of glowing gold; the radiator clanked and groaned—Beatrice was conversant with the secret life of radiators now—and there was a light, repeated tapping at the door. "Bee," Patrick said softly, as if trying not to wake her, though he was clearly trying to wake her. "Are you awake?"

She pressed her fingertips to her eyelids. "Yes," she said. "I'm awake."

"I brought you a cup of tea."

"Come in," she said. There was no clock in the room. How long had she slept?

The doorknob turned and the door opened, revealing Patrick dressed in sweatpants and a T-shirt, his hair shiny and damp and his face rosy, holding the steaming mug with the bag already in it. "Did you sleep well?" he asked.

"What time is it?" she replied.

"A little after nine," he said. He approached cautiously as she pulled in the spare pillow and propped herself against it. He held out the mug. The fragrance—it was the tea with orange peel she particularly liked—rose to her nostrils.

"This is thoughtful," she said, taking the mug. "I slept too late."

"It doesn't matter," he said. "I just got up myself and took a shower. Dad's been gone for hours."

She sipped the tea, smiling to herself as they both listened to what he didn't say: *We are alone in a room with a bed.* She patted the blanket. "Sit with me," she said.

He perched on the edge of the mattress, taking care not to jostle her mug. "You've aced it with Dad," he said.

Beatrice raised her eyebrows over the mug.

"He thinks you're grand."

"That feeling is mutual," she said. "He emanates kindness. I've never met such a man."

"He's a good one," Patrick agreed, passing his hand over the comforter, touching the fabric of her gown, a sleeveless slip, open in a V at the neck. "So this is what you wear to bed," he said. "What's it made of?"

"It's silk," she said.

"Beats the hell out of flannel," he said. Tentatively he pushed the comforter away a bit. "How far down does it go?"

Beatrice chuckled, sipping her tea. "It goes to my knees," she said.

He raised his fingers to her cheek, then, pressing lightly, followed the smooth cord of muscle down her throat to her sternum. Beatrice closed her eyes; she felt his touch clear through to her spine. She lowered the mug and his free hand came up to take it away, setting it on the nightstand. Still she kept her eyes closed as his fingers slid down below her breastbone, gently cupping her breast. He turned to her, bringing his free hand to the nape of her neck, holding her there between his hands, still pressing gently but firmly against the cage of her heart. "This is it, isn't it," he said softly. She opened her eyes as his lips grazed her ear.

"Yes," she agreed. "This is it."

꿎

Three weeks later, Beatrice and Patrick were married in a civil ceremony at Boston City Hall. Davey came on the bus, arriving early and returning to the Cape after a wedding supper at a seafood restaurant on the waterfront. The newlyweds took the trolley to the Copley Square Hotel, where they had a room booked for two nights; this was Davey's wedding present to them.

Beatrice sent a telegram to her mother from the hotel desk,

announcing the fait accompli. In the previous weeks she had exchanged a series of brief messages and endured one painful and expensive phone call during which her mother articulated her adamant opposition to the union. It was obvious, she maintained, that Beatrice's future husband was only interested in her fortune and she had but to disabuse him of the idea that she was rich and she would see how eager he was to marry her.

"I thought Marco had bankrupted us," Beatrice retorted.

"I am saving what I can," Maria said. "It's all I do, night and day, and no one will thank me for it."

Then Beatrice felt again the odd pang of sympathy for her bitter, solitary mother. "I will thank you," she said.

"You," Maria snapped. "Your thanks is to marry a penniless American so he can bleed us to death."

"He won't," Beatrice said. "He doesn't care about money. He wants to be a writer."

"Oh my God," Maria said. "Tell me you're not pregnant."

"I'm not," Beatrice said. "How dare you accuse me?"

"You're a fool," Maria said. "And he knows it."

"What's she got against Americans?" Patrick asked petulantly when Beatrice described this conversation. He had shown little interest in her family and knew only that her mother lived in Firenze, and that *Firenze* was the Italian word for Florence.

"It's not what she has against Americans," Beatrice answered. "It's what she has against me."

"I'm sure she loves you," Patrick said. "She'll get over it."

❧

The young couple moved into an attic apartment in a rambling, dilapidated, shingled mansion on Priscilla Street. They had a bedroom, bath, and tiny, minimal kitchen. The only furniture they bought was a mattress, a table, two straight-backed chairs, and two small desks Patrick found at tag sales. Beatrice purchased a stovetop *caffettiera,* a pound of good espresso, and the proper small cups from a shop in Little Italy. Now she looked forward to waking up before her husband, making her caffè at the two-burner stove, and sitting at the table with the morning paper. Patrick had been right—it was liberating to have a place of their own, to cook their own food and sleep in each other's arms. Outside the frozen world had thawed and the first tender leaves unfurled on the trees, like shy young dancers loosening their skirts. Crocuses, snowdrops, and grape hyacinth had come and gone, lifting their bright, hard faces above the melting snow, which drew steadily back from the walkways and streets like a tide going out. Rain was in the forecast. The sun gave off heat as well as light.

Beatrice wasn't given to nostalgia and reflection, but the rebirth of the natural world after the hardest winter she had ever known induced her to pause and consider her new American life. When she had arrived in Boston in the fall, it hadn't occurred to her that she would be married to an American by the spring. In fact, if anyone had suggested this possibility, she would have scoffed. But her trip to Italy for the Christmas break, though replete with sun and the familiar beauty of her home, had been like a plunge into an icy bath. It wasn't that her lonely life in America was better than the turbulent world she had left behind, but that it was emotionally safer. She confessed to herself that when Patrick lifted her up from the city sidewalk that January day, he was rescuing a woman who had fallen in more ways than one.

Patrick never asked questions about her family or her past; he maintained that he had fallen in love with her when she defended the honor of her inappropriate boots. He accepted her entirely at face value, a hapless foreigner who needed his help. The physical attraction between them was strong, and that too was a new country to her. His presence made her feel mysterious, desirable, and hungry.

Marriage had taken the edge off the erotic frustration and allowed her to observe her young husband with a clearer eye. She noted that he had little curiosity about the world she had left behind; indeed he had little curiosity about anything. For him, she concluded, she was born in that moment when he pulled her to her feet. And in a way he was right. She was not who she had been. The name her husband had supplied her with was Doyle. Bee Doyle. The pure ugliness of those two monosyllables appalled her.

⌘

Beatrice was accustomed to overconfidence in men, but in Patrick she detected an undercurrent of resentment and insecurity that surprised her, especially after meeting his indulgent and supportive father. Something curbed him, restrained him, and he was like a terrified wild animal chained to a fence; he kept bounding forward impulsively, as if this time he would escape. When he came to the end of his lead, the cruel shock of his powerlessness outraged him anew.

He graduated in June, without distinction. In fact there was a frantic scrambling near the end having to do with a paper he had failed to deliver on time and a professor who was so dissatisfied with his performance he threatened to derail the graduation process. This infuriated Patrick, and Beatrice endured an evening of alternating despair and petulance as she helped him rewrite the tardy exegesis and typed it on her Olivetti while he sat at their kitchen table finishing off a half-full bottle of whiskey.

His plan to find a job he could do in the evenings so that he could engage in his "real work" of writing during the day faltered at the start. He worked briefly as a waiter in a popular restaurant near Copley Square but soon fell out with the management and quit in a huff. After a few weeks of disgruntlement and fuming, he found a job as a bartender at a bar near the college. He made less money but got along well with everyone, and the atmosphere suited him. Bartenders, he told Beatrice, heard nothing but stories, and so he could look on his job as a resource for his writing. He was asleep when she went off to her classes at the college and gone when she came home to prepare herself a quiet supper. If she stayed up until his return, he regaled her with the evening's adventures, she drank wine, and he drank whiskey. They fell into their bed and had frenzied sex before falling asleep.

On his desk near the window he had set out his typewriter, a ream of paper, and a leather-bound notebook in which he kept ideas for stories. Beatrice had her own desk on the opposite wall, with a poster of the Tuscan countryside tacked up on the wall above it. Several months went by during which he presumably spent his days reading and writing, and she noticed that the page in the typewriter roll was occasionally filled and removed, but he said nothing about what he had written. Her own work proceeded at the little desk, and she churned out essays at a regular pace. Her professor encouraged her to submit her papers to journals, and at last one was accepted. Patrick congratulated her on this accomplishment with a bouquet of flowers and a bottle of sparkling wine. During the celebrations, he referred to the journal repeatedly as "your little magazine."

In December, when the college closed for the long winter break and the young couple set out on their first journey to her home in Italy, Beatrice Doyle was pregnant.

PART 3

The Mutual Friend

In the last week of my first residency in the limonaia, my colleague Ruggiero Vignorelli, who had recommended me to Beatrice Doyle, arrived for an extended stay at the villa. His friendship with Beatrice was evidently of long standing and his presence unremarkable and expected. One morning I came out into the dazzling sun to find Beatrice standing in the drive speaking to Anna Falco, who nodded agreeably over a thick stack of folded linens she held closely in her arms. As she turned to mount the staircase to the villa, Beatrice greeted me with the news. "Ruggiero is coming up from Rome this afternoon. Will you join us for dinner?"

"*Volentieri,*" I said.

She nodded, pursing her lips. My every pathetic effort at Italian brought out the encouraging teacher in her.

"Come at eight," she said.

I should bring something, I thought, and my brain worked over this problem for the rest of the day. Wine was pointless; Beatrice had a cellar full of the family vintage. Flowers also de trop, as the garden was a riot of blooms. I drove about the countryside taking wrong turns, stopping in one dusty, dreary, sun-baked little village after another to consult my map. It was a discouraging day. I spoke to no one, never found the landmark I was searching for, had a frustrating time finding gas for the car. When I did locate a station, the attendant was a rude fellow who was annoyed that I didn't have correct change. Later I realized he'd clipped me for 5,000 lira. Hot, tired, hungry, without a present, and sorely in need of kindness, I stopped at Beatrice's local bar near the villa and ordered a *tramezzino* and a coffee. The barista was polite—he knew who I was and why I was there—but uninterested. He occupied himself in a conversation with a garrulous man in an elegant suit sipping a glass of fresh grapefruit juice at the far end of the bar. I gazed at the refrigerated case against the wall; fig tarts, *millefoglie,* cannoli, and a special display of that strange and wonderful creation called the *semifreddo,* which is neither ice cream nor cake but somehow both. I finished my sandwich, caught the barista's attention, and met him at the case, where he treated me to the first glimmer of a smile as I dithered between the chocolate-striped *stracciatella* and the plain peach scattered with crushed pistachios. Beatrice, I recalled, liked the peaches I'd brought. *"Prendo questo,"* I said, pointing at the peach. He nodded his serious approval. *"Buona scelta,"* he said. *"Più semplice."* Well chosen, more simple. He slid the confection from the case and lodged it deep in a colorful carton complete with a gay red ribbon and a golden seal stamped with the name of the bar.

Done. I returned to the limonaia, stashed the dessert in the fridge, and collapsed on the bed, fanning myself with the map. As I drifted into a dream of more driving, I heard, distantly, the sound of a car turning in to the drive.

⌘

When I woke there was only the sweet sound of doves cooing in the eaves. The afternoon light flickered over the polished dark wood floor as the gauzy curtain at the window fluttered in the breeze. I had a few moments of that postdream uncertainty that resolves quickly to pleasure or anxiety depending on the answer to the question *Where am I?* Not, I thought, late for class. Not late for anything, but lazy and warm in Tuscany, with no more pressing obligation than a dinner with friends. I roused myself, descended to my rudimentary kitchen, and put the kettle on to boil. A glance through the glass doors told me that Ruggiero drove a red Audi coupe. It was snugged up to the Cinquecento as if to contrast German efficiency with Italian parsimony. The coupe gleamed; the Cinquecento, cloaked in dull matte bluish steel, leaned away as if it might collapse in the heat. It occurred to me that Ruggiero was my age, thus ten or so years younger than Beatrice.

Were they lovers?

I didn't know Ruggiero well. He was part of a set at our college who met in various configurations once or twice a week at a local eatery, a place with pretensions to Italian style: the salad was arugula and pear, the pasta came with mushrooms or shrimp cooked in olive oil. The group comprised two Italian professors, a painter from the art department, a psychologist, not on the faculty but married to a physics professor, the curator of the art museum, and myself. How they found each other I never knew, but if I wandered in of an evening in search of company, there they were, and the painter, an old friend, always encouraged me to join them. Ruggiero was the newest member of our faculty and something of a mystery. Rumor had it that he was divorced and seductive, though scrupulous about his relations with students—distant with the females, hostile to the males, and considered rigorous by all. One of my students told me the girls unanimously agreed that he was "hot."

This didn't surprise me. Ruggiero's hairline was receding, but he had strong, handsome features, so it didn't much matter. He was squarely built, a bit stoop-shouldered, the beginnings of a paunch pushing out over his waistband. He had a habit of thrusting out his jaw and widening his eyes that reminded me of Al Pacino. His English was fluent, his accent utterly charming. He was a film buff, and in our conversations he set me on the track of lesser-known works by Rossellini, De Sica, and Visconti, whose film *Senso* he considered the most sublime ever made. He liked me because I liked film and because he knew I was a novelist. One night I got into something very near a shouting match with the psychologist Mark Marker, who was extolling the virtues of psychotropic drug treatment for children under twelve. Though Ruggiero said nothing, I felt the admiring look he gave me from his corner of the table. As we were leaving, which we did in a group after vexing the poor waitress with a bill split six ways, he helped me on with my coat. "You are right," he said confidentially. "Mark is a menace."

⌘

At 8:05 I took my package from the refrigerator, crossed the drive, and climbed the steps to the villa. I found the heavy door slightly ajar, so I rapped my knuckles against the wood, waited a moment, and called out "Hello." Beatrice's voice rang out—"Come in"— and as I stepped into the foyer, she appeared in the dining room doorway, wiping her hands on a tea towel. I held out my package hopefully. "I brought some dessert," I said.

"Really," she said, looking skeptical. "This isn't necessary."

She turned back to the kitchen and I followed her. "It's a semi-freddo," I said. "Shall I put it in the refrigerator?"

"Yes, do," she said. She lifted a lid on a pot, looked in, and closed it again. "Ruggiero will like that," she said. "He's fond of sweets."

Various plates of the usual antipasti were spread about on the table and counters: artichokes, roasted red peppers, a bowl of ovoid mozzarella di bufala, dressed cannellini beans, toasts spread with chicken liver pâté. "Can I do something?" I asked, having carved out a space for my package in the crowded refrigerator.

Beatrice opened the oven, from which issued a delicious aroma of baking lasagna, reminding me I'd had nothing to eat but a small tuna sandwich, that I'd had a trying day, that I was tired, hungry, and relieved to be speaking English. "You can start taking out those plates," she said. "How was your day?"

I lifted the plate of artichokes and the bowl of cheese. "Not great. I kept getting lost," I said, stepping into the gloom of the dining room. The lamps all had 30-watt bulbs and stood scattered near the walls. The overhead fan was on, drowsily batting the air, and an oscillating standing fan whirred sympathetically near the head of the table. It was surprisingly cool and comfortable, definitively Old World, that world where the movement of the sun, now finally setting, brushing the western windows with a rosy glow, dictated the business of daily life. The hall leading to the rooms I'd never seen was nearly dark, and I peered into it as I laid the dishes on the embroidered runner. I heard a click, then footsteps; then, slouching toward me, the figure of Ruggiero Vignorelli materialized. Without hesitation he advanced upon me. "Ah, Jan, how nice to see you," he said, his hand outstretched in greeting. "Beatrice has told me she's grateful to me for sending you to her." I offered my hand and he held it briefly, firmly, between his own. "And she is seldom grateful," he said archly, "as you may have noticed."

I smiled and ignored the invitation to dismiss my friend as an ingrate. "I'm grateful to you as well," I said. "Beatrice has been very kind."

"Well," he said, releasing me, "it is a happy coincidence."

Beatrice looked out from the kitchen and addressed Ruggiero. "Open the wine, please," she said curtly.

He turned to the sideboard. "Your mother is in the chapel, praying," he told her. "She won't join us for dinner."

Our hostess only frowned at this information and turned back to the kitchen.

"Is there a chapel?" I asked.

"Oh yes," he replied. He took up a wine bottle and examined the label. "All these old villas have chapels."

Beatrice came in carrying three platters, one on her forearm like a waitress. "She'll wait until we're half done and come in wanting her coffee," she said. "I'll fix the caffettiera now."

So, I thought, at last I would meet the ancient mother, the bold woman who had charged off into a war zone to rescue her brother from an asylum, only to see him murdered in the driveway of her safe retreat.

Ruggiero opened two bottles of wine, Beatrice appeared with more dishes, and we three sat down, gathered at the end of the long table, with Beatrice at the head. The conversation was easy at first. Ruggiero recounted his arrival in Rome, where he had an apartment, and his encounter with his neighbors, who were in an uproar because the subterranean floor of the *condominio* had been taken over by a nightclub where live bands blasted brutal music late into the night and the youthful patrons congregated on the street outside, blocking the *portone*. There was nothing to be done about it; the new tenants had signed a lease, so the residents appealed to the mayor, hanging banners from the windows that read, "Petroselli, preserve the peace: close Fonclea."

Beatrice, quick to catch any confusion on my part, said, "Petroselli is the mayor. Fonclea is the club."

"I see," I said, shoveling a sizable portion of lasagna onto my plate as Ruggiero thoughtfully refilled my glass. He asked what sights I had been seeing, what towns I had visited, and I named a few. Siena, I said, was my favorite; all agreed it was a city of surpassing architectural interest and beauty, yet up-to-date, with excellent shopping and dining potential. Ruggiero suggested we all go to the small restaurant on the island in Lake Trasimeno where, for not very much money, we could eat fried fish caught in the lake. Beatrice opined that the ferry from Passignano was the best one to take, as there was an excellent ceramic shop near the landing. The conversation was so superficial and generic that my thoughts drifted and I busied myself with trying to detect some hint of the level of intimacy shared by my new Italian friends. They were comfortable with each other, but not, I thought, in the way lovers were. I was so absorbed in my speculation that I failed to notice the subject had turned to politics. The matter was doubtless being raised at dining tables all over the country: the recent election that had resulted in the elevation of Benedetto Craxi as the first socialist prime minister of the nation. Ruggiero supported Craxi, who had achieved his position through a clever jockeying of coalitions, a maneuver designed to keep the communists out of the government and sideline the Christian Democrats. Craxi was a fixer, practical and experienced; he was also pro-Palestinian and would stand up to the Americans.

Beatrice was having none of this. In her view Craxi was a puppet of Andreotti and in love with money. He would conduct business as usual in a government already awash in corruption. She further maintained the Enrico Berlinguer, the head of the Communist party and a long-time rival of Craxi, was a cultured and honest man who had stood up to Brezhnev and was committed to Eurocommunism.

I applied myself to my wine, as I knew little about Italian politics beyond the fact that the government was made up of volatile coalitions that rose and fell, merged and fractured and merged again like the murmuration of starlings I'd seen harrying the skies over certain streets on winter evenings in Rome. Beatrice was sputtering, and Ruggiero had resorted to slapping his open palm against the table, repeating, "You are not informed, you are not informed," in the practiced manner of a professor outraged by an obdurate student. They weren't listening to anything outside their argument, but I heard a sound from the hall, the brush of leather against marble, punctuated by a muted tap that I correctly identified as the rubber tip of a cane. In the next moment the severe old woman I'd watched going back and forth to the other side of the villa appeared in the doorway. Her fierce black eyes darted over me, past the gesticulating Ruggiero, and closed, like the clenching claws of a hawk diving in for a kill, on the startled, undefended face of her daughter.

Ruggiero pushed back his chair and rose to his feet. *"Signora,"* he said, *"venga a sedersi con noi."* He pulled out the chair next to his own, gathering her toward him with his free arm. Beatrice rose more slowly, her brow contracted in an expression I couldn't translate; was it concern or impatience? She murmured a phrase containing the word *caffè* and retreated to the kitchen. Her mother's eyes didn't leave her, fixed on her back until she disappeared. Then this lady turned upon Ruggiero, approaching him with the steady gait I'd noted from a distance; my eyes were drawn to her shoes, neat black pumps with low heels and a raised flap at the front, like loafers. She was dressed all in black, unadorned but for a pair of diamond studs flickering from the thick flesh of her earlobes. Her hair was black, thin, drawn into a knot at the nape, and her face was all bones, with taut yet wrinkled age-spotted skin, colorless lips, and a pronounced chin. She must have been like her daughter once, not beautiful but arresting. And like her daughter she gave off a strong vibration of willfulness. She settled into the chair Ruggiero pushed in for her, folding her hands on the cloth, ignoring me entirely as I studied her across the table. Her posture said, *I am waiting to be served.*

Ruggiero smiled ruefully at me over her head. "Have you met the signora?" he asked.

"I haven't had the pleasure," I said.

He spoke to the old woman in Italian, explaining that I was a *professoressa* and a colleague of his at a college in America and that I was staying for some weeks in the limonaia.

"Lo so," she said flatly. I know. Her eyes flickered over my form, landing nowhere. It was like being vacuumed.

"È un piacere conoscervi," I said. It's a pleasure to meet you. But was that pronoun *vi* or *ti* or *la*? The slight tremor at the corner of

her mouth made me think I'd made the wrong choice. Ruggiero seemed not to care. He spoke Italian slowly and clearly, and I was able to understand him better than anyone I'd met. He said she had been staying in Firenze but had come out to the villa for the summer, as it was cooler here.

I stuck with English. "I was in Firenze a few weeks ago," I said. "And it was truly a furnace. A very noisy furnace. The signora must be enjoying the peace and quiet of the villa."

Ruggiero translated this dutifully, and the old lady cast me a hard look. Had I said something impertinent? *"La tomba è silenziosa,"* she observed coldly.

"The grave . . ." Ruggiero said.

"Is quiet," I finished. "I get it."

Later, as I lay in my comfortable bed in the limonaia, stuffed with food and woozy from wine, this phrase from Beatrice's elderly mother came back to me: the grave is quiet.

Above all, I treasured quiet. Had I believed in God, a convent that required a vow of silence would have greatly appealed to me. Not, I thought, total silence; I enjoyed the sounds of nature— birds, the rain, the sea, even the buzzing of bees—and I loved music, but the clatter and crash of the modern world vexed me. I had imagined—no, I had assumed—that this old woman, who skipped dinner in order to commune with the divine, would share my attraction to solitude, but she'd seen through me, reproved me, and dismissed me. *Oh, yes, you want quiet; life is too noisy for you. Well, you'll have silence soon enough and for eternity.* She ignored me after that, nor did she have much to say to anyone.

Beatrice served her an espresso, which she sipped slowly, savoring the bitter blackness of it. "She drinks eight cups a day," Ruggiero informed me, smiling down upon the diminutive lady as if her caffeine addiction constituted an accomplishment. They exchanged a few words I didn't understand, but I noticed that her eyes rested softly on his face, without the acute penetration she fixed upon her daughter. Beatrice was dutiful, serving the coffee from behind, taking the empty cup away without comment. When she had finished the old lady stood, pushing back her chair as Ruggiero leaped up and handed her the cane he'd propped against the sideboard. *"Buonanotte,"* she said to him, and made her tapping way back into the darkness from which she had come.

Beatrice brought out the semifreddo and set it down next to Ruggiero, who gave a small exclamation of pleasure. She brought a serving knife and three glass plates from the sideboard and set them next to the confection, announcing, to my great delight, "I don't usually eat desserts, but I'll have a small slice. You've made a good choice. Not too sweet."

⁓⁓⁓

The next morning I slept late, and when I got up I saw that the Audi was gone. Ruggiero and Beatrice had doubtless ventured out to the bar. I fixed myself a pot of tea and made toast in the fifties-era toaster with its twin wire cages in which the bread was raised and lowered by Bakelite handles. It was an overcast morning with a light breeze, warm and inviting, so I set my breakfast out on my little terrace, bringing along my notebook and the Mussolini biography. I made some notes about the dinner party and then turned to the biography, where I learned that in 1919 sixteen rival political groups used the word *fascio* to describe themselves. The biographer concluded: "Ranging from anarchists to restless bourgeois university students, these 'fascists' had nothing in common except their name."

So Mussolini didn't coin the word. I finished my tea and went inside to use the bathroom. Once upstairs I decided to change to a light sweater. Then I made my bed and put the shirts I had washed and hung on the windowsill away in the dresser. When I came downstairs, a man was standing at the glass doors looking boldly inside. He saw me but made no movement, simply including me in his scrutiny. It was Luca Salviati, and I noticed he was holding my notebook loosely at his side. Had he been reading it? *The nerve,* I thought, crossing quickly to the door and pushing it open forcefully. "Can I help you?" I said.

"Perhaps I am helping you," he said, backing away and holding the journal before him like a talisman. "The breeze must have blown your book off the table. I found it on the ground."

I fairly snatched the notebook. I thought his story unlikely; the breeze was weak, and my notebook had a spiral spine and thick cardboard backings. But I didn't challenge him. I set it back on the table, turning away from him.

He scooted in close beside me. "I notice you are reading about Mussolini," he said. "That's an unusual subject for an American tourist."

"I'm interested in the period," I said.

"I wonder why," he replied.

"It strikes me that what happened in Italy during the war was very different from what happened in the rest of Europe."

He pressed his lips together and his gaze turned inward. "Italy is very different from the rest of Europe," he said.

"Obviously," I agreed. I was thinking about his father, Marco, the fascist who managed to squander a good portion of his patrimony. Marco was on the roof that night the Germans blew up the bridges, but where was Luca? He was a few years older than Beatrice, perhaps seventeen or eighteen at the time. Did he admire his father and share his adoration of Mussolini? Was he perhaps out in the streets in a black shirt, assisting the Germans in the destruction of his city? The moral conundrum of that night in that city in that war was so complex it required sudden choices everyone involved might only want to forget they had made. Had Luca decided to study psychology in self-defense, or as an escape? He had no children, and not by accident. Just as his cousin had done, Luca rested his hand across the cover of the book on my table, his long, manicured fingers obscuring the domed forehead of the Duce. He read the author's name and raised his eyes to mine. "This is written by an American," he observed.

"Actually," I said, "he's a Brit."

"Oh," he said. "Not so far afield. Not an American or an Australian."

"The Australians fought in Italy during the war," I said.

Just the trace of a smile. "They came from all over the world to fight in Italy."

"Americans see themselves as liberators," I said. "But you know that."

He nodded. "Yes, I know. They saved us from ourselves and we are all very grateful." This last bit was so patently insincere that I rolled my eyes.

"And the former fascists?" I asked. "Were they grateful?"

This brought an expression of genuine amusement to his features. His eyes grazed mine, just short of engagement, then settled wistfully on the Duce's photograph. "But surely you know there were no fascists in Italy," he said. "Italians were all partisans."

I laughed. "So I've heard," I said.

"It was this man," he continued, pointing his index finger at the brooding Duce on the cover of my book. "Only this man, all by himself. He rose to power and transformed a backward, dissolute country into a fascist state. For twenty years he controlled it all. The people adored him. Hitler admired him. He was a tyrant, an unrepentant dictator. He was to blame for it all. Isn't that what your British historian says?"

"No, he doesn't," I said. "I think he sees Mussolini as an opportunist who rode a wave, but he didn't make the wave by himself."

"And who made the wave," Luca asked, "according to your British historian?" He was baiting me, superior and indulgent at the same time. He could no more credit a British view of Mussolini than I would have an Italian's view of Franklin Roosevelt.

I shrugged. "I don't know. I've only read a few chapters."

At this point the distant sound of a motor grew rapidly nearer, and we both turned toward the gates. The Audi burst into the drive, swerving widely to pull up alongside the Cinquecento.

"Here is my cousin and her friend," Luca observed.

"Do you know Ruggiero?"

"He is here in the summers," he said.

The engine sputtered and died, the doors of the coupe flew open, and Ruggiero stood up on the driver's side. Beatrice, I noticed, never exited a car just because it had stopped. She appeared to be looking for something, bending forward in the seat, then reaching into the back and pulling out her purse. At last she stepped onto the drive, holding the purse in one hand, a paper bag I recognized as from the bar—her mother's cornetto, I assumed—in the other. Seeing us, she raised the bag toward the villa, turned to slam the car door closed, and headed up the steps. Ruggiero also faced us briefly, with a wave of one hand. *"Buongiorno,"* he said.

"Buongiorno," I cried out. Luca only nodded, casting Ruggiero a wintry look. Ruggiero lingered for a moment, deciding, I thought, whether to engage us or escape us. He was a sociable man, though private about his personal life, so he was torn. Luca, ignoring him, turned to face the limonaia and said, entirely apropos of nothing, "Do you like this little place?" Across the drive Ruggiero got the message, carefully closed the door of his expensive car, and followed Beatrice up the staircase.

"What?" I said coldly.

"It seems to me cramped and hot," he observed. "I don't understand this passion for turning outbuildings into living quarters."

"You don't approve," I said.

"It's so unnecessary," he concluded.

Neither of us acknowledged what I knew he was thinking: *And now we have Americans living in the driveway.*

"I like it very much," I said.

"Well," he said. His eyes traveled up to the low-ceilinged second floor, over the brick-colored tiles on the roof, and beyond to the steadily darkening sky. "I believe we will finally have some rain," he said. And with that he tapped his heels together in the military manner, or, I thought, like Dorothy trying to get back to Kansas, and set off across the drive to his own front door.

⤷⬥⤶

Luca was right; the rain started an hour later and swept down with such force that I decided to stay in for the day. I had plenty of food and books to read, journal writing and grammar exercises to keep me busy. The rain closed me snugly inside the limonaia; I couldn't see beyond the terrace. I left the door ajar to hear the sound. It rained hard and steadily until noon, then subsided gradually to a fine drizzle. I stepped outside to see how muddy the drive was.

Not too bad, as it turned out. Standing water in a few potholes and soggy on the verge of the garden, but the dirt was so thoroughly and anciently packed and hard that it shed the rain like a taut canvas. As I looked toward the villa, the big door opened and Beatrice backed onto the landing, her arms wrapped tightly around a heavy bundle of linens. She attempted to turn in the narrow space, an edge of sheet pulled loose, and a few napkins dropped onto the step. She uttered an oath. Where was Ruggiero? I wondered.

"I'm coming," I called, dashing out into the misty rain. I hurried up the nearer staircase and met her at the top. "Let me help you," I said, picking up the stray cloths near her feet.

"Thank you," she said. "You are a lifesaver. I have to get this into the car and take it to Anna Falco. Please close the door behind me."

I did as she asked, then hurried back down the left staircase to meet her at the foot of the right. She glowered at me over the unwieldy bundle. "Now, if you will open the car door," she said.

I went to the car and threw open the passenger door. Beatrice

approached, assured and steady in her narrow-heeled shoes, bending and backing up at the same time as she deposited the shape-
shifting load onto the seat. "It's like a dead body," she said, shaking
out her arms. I threw the two napkins I'd rescued onto the pile and
closed the door while Beatrice crossed to the driver's side. "If you
will squeeze in the back, we will go and see Anna together," she
said.

There was only a narrow space between the hard little seats, one
of which was occupied by the unwieldy bundle. "*Squeeze* is the
operative word," I said as I clambered across the driver's seat on my
knees and fairly dived onto the hard bench seat in the rear.

"Fortunately, you are not a large person," she said. She slipped
into the driver's seat and pulled the door behind her. As she started
the engine and we burst out through the gates, I occupied myself
in finding an angle that would accommodate my knees without
pressing them into the back of the seat. I knew the trip would be a
short one, as Anna Falco sometimes walked to the villa. "This car
is like a character," I said as we hurtled past the field of sunflowers,
then turned in to a long, rock-strewn, potholed, uphill lane that
curved gently until Beatrice took a sharp right turn and I could see
the house.

It was the typical Tuscan farmhouse touted in every tourist
brochure, a gray stone box with a red tiled roof. An awning con-
structed of a steel frame covered in rushes jutted out over the stone
terrace that ran the length of one side. On the other side, an enormous, ancient olive tree shaded a smaller brick terrace. The upper
windows glittered as we approached. I realized the sky was clearing
and a few sun rays had broken through to pick out the glass. Beatrice cranked her window down and the damp, warm air rushed in.
The road had leveled to a wide plain of dust and brown grass. Two
vehicles were parked there, a Fiat Panda much like my rental and
a battered truck with a wooden-slat-framed bed that looked like

it could be useful for transporting sheep. The hood of the truck was open, and as we passed, a man bending over the engine and partly hidden from view stepped back, raising one hand high, as if, I thought, to stop us.

He was small and wiry, dressed for what he was doing, physical labor—an oil-stained shirt with sleeves rolled up to the elbows, a workman's faded pants, and sturdy, mud-spattered boots. His eyes were dark, and his thick black hair was swept back and oiled into a pompadour. This, combined with his neatly trimmed mustache, gave him a nineteenth-century look. He was frowning deeply— perhaps the engine presented some insurmountable problem—and he regarded us from beneath his brows with a combination of suspicion and indifference.

Many years before in Milan I had admired a painting by Giuseppe Pellizza da Volpedo titled *Il Quarto Stato*. It depicts a worker's strike at the beginning of the twentieth century. In the background a vast roiling sea of humanity, men, women, children, some shod, some barefoot, advances toward the viewer. In the foreground, two men and a woman holding a baby stride ahead of their fellows, leading them into the light. The full-bearded man at the center of this trinity wears a vest and a soft-brimmed hat; his eyes are sad but determined, his stride purposeful. It wasn't a strong resemblance, but something about this living man who stepped back from his truck and raised his hand, palm out, as if to waylay our approaching car reminded me of the man in that painting. It was the sense of there being a mass of frustrated human ambition behind him.

"*Ciao,* Beppe," Beatrice called out to him, flapping her hand wearily out the window as we passed.

"*Ciao, signora,*" the man replied. He noticed me, jammed in the back seat behind the laundry, and his sullen expression changed to a wide, delighted grin. He leaned away from the truck, his eyes fixed on me as I bounced about, holding my knees in both hands. He was laughing as we made a final curve and I could see him no longer.

When we came to rest at Anna Falco's front step, I asked Beatrice, "Who is that man?"

"Beppe Bottini," she said. "He works for us. Everyone here has worked at the villa forever."

Anna Falco opened the farmhouse door and stepped out to greet her family's employer. She had a friendly, easy manner, and she exchanged obligatory air kisses with Beatrice. The two women occupied themselves with removing the linens from the car seat, transferring them into a deep wicker basket Anna produced from behind the door. Neither of them watched me as I extricated myself, with much twisting and squeezing, from the torturous back seat. When I stood firmly on the ground, Anna turned toward me at the door, gesturing for me to follow.

"Come inside," Beatrice said. "We'll have a glass of *vin santo* with Anna."

I followed cheerfully enough, wiping my feet on the doormat. As I stepped into the entry, a large gray cat burst out from the gloom and dashed past me into the yard, startling me so that I gave a shout. This amused Anna and Beatrice, who had gone ahead, each holding a handle of the basket between them. Anna said something in Italian from which I extracted the word *gatto*. Beatrice said, "That's Piccolo. Anna is saying that he delights in scaring people."

The room we were passing through was simply furnished: a few armchairs, a chintz-covered couch, side tables. A heavy old television on a rolling metal stand faced the couch from a corner. Beyond this was the dining room, largely occupied by a rectangular table, farmhouse chairs with woven rush seats, and a massive sideboard. I noticed a collection of framed photos propped on the highest shelf, but the room was too dark to make out much about them. Otherwise the walls were bare white plaster, the floors polished dark gray stone throughout. Anna and Beatrice went ahead of me into the bright light of the kitchen, where the double doors stood open to the smaller terrace. It was a long room, with white tile counters on two sides. A brick oven with an open hearth occupied half the back wall. The oversized sink, with one of those clever wooden drying racks attached to the wall above it so that the dishes drained directly into it, stood in a central position, while the refrigerator, a vintage model with the freezer inside, was tucked into a corner like a shameful addition. I noticed all this after the fact, because my first consideration was a square table with a checked cloth near the open doors at which a very old man dressed neatly in loose cotton pants and a soft, sky-blue flannel shirt sat looking at me with an expression of childlike curiosity.

"Jan," Beatrice said. "This is Anna's father, Stefano." Then she addressed a stream of Italian at the old man, in which, to my satisfaction, I isolated the word *amica* as well as my name. She had called me her friend. Stefano nodded; I stretched out my hand and said *"Piacere."* He regarded my hand and nodded again.

"He's a little confused these days," Beatrice said to me. Anna disappeared into the dining room, returning at once with a bottle and four glasses on a wooden tray. The old man's face brightened at the sight of the tray and he adjusted his chair, laying his palms flat and wide apart on the table as if to specify the space he called his own. Then followed the charming ritual of the vin santo and the biscotti, which is dear to the owners of all the smallhold farms of Tuscany, particularly when they are visited by foreigners and those locals they deem to be their social superiors. When the glasses were filled and the plate of hard cookies set on the table, Beatrice and Anna tapped their glasses and said *"Cin-cin"* to each other. The old man held the stem of his glass carefully, gazing into the reddish liquid with evident pleasure. His free hand scrambled across the cloth and snatched a cookie from the plate. *He doesn't get dessert wine and a biscotto every day,* I thought.

Anna and Beatrice fell quickly into a complex conversation. I could make little of it, and Beatrice didn't bother to translate. I heard the names Luca and Mimma exchanged with unmistakable irony, as adults who know each other well talk about politicians and naughty children; it was a tone that included the implication *What can you expect?* I sipped the sweet holy wine, which reminded me of taking communion in the Episcopal church when I was a girl, and watched the old man break his biscotto in half and dip one part into his glass. He raised his eyes to mine and gave me another nod. I smiled and nodded back. The phrase "a nodding acquaintance" drifted across my consciousness. I reached for a cookie.

I was facing the open doors, and I could smell the musty damp bark of the enormous olive tree that shaded the terrace so thoroughly the table and chairs scattered beneath its cover were dry. What I liked about Italy, I thought, was this openness to the outside. Shutters, not screens, open doors, talking to neighbors through open windows, outdoor furniture that never comes in, the occasional bird flying in one window and out the other. The door framed an in-between world—a tree with a stone floor beneath it. Beyond the steady flow of conversation between Anna and Beatrice and the crunch of the hard biscotto between my jaws, I heard the sound of footsteps passing along the side of the house. In the next moment an attractive young man appeared, so perfectly still and poised on the threshold that he seemed to have materialized from the air. He was dressed in a dark gray suit over a beige linen shirt, no tie, soft black leather city shoes—attire that struck me as entirely out of place in this farm kitchen. His complexion was pale and delicate, his hazel eyes, behind wire-rimmed glasses that magnified them, thinly lashed and myopic; his hair was thick, neatly combed from a side part, neither brown nor blond but somewhere in between. He had a pretty, girlish, soft-looking mouth and a slightly receding chin. All this I took in later, but what I noticed in my first sighting of Leonardo Falco as he paused in the doorway of his mother's kitchen was the mysterious and enormous calm he seemed to emanate from every pore. He looked in at us, his eyes passing from one to the other, from a secure and inviolable distance. He was, I thought, perfectly and entirely self-possessed.

His mother and Beatrice broke off their conversation. "*Ecco* Leonardo," the old man said, the first words he had spoken in my presence. His eyes, which had been until then slightly dazed, brimmed with pleasure. Anna rose from her chair and advanced upon Leonardo as he stepped inside, bending his head down to receive her pecks on each cheek. "This is Anna's son, Leonardo," Beatrice said to me, and then she addressed him with a greeting and the presentation of her *"amica, una professoressa dagli Stati Uniti,"* which he acknowledged by putting out his hand to me. I rose halfway in my seat, stretching out my arm to reach his hand over the table. Briefly we grasped each other; his grip was firm. I said, *"Piacere,"* which seemed to satisfy all present. "We won't stay much longer," Beatrice advised me.

Leonardo took a chair but declined a glass of wine. There followed a brief conversation with Beatrice and his mother which ended abruptly when, evidently activated by some mutually agreed-upon signal, everyone but me and old Stefano stood up. Anna began pulling in the glasses and setting them back on the tray. Beatrice made for the door. I pushed back my chair and followed along, through the dining room, with Anna catching up to guide us to the drive. More kisses and murmurings; Beatrice and Anna had clearly settled some matter relative to the cousins, and we were back in the Cinquecento, this time with me and not the laundry in the passenger seat.

⟡

As we rattled back along the rutted lane, Beatrice leaned forward in the narrow seat, concentrating on avoiding rocks and potholes. My thoughts drifted to the family at the farmhouse. "That was nice," I said. "Thanks for bringing me."

"I thought it might be of interest to you, as a writer," she said. "And of course they are curious about you."

As a writer, I thought. It amused me that Beatrice credited me with powers of observation, which in her view must require constant exercise. "Anna was kind to me the day I arrived," I said.

"She is an excellent person. She told me my cousin turned you away at the door."

"She couldn't understand my Italian," I said.

Beatrice snorted. "Oh, she understood you well enough. She and Luca don't approve of my renting the limonaia."

"Why?" I asked.

"Well," she said, pausing as she swerved the car past a small boulder in the road, "they don't much approve of anything I do. When I'm here. Because I'm not here most of the time." We had come to the main road. Shifting gears and craning her neck in both directions, Beatrice steered onto the smooth asphalt.

"And Mimma never leaves," I observed.

"Exactly," Beatrice agreed. "When she was young, my side of the family had the whole villa. She was stuck in the city with her creepy brother, her silly mother, and her brute of a father. She has envied me her whole life."

"Her father was Marco," I said.

"You have a good memory."

"I'm working it all out," I said. "Now I'm wondering about Stefano. He must be close in age to your uncle Sandro."

"Sandro was several years older. But as a child he and Stefano were great friends. My aunt told me they roamed all over the countryside together. Sandro loved the villa."

"Is that why your mother brought Sandro here in the war? Because she knew he loved the villa?"

Beatrice shrugged mightily. "Who knows why my mother does anything?" she said. "Even God does not know."

We had arrived at the gates of the villa. As the car careened into the drive, Beatrice said sharply, "What's going on here?" She braked, turned off the engine, and threw open the door. On a grassy patch between the cars and the villa, Luca and Ruggiero faced each other, both gesticulating fiercely and speaking at the same time. Mimma cowered behind her brother, grasping her headscarf between her hands and emitting a high-pitched whine that sounded more like a distressed housecat than a human. My eyes were drawn upward by a motion. It was Beatrice's spectral mother leaning on the landing rail, muttering darkly and batting the air up and down with an upturned palm, as if to bring to the attention of the angels safe in their heaven this human folly here below.

Beatrice launched into the argument, leaving Ruggiero to join me near the cars.

"A pipe has burst in the cousins' bathroom," he explained. "Water is pouring into their dining room. No one knows how to turn off the water."

"How awful," I said.

"Luca has pointed out to me repeatedly that he is a doctor and not a plumber."

"That's helpful," I said. We exchanged smirks.

Beatrice abandoned the argument, dashed up the stairs, and disappeared inside. Luca turned on his sister, smoothly transferring his outrage to her, which served to exacerbate her wailing. Beatrice reappeared on the landing, brandishing a key. Her face was flushed and her eyes flashed fury as she rushed past her mother, who ignored her. "It's in the cantina," she announced as she passed us, heading for the big arched doors behind the staircase.

"Ah," said Ruggiero, following her. "It's in the cantina."

In spite of the anger, the excitement, and the urgent need to stanch the flow of water into the cousins' dining room, my only thought was, *Great, now I get to see the cantina.* Beatrice opened the heavy paneled door. Inside she fumbled briefly for a light switch. Then, as various low-watt bulbs placed in strategically useless locations dimly illuminated the cavernous room, I followed Ruggiero inside.

The cantina was an unspectacular, though vast and impressively vaulted, stone room, damp and largely empty. Mysterious jars and large cans stacked on cheap metal shelves at one end leaned ominously toward a trestle table heaped with broken appliances, discarded pots and tins. Near the entrance a few barrels, presumably filled with olive oil, huddled like conspirators next to two wooden racks designed to hold several dozen wine bottles. I noted with pleasure that one rack was completely loaded and the second nearly full; we wouldn't be running out of wine at the villa anytime soon. A gathering of farm machinery, like iron monsters at a club meeting, sporting giant combs and rollers for subduing the soil, and a threshing device the size of an ox constituted the rest of the cantina's furnishings. Beatrice marched directly to the farthest wall, where a thick pipe, black with grime, rose through the stone floor to the lowest point of the vault and then took a sharp right turn into the wall. This was Beatrice's destination, and I followed her while Ruggiero interested himself in the farm equipment. Near the base of the pipe, a rusty valve with a thick hexagonal bolt gave the impression of ancient desuetude. Beatrice took up a heavy wrench from a crate against the wall and set to work. "Can I help?" I asked, though clearly I couldn't.

"No, thank you," she said. She fitted the wrench over the bolt. "This is a one-woman job." Then she grasped the wrench handle in both hands and pulled with all her strength. To my surprise the bolt turned, stiffly at first, then more easily. When the wrench handle was all the way down, Beatrice refitted it to the bolt and pulled again, until, halfway down, she could pull no more. The valve was closed.

"*Brava!*" I exclaimed. "*Forza ragazza!*"

Ruggiero wandered over as if he'd just noticed our presence. "Any luck?" he inquired.

"It's closed," she replied. "No thanks to you and Luca."

He bristled. "How could I possibly know where the water main in your house is?"

"Luca knows," she said. "He's just being a prick."

I was reminded of how thoroughly fluent Beatrice's English was.

"Now what?" asked Ruggiero. "I suppose there's no water in the entire villa."

"Now I call Anna and she sends Beppe," Beatrice said. "He's in her field fiddling with the truck."

We three filed back into the villa, where Beatrice called Anna from the kitchen phone while Ruggiero and I sat in the dining room. Beatrice's mother came in, said a few words to Ruggiero on the subject of the *tubi,* and went out again. "She is convinced that Luca broke the pipe on purpose," he said.

"Why would he do that?" I asked.

"Because he wants to make life more difficult for Beatrice," he said.

Beatrice concluded her high-volume conversation and joined us at the table. "He will be here in a few minutes," she said.

"Shall we have a glass of wine?" Ruggiero suggested.

"Definitely," said Beatrice. "My nerves are in shreds."

Ruggiero chose a bottle from the sideboard and brought it to the table. I went to the kitchen for the glasses; we pulled out our chairs and sat down companionably. "Your mother opines that Luca broke the pipe on purpose," Ruggiero informed Beatrice as he filled her glass.

"I wouldn't put it past him," she replied. "But it's probably not true. The pipes in this house are crumbling; they are ancient. Beppe patches them all together, but we really need a whole new system, which would cost a fortune."

"So you think he'll be able to fix it?" I asked, though obviously she did think that.

"Oh yes," she said. "He does it all. Plumbing, electricity, gas, stone work."

"A valuable man," Ruggiero observed. We were quiet then, sipping our wine, considering the wonder of Beppe as our eyes casually combed the walls, the ceiling, the floor for signs of imminent collapse.

"He's a thief," Beatrice said. We all heard the crunch of tires on the gravel, the hiss of brakes as the vehicle came to a halt. "But thank God, here he is," she concluded.

We drained our wineglasses, pushed back our chairs, and went out onto the landing without speaking. Beppe was stepping down from a small Chevy van, once white but two-toned now from dust and splattered mud. The sun had come out, and it lit his inquisitive face as he gazed up at the three of us, his hands propped on his narrow hips. "*Ciao,* Beppe," Beatrice said, going down to meet him. Before she reached the drive, Luca and Mimma appeared from under the bower. At the sight of Beppe, Mimma, still distraught and weeping, pushed ahead, but Luca caught her elbow and led her along, greeting the handyman with a formal "*Salve,* Beppe."

"*Buona sera, signore,*" said Beppe. Beatrice joined the group and apprised Beppe of the problem. At the mention of the tubi, Mimma clapped her hands to her face and commenced her high-pitched keening. Luca spoke sharply to her, and Beatrice opened her hands to the air in a gesture of hopelessness. Beppe moved closer to Mimma. "*Poverina,*" I heard him say as he reached out to pat her shoulder tenderly. She lowered her hands and raised her sad, blotchy face to him, gasping for air. "*Poverina,*" he said again. "*Poverina signora, non pianga.*" Poor lady, don't cry.

He pulled a folded patterned handkerchief from his pants pocket, shook it loose, and pressed it into Mimma's hands. She accepted, bringing the cloth to her eyes with a little moue that was absurdly, horribly coquettish. "*Grazie,*" she said weakly.

"Amazing," I said to Ruggiero on the landing. "He's calmed her down."

Ruggiero nodded. "Beppe is quite the character," he said.

"Do you think he's a thief?" I asked.

"Oh, definitely," he said. "And one who knows more about this family than they know about themselves."

At the time, I thought Ruggiero was spreading his insider status on a bit thick, but as it turned out, this observation would prove to be prophetic.

⌘

I spent the last two days of my first stay at the Villa Chiara almost constantly in the company of Beatrice and Ruggiero, but I was never able to penetrate the exact nature of their relationship. They had met in California during a period when they were both teaching at UCLA. Beatrice was a single mother with a son. Ruggiero was married at that time, his wife was from Sardinia, and they had no children. When Ruggiero divorced, he wanted to leave the West Coast and he took a position at my college in Pennsylvania. A few years later Beatrice moved to the small college in New York where she was still employed. These two institutions are just far enough apart to make day trips impractical, so the two friends fell into the habit of visiting in Italy, where they both naturally spent their summers. They appeared habitually comfortable with each other, shared various interests, and were constantly planning outings to see art or attend concerts, but they especially enjoyed driving out to try different restaurants, some new, some old favorites where they were welcomed by cheerful staff. Their manner with each other was more accepting than affectionate. Ruggiero was occasionally dismissive and even combative. He liked to run the show. He was pleased that Beatrice had taken a shine to me, as I was, I understood, a kind of offering he had made her: the paying guest who was also, in some ways, an equal. If I had been an unsatisfactory companion—and I suspected that Beatrice could be exacting in her requirements for that post—his own amour propre might have been adversely affected. The fact that I was a writer and had published books—not bestsellers but favorably reviewed—gratified them both. Whenever I solicited an anecdote about their lives or the history of a place, they brightened, coming to attention in that way children do when they realize an adult is actually interested not just in what they have to say but in how they say it. They made an effort to tell the story well.

Once Beppe had repaired the pipes and the cousins had retreated to their domain, Ruggiero proposed an outing to the restaurant on a little island in Lago di Trasimeno, about a ninety-minute drive from the villa. The next morning we set out in Ruggiero's car. Beatrice had been there years before and remembered it as a charming setting. Very few people, all elderly, lived on the island, though there was a small hotel that couples sometimes booked for weddings, several restaurants, and a ruined castle. Saint Francis of Assisi had passed a Lenten period there and performed a miracle in the boat that ferried him out from the mainland. A shining school of fish leaped over the boat, welcoming the saint. "They knew it was Lent and he would be fasting," Beatrice said as we sped along the winding road to the lake. "So he wouldn't eat them."

"That was too bad for him," said Ruggiero, "as they are delicious."

"A little bony," said Beatrice.

"*Persico,*" said Ruggiero to me. "In English they are called pearch."

"Perch," I said from the back seat. "Very bony."

Beatrice snorted, flashing her eyes at me. "You see," she said to Ruggiero, who made no reply. We left the highway and descended to a two-lane road that cut through low hills on one side and miles of marsh grass on the other. "Look," said Beatrice. "There is the *lago.*"

And indeed there was the lake, blinking like an enormous silver eye fringed by the rustling grasses of the marsh. Briefly we turned away from it, following a road that funneled us through the outskirts of scattered farmhouses and olive groves and into the bustling center of Passignano, the oversized village that fronts the shore of the ancient Lago di Trasimeno. We passed a lovely walkway winding along the shore and then the Hotel Lido, with its open-air dining room, like a dance floor scattered with tables and chairs, and equally scattered diners lifting glasses of white wine, consulting waiters in white jackets, or ogling the trays of fish and pasta held aloft by other waiters passing nearby. The main street was almost absurd in its quaintness, its colorful restaurant awnings and narrow shops, including the popular ceramic dealer, where casserole dishes, pitchers, plates, enormous bowls of all sizes and colors, painted with scenes or fruit or intricate designs, were displayed on red cloths stretched on the pavement from the shop door right down to the street, so that passersby had no choice but to pick their way among tempting crockery to get to the other side. On the water side, I saw the ferry pier, blinding white, jutting out into the placid lake, with a ticket booth at the end the size of a small house and benches along the walls next to the open doorway. Ruggiero drove past it and pulled into a public parking lot. We passed a shabby, possibly sinister attendant leaning against a light pole, moodily smoking a cigarette. When we were all out and Beatrice and I turned toward the pier, Ruggiero hung back to have some heated words with this fellow, doubtless about the parking fee and how and when it must be paid. Beatrice and I went ahead to the walkway, gazing out over the water at our destination, the picturesque Isola Maggiore, the only inhabited island of the three in the lake. It had, as islands do, a startling resemblance to the back of some large animal, a dragon or a huge green bear, rising above the water, glinting gold in the sun, a shimmering mirage in the calm dark blue of the lake. "It looks like an enchanted place," I said.

Beatrice nodded. "It is medieval," she said. "You'll be surprised at how much stone is there. It used to be famous for lacework, and there may still be a few old women who do that and make a tiny living selling their wares to tourists."

Ruggiero joined us. "These people are gypsies," he said. "They charge you to park your car and then they steal from your car while you're gone."

"Is that true?" I asked.

"Why else would he be so insistent that he is not responsible for anything that happens to the car?"

I considered this as we made our way to the pier. In Rome, years before, I'd been robbed by gypsies twice. Once a gypsy had cursed me because I wouldn't give her money. They were mostly women in the city, often holding babies, accompanied by children who could skillfully relieve tourists of their wallets without their knowledge. I'd watched Roman matrons beat back a gnarly old gypsy and her companion, a younger woman carrying a baby, who were trying to board a bus. The gypsies fascinated me. They were like flocks of exotic birds, swathed in yards of colorful fabric and headscarves rolled down over their foreheads so that all one could see was their quick, defensive eyes. I thought of them as city dwellers who wouldn't be able to tolerate the fresh air outside the metropolis. They were constantly being abused, pushed away, held back, turned out, so they were always on the move. During the war they were routinely rounded up by the Nazis and sent to concentration camps, where many thousands of them died. One rarely saw the men, though I assumed they controlled the women. Why would a gypsy be out here at a tourist town robbing cars?

We arrived at the pier, and as we walked out to the ticket booth I could see the ferry plowing steadily toward us, as if on clouds instead of water. It was a double-decked boat, the top open on the sides. Passengers leaned against the rails, milled about among the seats. The lower deck was lined with windows that reflected the flickering light from the water. There was a festive air about it that lifted my spirits. In years to come, nothing of particular import ever happened to me on either end of the ferry ride between Passignano and the Isola Maggiore, and perhaps because of its experiential blandness, its unsullied isolation from everything else in my life, I returned to Passignano whenever the opportunity presented itself, and each time, while I gazed across the water at the smart little vessel coming to take me to the island, the same lightness came over me, as if I had shrugged a weight from my shoulders, and I was once again eager to join my fellow tourists on the upper deck.

We three filed on and found seats near the front. As the metal gate swung closed, the engine rumbled somewhere down below and the prow pushed out into the lake. A few children dashed past us to stand at the rail, shouting to their parents joyfully. The island resembled a magical forest floating in a haze before us, vague and small at first but gradually expanding in all directions so that it seemed to be rushing toward us to enfold our little boat in a deep green blanket lined with a thick trim of blue silk at the edge. A dot of gold near the highest point began to spread, defined by the steady illuminating rays of the sun as stone, as crenellated, as a tower. "Is that a castle?" I asked Beatrice.

"It is," she said. "It's not so very old, but it is abandoned."

Ruggiero, who had a considerable knowledge of the place and was eager to inform me, took over. "It was built in the late nineteenth century," he said. "It's called the Castle Guglielmi, after the family. Now it belongs to the city of Perugia. I believe there are plans to turn it into a grand hotel and spa, but these plans are continually falling through, as are the ceilings of the many large rooms inside."

"Is it open for visitors?" I asked.

"Sometimes yes, sometimes no. We will try our luck after lunch if you are curious."

"I am," I said.

Now the verdant island that had been before us was above us and the tower disappeared beyond a crescent of willow trees sweeping their fountains of soft green branches down to the water line. The ferry angled to come up alongside the pier and our fellow passengers roused themselves, pulling in their bags and cameras and water bottles, their sun visors and sandwich wrappers, standing in small groups, a family here, a couple there, children breaking out for the stairway. We joined them and went down and out into the bright sunshine, where a bevy of return passengers stood waiting in a tightly packed crowd behind the gate.

"Italians don't like to queue," I observed to Beatrice as we descended the wooden gangway.

"This is true," she agreed.

Before us the town, ancient, yet fresh and bright, opened before us like a movie set. The stones below our feet and all along the wide piazza were of the same hue, the comforting pale gold of homemade bread fresh from the oven. Indeed I had the sensation of being set adrift among enormous loaves of bread, with windows and doors cut into their sides just for the novelty of the effect. A big loaf with a green awning and tables set out in the shade of an oak tree attracted many of our fellow passengers. Others set off down the wide pedestrian street, which wound this way and that among the loaflike houses. Some walked briskly, intent on destinations; others loitered, gazing about as if lost and clearly disconcerted by the paucity of shops. The children ran and no adult called to stop them. There were no cars, no *motorini,* no marauding child-nabbers, no dangers of any kind, and so they ran, shouting to each other, their sneakers rapping softly against the wide, warm golden stones beneath their feet.

"This is marvelous," I said to Ruggiero, who was directing us by staying a step or two ahead.

The hotel was not ancient but it was old, perhaps last decorated in the sixties and now shabby, yet also clean and welcoming, with heavy furniture and light, bright open windows. I followed Ruggiero and Beatrice into the dining room, which was small, perhaps twelve tables covered in salmon-colored linen cloths. Ceiling fans whirred gently overhead, arranged in a diagonal line across the room. Two couples were already dining, one next to a window, the other near the open doors. After some consultation with Ruggiero, a waitress dressed for the heat in a sleeveless top and cotton skirt seated us by a long window that looked out onto a wall covered by bougainvillea. I'd been expecting something more open and touristy—a pier perhaps, over the water, where we could see the fishermen chugging about in their boats laden with fish—and I was relieved by the simplicity of this place, the soft murmur of the other diners, the caress of warm air generated by the fans, the frank manner of the waitress, who, after seating us, left just long enough to take up bottles of water and wine and return to the table. There was no menu and Ruggiero ordered for us, asking me only whether I preferred spinach or escarole as a side. A boy of perhaps twelve came out from behind a screen that blocked the entrance to the kitchen, carrying a basket of bread. He was a lean youth with laughing eyes and an easy confidence. He exchanged a joke over some small matter with the waitress as they crossed each other on their paths to and from the table and the kitchen.

Ruggiero poured out white wine and we touched our glasses. *"Cin-cin,"* he said.

Beatrice took a small sip, her eyes wandering over the room. "I haven't been here in years," she said. "But they haven't even changed the tablecloths."

"No," Ruggiero agreed. "It's as if time stopped here and decided not to go on."

Beatrice nodded. The waitress emerged from the kitchen holding a tray laden with dishes. "The last time I came here was with my husband," Beatrice said. "When David was just walking."

This was the first mention Beatrice had made of her husband, and I was curious to hear more on the subject. "Did he like it?" I asked.

"My husband?" she said, recollecting herself as she was then, the same woman but different in this unchanged room. A smile played about her lips, but not a cheerful smile, and her eyebrows lifted slightly, her eyes charged with irony. "He said it was the dullest place on earth."

Ruggiero chuckled.

"Bahr none," Beatrice added.

"Bahr none," Ruggiero repeated. "That's such a descriptive expression."

"Had he much experience to bar?" I asked.

"No," she said. "He was as provincial as a cow. I was too, I suppose. We were both very young."

The waitress arrived with our soup: three identical bowls of minestrone, with a broth that was nearly clear. She set them before us, murmuring, *"Buon appetito."*

I took up my spoon. "How did you meet?"

"We met in Boston. We were both students at Boston College. I was a graduate student, just arrived, and he was a senior, two years younger."

"Was he from Boston?" I asked.

"Wellfleet, on Cape Cod, born and bred, as he would have said," Beatrice replied.

"Truly a phrase-maker," Ruggiero observed.

"It was all new to me," Beatrice said. "But it became old very quickly."

"And he was Irish, I take it," I said.

"Patrick Doyle," she said. "Irish and proud of it, though of course he knew nothing about Ireland. He had a thick accent; I found it charming."

"Pahk the cah in Hahvad yahd," said Ruggiero.

"It was the fifties. We hadn't all heard John Kennedy yet."

"What was he studying?" I asked.

"He was studying not much," Beatrice said. "He fancied himself a writer. He was going to out-Hemingway Hemingway. He wanted to go to Paris, but of course he had no money. His father was an oysterman on the Cape. At the time that seemed romantic to me as well."

"An oysterman?" I said. "On Cape Cod?"

Ruggiero was grinning over his soup spoon.

"What did I know?" protested Beatrice.

"You fell in love with the son of a poor oysterman," Ruggiero said.

"He was good-looking. Black Irish, they call it. Fair, fair skin, black hair, dark blue eyes. Allergic to everything. A mosquito bite was a health issue. Poor David inherited that from his father."

We ate our soup thoughtfully, considering the curse of fair skin.

"Were you married in Boston?" I asked.

"Yes," Beatrice said. "Quickly and quietly. When it was over, I phoned my mother and his father took us to dinner at a good restaurant. We had a room in a hotel for two nights—that was the honeymoon. On the way there he stopped and bought two bottles of whiskey. That should have been all I needed to know."

"This is a depressing story," I observed.

"He could be very charming. But when he was drinking he became weepy and filled with self-pity. That night he paced around the room, drinking the whiskey from a bathroom glass and whining, "I must be crazy, God help me, I've married an Eye-talian.""

Ruggiero laughed. "You've never told me this story," he said.

Beatrice shrugged. "It was all so long ago."

Patrick in Italy

In the brief course of their courtship and marriage, Patrick Doyle had learned very little about his wife's family. He knew that her father had passed away when she was a child, that her uncle had recently dropped dead in the street, that her mother and her aunts lived in Florence, a city he associated with writers he disliked, Henry James and E. M. Forster. He had seen pictures of the Ponte Vecchio and Piazza della Signoria, both of which he dismissed as "too ornate." Like many of his fellow Americans, his first trip abroad was an exposure he both anticipated and dreaded. He would rather have gone to Paris. Beatrice promised a side trip to Venice, where they could dine at Harry's Bar, famously frequented by his idol, Ernest Hemingway.

Beatrice was eager to be in her homeland, though she knew the likelihood that her family would welcome her American husband was slim. In her absence, her mother had completed the grand derangement caused by Marco's death. The ancient, spacious, elegant palazzo, with its worn stone steps where five could walk abreast, the marble columns and floors, wide halls and frescoed ceilings, the dining table that seated sixteen beneath a ponderous chandelier suspended from the vaulted ceiling, the Persian carpets, high-backed leather chairs, floor-to-ceiling recessed bookcases, and carved plaster cornices in her grandfather's library, the courtyard where water bubbled eternally in a deep stone bowl, the roof terrace with its view of the Duomo and the Arno—all this had been sold; it was still there, but gone, and Beatrice's heart ached at the thought of standing on the street before the bolted doors with all access permanently and irrevocably prohibited. Perhaps it was just as well that her husband and their child would have no palpable sense of what the family had lost.

Maria had recouped and regrouped, bought and sold, shifted and consolidated, as had many of her neighbors. The rebuilding after the war had turned the ancient city, especially near the Arno, into a wonderland of scaffolding. Now it was complete, and all manner of new arrangements were possible. Maria had purchased two floors of a former grand palazzo on the Arno, and it was at this reduced lodging that Beatrice and her American husband presented themselves. After the short climb from the street, the newlyweds entered the lofty foyer. Patrick frankly gasped for air. The spacious, high-ceilinged rooms, the wide loggia overlooking the river, the abundance of marble, frescoed ceilings, rich carpets, and tapestry hangings, the artfully displayed family antiques from the Salviati palazzo, astounded him. "Why didn't you tell me, Bee?" he whispered. His eyes traveled nervously from the Baroque plaster cornices down a line of gilt-framed paintings and settled on the plush silk-upholstered settee positioned in a shallow alcove near the window.

"Tell you what?" she said. Though of course she knew what.

"That you're rich." His tone was accusing, bordering on pique.

"Would it have made a difference?" Beatrice asked. But she was thinking, *We're not as rich as we were.*

An inner door opened and her mother, dressed in black, her hair bound in a tight knot at her nape, her mouth set in a habitual frown, her flat black eyes as shiny and crafty as a raven's, advanced upon them. Beatrice stepped forward and the two of them exchanged quick kisses on either cheek. Her mother's strong hands gripped her forearms, holding her in place. *"Mamma,"* Beatrice said as she was released from the maternal welcome. *"Ecco Patrick, mio marito."*

Patrick Doyle stuck out his hand and said, "Pleased to meet you, ma'am."

⁓ֆ֍ֆ⁓

In the days that followed, Beatrice found herself the object and the subject of severely conflicted emotions. Her mother, who had railed against every decision her daughter had ever made, now regarded her with a combination of pity and scorn. Often demanding, never approving, Maria was now merely distant, offering neither advice nor censure. She expressed an interest in where the baby would be born—the child was, after all, heir to the Salviati estate—but the announcement that the young parents had agreed upon Boston as the proper locus for the event provoked barely a rustle of the maternal feathers.

Patrick, accustomed to his role as the knowledgeable guide, the interesting young man at ease in a world he fairly owned, the rescuer, the lover, now the husband of a woman he knew nothing about, was out of his depth in Florence, and like a desperate pup tossed into a river, he paddled in pointless circles, just trying to stay afloat. He had never left his own country, never felt himself a foreigner, never stepped into a street where, should he lose his way, no passing stranger could set him right. "I'll pick it up," he said when Beatrice suggested he listen to language tapes before the trip. On their first outing, a simple walk to the Ponte Vecchio, a sullen belligerence settled over him, and he made no effort to disguise his wounded amour propre. High-spirited Florentines surrounded them, ignored them, chattering among themselves in perfectly impenetrable Italian. "I can't believe no one speaks English here," Patrick said.

It was a clear, chilly day in early January, with no edge to the cold, but many of the passersby were wrapped in absurd fur coats and oversized cashmere scarves. When they passed a bar with a glassed-in terrace, Beatrice suggested a stop for refreshments. He was quick to agree, dropping into a cane chair as the waiter approached, flourishing a small round tray. "Would you like a coffee?" Beatrice asked. Patrick glanced about at their fellow patrons, bumptious and voluble, sipping from their tiny cups, tearing at crescent rolls or stabbing forks into plain brown tarts. "I'll have a beer," he said. She ordered for them both. A beer, a caffè macchiato. The waiter smiled at her, recognizing her as a local with a pretty American boy in tow, or so it seemed to Patrick, who shot the fellow a warning look so completely uncalled for that he pulled in his chin and backed away.

Beatrice missed this exchange. She was watching two young women who were teasing an old gentleman, doubtless, she thought, their grandfather, at the next table. The old man smiled benignly as the two women argued about whether he would prefer his cornetto plain or with almond paste.

"It's so good to be home," she said.

Patrick followed her eyes. The women were both stunningly beautiful and very clearly apprised of and emboldened by that fact. Why were they petting and fussing over a doddering old fellow in an oversized wool coat? Were they prostitutes?

The waiter appeared and lowered the tray of drinks with an expression of studied indifference. Beatrice spoke to him as he placed the espresso before her. He smiled, his eyes taking her in brightly; quipped a reply; they both laughed. He set the beer in front of Patrick without looking at him and turned away.

"What's so funny?" Patrick asked. He sipped the beer, which was warm.

"Just pleasantry," Beatrice replied.

"What did you say?"

Beatrice felt a flush of blood rising to her face. She had remarked that it was a bit early and a bit chilly for a beer, but she knew better than to let Patrick even suspect that she had engaged a waiter in a disparaging remark about him. Indeed, she blushed that she had been so thoughtless, that she had, in essence, talked behind his back right in front of him. Her brain buzzed, seeking a safe reply—seeking, she understood, a lie. She glanced past him to the street, where a woman in a full-length mink sported two shopping bags and a collie. "It was nothing," she said. "I said it was cold outside but lovely and warm in here."

Patrick looked puzzled but not incredulous. "And what did he say?"

Another panicked search; a quick recovery. "He said it was best to look at cold weather through glass."

"It's not that cold," Patrick protested, sipping his beer.

"No," Beatrice agreed. "There's never any helpful ice here to fall down on and meet your husband."

This pleased him.

⳾⳾⳾

The plan was to visit Florence for two weeks, with side trips to Venice and Pisa, as Patrick had professed a desire to see the Leaning Tower. After that they would spend two weeks at Villa Chiara, where the aunts would welcome them and Patrick would have a quiet place to work on his novel.

Five days of his mother-in-law's hospitality was more than enough for Patrick, and he was eager to see Venice because, he explained, he was always happiest near the sea. On the sixth day they packed two small bags and headed for the Florence station. They took the train to Santa Lucia station and then the vaporetto along the Grand Canal and under the Accademia bridge, debarking at the stop in Dorsoduro near their hotel. On the water, Patrick revived; it was his element, and the nervous, awestruck tourists packed into the chugging little boat amused him, though in truth, as the magical vista of the ancient city opened before him, his jaw dropped open and he breathed a sigh of wonder. Beatrice, smiling, watched him, her hand resting on his arm. "It's lovely, isn't it?" she said.

"It's wonderful," he said, covering her hand with his own.

At the hotel he opened the arched casement window of their room and leaned out to watch a gondola passing along the canal just below. "Why can't we just stay here?" he asked.

Seated on the edge of the creaky double bed, Beatrice was having the same thought. The sound of water lapping endlessly, the damp, chilly, salt-saturated air that poured in over the windowsill, the echo of distant voices, a shout from the pavement, the throaty song of a gondolier, the chatter of birds in the piazza, all served to sever the traveler from every place in the world that was not Venice. "We could skip Pisa," she said. "The tower actually looks just like it does on the postcards."

He turned, smiling boyishly, as he had not smiled during the difficult week in her mother's apartment. "To hell with Pisa," he said. He bent over his knees and commenced pulling at his shoelaces. "How's the bed?" he asked.

She dropped back on the mattress, which didn't give beneath her. "A little hard," she said, kicking off her shoes.

Patrick stepped out of his shoes and pulled his sweater over his head. "Let's soften it up," he said.

Later, when they lay side by side, satiated and lazy, gazing up at the cracked ceiling with its faded fresco of clouds and cherubs, Patrick mused, "I wonder if he's here now?"

Beatrice knew her husband well enough to guess who "he" was, but she gave him the opportunity to say the revered name. "Who?" she asked.

"Papa Hemingway."

Beatrice smiled. "It's possible, I suppose," she said.

In fact, Ernest Hemingway was holed up in Havana, wounded,

drunk, and angry, and there were no photographs of him on the walls of Harry's Bar. But the waiter spoke English and offered Patrick a few stories about the great writer, his favorite table, and the very dry martini called a Montgomery, which Hemingway drank because the owner, Signor Cipriani, had invented it especially for him. He told of how Hemingway and his wife had arrived at the Gritti Palace not so long ago, having survived two plane crashes in Uganda, and how, though the intrepid writer's ribs were broken and his skull burned and cracked, he insisted on taking his accustomed place there, in the corner, raising toasts to his friends and upbraiding his wife for worrying about his health.

"He lives hard," Patrick averred. "He won't ever go easy on himself or on his work."

Beatrice studied the menu while the waiter went to the bar to order her glass of white Veneto wine and the first of the four Montgomerys Patrick would have with his meal. By the second, when the waiter brought out a platter with a whole fish splayed across it, Patrick declared Venice the only place in the world where a writer might do his best work, and this was because the sea penetrated the very pores of the city.

"That's an interesting idea," Beatrice said.

The waiter set the platter on a side table. Taking up a knife and spoon, he began expertly separating the head from the body.

"What's he doing?" Patrick asked Beatrice, though the waiter understood him perfectly.

"He's cleaning your fish."

"Stop!" Patrick exclaimed, to the surprise of the waiter, who raised the knife and spoon over the fish, his eyes wide and focused on Patrick.

"Give it to me," Patrick demanded. "I'm damned if I need someone else to clean my fish."

"As you like," said the waiter, lowering the dish in front of him.

Patrick went at it with his too-large knife, pushing aside the head and working the blade tip along the back spine. The waiter stood by, holding the utensils before him, as there was now no place to set them down. He exchanged a look with Beatrice, which she understood. Amusement, laced with sympathy.

"Can we get some potatoes with this?" Patrick said testily.

⟡

Patrick had little interest in looking at paintings or churches, though he did marvel at the tidal patterns left by the sea on the stone floor of San Marco. "So the water just rolls right into the church," he said.

"Actually," Beatrice told him, "it rises slowly. Here it bubbles up from the drains. People go swimming in it. It's called *acqua alta*."

"Meaning?" he said, with the tinge of impatience that colored every chance encounter with his wife's native tongue.

"High water," she said. "They put up platforms to walk on, but most people just wear boots."

"What a crazy place," Patrick concluded.

They took the boat to the Lido, which Patrick pronounced a poor facsimile of a beach. The big hotels were shuttered for the season and only a few hearty tourists wandered along the shore, clutching their coats closed against the ceaseless wind. The sand was brown and coarse, dingy compared to the dramatic white dunes of Cape Cod. The bathing cabins lined up in long, orderly rows, each with a padlocked door and dull tin roof, were in need of paint. "It looks like a prison camp," Patrick observed.

"There is something seedy about it," Beatrice agreed.

Patrick strode away from her to the edge of the water and stood for some moments looking out at the cloud-enshrouded sun. When he came back to Beatrice, his expression was determined. "This is not my ocean," he said.

Another day they went to Murano to see the glass-makers, and one chilly morning they walked the length of the Zattere, all the way to the customs house. On the last afternoon they set out on Riva degli Schiavoni and explored the residential Castello neighborhood, stopping at a small trattoria that Patrick praised for its pasta with clams and Beatrice for its seclusion and discreet service.

They had never enjoyed sex so often and at such length, passionate and playful by turns. Patrick said it was because she was pregnant, so he never had even the slightest anxiety that she might become so. "But it's weird," he said one evening after a particularly athletic encounter, "I feel like we're not alone."

Beatrice laughed.

"No, I mean it. The baby may have some deep memory of Venice. He may be terrified of Venice. Just the thought of it could give him migraine headaches." He clutched his head between his palms, groaning, "No, Papa, no, please. Not Venice. My poor head." Then they both laughed until tears stood in their eyes.

The Venetian honeymoon. The honeymoon of the pregnant bride. They would call it that. Were they happy? She wasn't sure. She consciously made an effort to be for her husband what he had been for her, an enthusiastic guide to the places she loved, and she was honest enough to recall with dismay how underwhelmed she must often have seemed to him, how critical and dismissive of the simple charms of Boston, of the rugged beauty of Cape Cod, which she had found too windy, too raw. But when Patrick scoffed at the treasures of the ancient world, when he dismissed churches packed with priceless art as "monuments to superstition," when the beach, when even the ocean, couldn't compete with the dreary, chilly little world he came from, she felt he lacked important powers of discernment. His inability to speak the language increased his defensiveness and made him dependent on Beatrice in ways he found intolerable.

After the trip to the Lido, he was rough with her in the hotel room bed, which made her fight back and call him a brute; then he was confidential and tender, holding her gently, stroking her back while he speculated about their future, their baby. "We'll have to find a bigger apartment," he said. "It would be good to have a yard." They discussed names, agreeing on the name for a son, David, after Patrick's father.

What they didn't discuss was money. Beatrice had the sense that this conversation was being held at bay. They had a joint account at the bank in Boston, his earnings and her fellowship money, but Beatrice knew Patrick now assumed she had an income of her own that she'd purposefully told him nothing about. It was a confrontation they had tacitly agreed to postpone. Venice was a distraction, a lark, an escape from the reality of who they were and what they must become. The conversation about money, Beatrice thought, should take place on solid ground, not in this fantastic watery world of mist and shadow.

It should take place, she concluded, at Villa Chiara.

⌘

They took the train from Venice to Florence, then changed at Santa Maria Novella for Siena, where Beatrice's Aunt Valeria waited for them with the car. Patrick was charmed by the Italian trains; the compartments reminded him of foreign films he'd seen, and he enjoyed standing in the passage, feet planted firmly apart, gazing out the window at the passing scene. It was all men there, most smoking cigarettes and studiously not speaking to each other. This man's world suited him.

Valeria, the more affectionate and emotionally stable of the aunts, had aged markedly in Beatrice's absence, and the sight of her on the platform, stoop-shouldered, painfully gaunt, tightly wrapped in her red wool coat with the unfashionable pink knitted cloche hat she'd made herself crushing her still-blond ringlets flat against her forehead, brought a sigh to Beatrice's lips. "Poor thing," she said as Patrick wrestled the luggage down the narrow steps from the train. Valeria spotted her, raised her hand, and approached, smiling brightly, birdlike in her sprightly intensity. Aunt and niece embraced, murmuring endearments, and when they parted Beatrice held her aunt's hand as she introduced her to Patrick, first in Italian and then in English.

"Pleased to meet you," Patrick said, looking at Beatrice. Valeria said something in Italian, also keeping her eyes on her niece. "You're pleased to meet each other," Beatrice said. "Let's go on to the car."

The car was a Fiat sedan with just room enough in the trunk for two of their bags. Patrick squeezed the smaller cases into the back seat and climbed in beside them. After a brief exchange, Valeria got in on the passenger side and Beatrice crossed in front of the car to the driver's seat. Soon they were hurtling along the Strada Statale, the two women talking animatedly while Patrick stared out the window, trying to let the Italian words flow past him without getting into his head. They left the highway and descended to a narrow two-way country road that ran between low hills flanked with farmhouses, winter fields mowed to flat gold, and vineyards pruned to rows of dry sticks attached by lines of wire strung between posts. The only green was the somber dark foliage of the cypresses gathered in close groups like sentries near the farmhouses. The houses were all alike, of various sizes, painted stucco or ocher stone, with pergolas or terraces attached and the same brick-red tile roofs dusted with snow.

At last, after nearly a mile of flattened sunflowers on one side and an unbroken stone wall on the other, Beatrice called out, "Here we are" and turned abruptly in to an open gateway, braking sharply to a halt before the long, pale front of Villa Chiara.

Patrick stared blankly through the window, taking in the peculiar triangular staircase with its rectangular viewing area at the top. As he watched, one of the oversized doors opened and a tall, dark-haired woman dressed all in white stepped out and advanced to the rail, where she stood very still, her palms resting on either side, elbows bent, looking down at the car.

"*Ecco Celestia,*" said Valeria as she opened the door and stepped out onto the drive.

"Aunt Celestia is a little strange at first," Beatrice said to Patrick. "A bit of a recluse."

"She looks like Emily Dickinson," Patrick said.

Beatrice turned in the driver's seat, smiling back at her husband. "That's a good comparison," she said. "She's very shy of men, but she'll be fine if you're kind to her."

"She won't know if I'm kind or not," he said, "since she can't understand a word I say."

"She knows who you are," Beatrice assured him. "They're both excited that you're here, and they know you're a writer. They had my grandfather's library cleaned and supplied the desk themselves in your honor. No one has used it for years."

"How do they know I'm a writer?" Patrick asked.

"Valeria said my mother told them."

"Really," said Patrick. He climbed out of the car and turned to pull out the cases. When he looked up at the villa again, he saw that Celestia had retreated into the darkness beyond the open door.

At that time the house was undivided, and the impression of vastness was increased by there being so many unused rooms, flowing one into another on either side of the dining room. On one side, they passed through a comfortable sitting room with a deep, empty, cold fireplace. Beyond this were two closed doors and two steps down to the bedroom and bath the aunts had prepared for their young guests.

On the other side, a wide stone hall led to the aunts' bedrooms, with a bath between, followed by the chapel, in which one or the other of the sisters was often lost in prayer. Beyond this, in a world unto its own, two casement doors opened into the library, once the refuge of the revered Giacomo Salviati.

Villa Chiara had been a summer house for the family, Beatrice explained to Patrick, hence in the library the book collection was small, the windows large. A green leather-topped table dominated the center of the room. This was the desk the aunts had prepared for Patrick, complete with an unopened ream of paper, a box of ball-point pens, another of pencils, and two kinds of erasers, kneaded and hard. An Olivetti typewriter occupied so small a space on the vast surface of the table that it appeared to be afloat in a sea of green.

"Ah," Patrick said. "An Olivetti."

Beatrice chuckled. Patrick used a Royal typewriter his father had given him in high school. He considered her Olivetti an inferior machine in every respect. "I don't know where they found it," Beatrice observed, examining the machine. "It looks fairly new."

Patrick turned away from the machine and went to a window, where he stood looking into an enormous cypress someone had planted too close to the house a long time ago. An agitated bird he didn't recognize picked its way among the branches. "It's very quiet here," he said. "It's like a tomb." He looked back at his wife.

Beatrice stood at the table, unnaturally still, her hands stretched across her expanded girth, her eyes unfocused, inward, as if listening. A beam of sunlight passing through the upper panes of a window shattered over her hair, her shoulders, and her hands, so that she appeared to radiate light.

"Are you okay?" Patrick asked.

She raised her eyes to her husband, her lips slightly parted, her eyebrows lifted in an expression of mischievous glee. "He kicked me," she said.

⌇⌘⌇

Dinner was a tureen of bean soup with bread in it, followed by a plate of cheese. There was nothing to drink in the house but wine and limoncello, so Patrick drank half a bottle of each. Valeria exchanged local news with Beatrice, who translated to Patrick until he begged her to stop. "It's all about people I don't know," he complained. Celestia, wrapped in an ecclesiastical white cape with slits for sleeves, sat straight-backed and silent, ferrying large spoonfuls of soup to her puckered lips with the concentration of a brain surgeon. Her sister spoke to her once, which provoked her to set the spoon down in the saucer, pat her lips with the napkin, and murmur a monosyllabic reply. Patrick, lifting his glass, gazed at her in frank wonderment. Not once during the meal did she allow her eyes to stray near him.

At last the young couple retired to the cold, high-ceilinged bedroom with its stone floors and deep-silled windows, so devoid of furnishing that their voices echoed and Patrick affected a conspiratorial whisper. The room, Patrick observed, was "as dark as Egypt." Beatrice felt her way to the bedside and switched on the lamp. The paltry blob of yellowish light it cast straight down onto the table made him laugh. They shed their clothes on either side of the high tester bed, climbed in beneath the stack of wool blankets, and clutched each other like runaway children. "This place is so bizarre," he said.

"It's just a house," said Beatrice.

"The aunts are weird," Patrick concluded.

Beatrice chuckled. "Wait until you meet the cousins," she said.

"Are they coming here?"

"No," she said. "They live in Lucca."

Patrick thought that with luck he would never meet the cousins. He raised his head and kissed his wife, softly at first and then greedily, possessively, and she responded with equal ardor. Moving together through the familiar rhythms of their lovemaking comforted them both, as if their mutual passion threw up a solid barrier that blocked the antagonistic claims of family, culture, and nationality. For a little while they belonged to nothing but each other.

When they were still, drifting to sleep, Patrick's lips pressed light kisses against her cheek, her ear, her clavicle, and she whispered, "I love you, I love you." She felt the faint stirring deep inside her, the little fish of a baby flailing in the dark night sea of her womb. She pressed her palm against her abdomen, rubbing it gently. "I love you," she said again.

⌛

In Florence their sleep had been fitful, but at Villa Chiara a deep, dreamless slumber possessed them until well into the morning. "I always sleep well here," Beatrice observed when they woke. She pulled in the clock from the nightstand.

"It's because the room is so cold," Patrick said, rubbing his eyes with his fists. "What time is it?"

"It's ten o'clock," she said. "The aunts will think we've died."

"I'm starving," said Patrick.

In the kitchen the woodstove poured out a welcoming and continuous tide of heat. The aunts were nowhere in sight. Patrick examined the stove while Beatrice opened the refrigerator and took out eggs, bread, prosciutto, a plate of chopped spinach. "I'll make you a big American breakfast," she said.

"How old is this thing?" Patrick asked, lifting the wooden handle of a flat iron burner and peering into the firebox below.

"I have no idea," Beatrice said. "Very old, I'd guess."

He bent over the front, opened and closed the heavy iron and glass door. "It's a beautiful thing," he said.

This amused Beatrice. Rococo cornices and frescoed ceilings did nothing for Patrick, but an ancient, serviceable stove touched his practical New England heart. He took up a split log from the neat stack in the bin next to the stove. "Who chops the wood?" he asked.

"The caretaker does it," Beatrice replied. "It comes from the grounds. There's a bit of forest at the back, and it provides enough for us all."

"The cah-taker," Patrick repeated, pronouncing it Bostonially.

"It's a family," Beatrice explained. "The Falcos. They've been with us forever. We'll go for a walk after breakfast, and we may meet one of them."

Patrick shoved the log into the fire and carefully closed the door. "So do we own the Falcos?"

"Please," Beatrice said. "Don't be ridiculous. They are our neighbors. Anna is my friend."

"Right," Patrick said, rising from his admiration of the stove. He surveyed the plates Beatrice had set on the table. "More of this strange ham," he said. "How do they get a pig to come out like that?"

❧

"I'm going to take you all the way there," Patrick had said that first day, when he found her flat on her back on the ice. Walking had been how they found each other. "Take a walk with me," Patrick said whenever she was exasperated with him, and they would follow some well-worn path around the park or along the waterfront, talking it out, revealing themselves to each other, because, Beatrice thought, they were still, after nearly a year, such strangers. "Let's walk through the vineyard," she said now, as they stood side by side on the drive. She was wearing the "immortal" boots, as Patrick called them, and a thick American wool sweater he'd given her at Christmas. It was a cold, bright day, and the ground was brittle underfoot but not frozen. He wore a soft black leather jacket, jeans, and sneakers, all he would need, he maintained, for what Tuscany had to offer in the way of winter. They passed the limonaia, closed up now, sheltering enormous pots of leafless trees, and set off into the garden.

"So how big is this place?" Patrick asked, by way of an opening.

"About two hundred and fifty hectares," Beatrice replied. "Some of it here, some across the road."

"What's a hectare to an acre?"

"Nearly two and a half."

"Bigger?"

"Hectare is bigger, yes."

Patrick did the arithmetic. "Wow," he said. "How many people live on it?"

"I don't really know. A lot of it is tenant farmers now. Some of them own their houses and some land, others rent, more or less."

"More or less?"

"They turn over a percentage of their profits to us. We maintain the buildings."

Patrick nodded.

"It's a very old system," Beatrice said.

They had come to a gate, propped open with a pitchfork. Beyond it, long lines of neatly tied, leafless grapevines stretched uphill and down in every direction. Patrick followed Beatrice, who struck out on a dry path along the edge of the field. "So all this is yours," he said. It wasn't a question.

Beatrice paused until he drew up beside her. She tucked her hand inside his elbow. "It belongs to my family," she said. "It's not mine. I don't have anything to do with it. It's a business. And these days, sadly, not a very profitable one." They walked on, steadily uphill. "There are a lot of families like mine now," she continued. "Once they were rich and powerful, but the war bankrupted the government and destroyed a lot of property. In our case my uncle was profligate and made bad investments. When he died my mother had to sell the palazzo that had been in our family for almost five hundred years."

At the crest of the hill, Beatrice paused again. They looked out over a landscape of cultivated orderliness, attenuated vineyards giving over to smoky olive groves and ashen stands of oak. A neat line of cypresses pointed to the crest of another hill, where the ocher wall of a farmhouse showed through a cluster of pine; all was gray and brown, with only the dark gray-green of the evergreens for color. Beatrice sighed, leaning against her husband's side, and he looked down at her, feeling through his arm the wave of contentment that passed through her at the sight of her ancestral lands.

"You're an aristocrat," he said.

She blew out a puff of air at the charge. "I suppose I am," she agreed.

"And this place has everything in the world to do with you."

"That's true," she said.

She had thought to go into some detail on the subject of her family's financial situation. To her surprise, Patrick had penetrated to the heart of it; her family and their property, this property, had everything to do with her. If he understood that, she reasoned, what else was there to say? And in fact she had sketched for him everything she knew about it. They walked on, down the hill and across a mowed meadow, golden in the sun and lined with dark ilex shrubs. This gave onto a kind of lane; hard, bare ground forked in two directions, one meandering uphill to the farmhouse they had seen from the distance. Beatrice took this uphill path.

"Is this where the cah-taker lives?" asked Patrick.

"No," she said. "They're off the main road, across from the villa."

"Who lives here?" he asked. But as they approached Patrick guessed the answer to his question. The shutters were tightly closed, and a thick softwood vine had escaped a trellis and now blocked the upper portion of the door.

"No one," Beatrice said. "There were tenants before the war, but the father was killed and the wife took the children back to her family in Genova. The fields got parceled out, and no one needed the house, so it just sits here."

"It's a nice-looking house," Patrick said. He walked across the front and looked out over the fields behind it. "This is definitely the middle of nowhere," he said.

That, in a phrase—in a nutshell, Beatrice thought, because it was an English expression that amused her, and for which there was no close Italian approximation—was Patrick's verdict on Villa Chiara. It was nowhere. There was nothing to see but fields and trees, nothing to do but eat. The aunts, he pointed out, never even turned on the lights; like cows, they went to bed when the sun set. When Beatrice encouraged him to take advantage of the library to work on his writing, he scoffed at the idea.

"Writers live in the world," he said. "They don't sit at a desk in a frigid room waiting for inspiration, they go out and find it. They talk, they argue, they size up the competition, they go to the desk in a white heat."

A few years later, after two failed suicide attempts and several rounds of electroshock therapy, Patrick's idol, Ernest Hemingway, shot himself on an isolated estate in Idaho. Patrick claimed the great writer's wife had insisted they move there. She wanted him to herself. She had taken him out of the world so that he could work in solitude, and that solitude had killed him.

PART 4

PART 2

A Ghost Story

On my last night at Villa Chiara, I dreamed of Beatrice's
mad uncle Sandro. At least I thought it was him in the
dream. I woke to an insistent rapping on the glass pane of
the kitchen doors, oddly syncopated with the ticking of the ceiling
fan. It was near dawn; a mauve, silky light coated the furniture and
slicked the stone floor. I sat up, drowsy and confused, feeling about
the pillows for the T-shirt I'd pulled off in the night, tightening the
drawstring of the linen shorts that doubled as my pajamas. "Coming," I muttered, making my way to the steps. Whoever was at the
door could see me descending—bare feet and legs first, then trunk,
and finally my sleep-shocked head—but the rapping continued.

A man, dressed all in white—even his hair, sticking out wildly in
uncombed tufts over his ears, was white, and his complexion was
sickly pale. His eyes, colorless in the early-morning light, stared
fixedly but not at me. I had the impression that he was blind. I
approached the door, presenting myself bravely. "What do you
want?" I asked.

He continued the mindless rapping against the glass. *He's in shock,*
I thought. "Who are you?" I asked, and as I spoke the answer came
to me: *This is Sandro.*

I woke up. For some moments I lay still, absorbing the details of
the dream. It was childishly obvious, as my dreams often are, yet

vivid and sensual; my feet felt cool from the stone floor, my T-shirt had ridden up to my breasts; I hadn't taken it off, so putting it on was part of the dream.

Beatrice's uncle Sandro. Why would he be knocking on the limonaia door in the driveway where he was shot? Was he looking for me or someone else? Or was he just a lost ghost wandering in the dawn?

He was looking for me, I concluded, drifting back to sleep. He came to say, "Remember me."

As I packed my suitcases, checking under the bed and in the deepest recesses of the wardrobe, I felt a pleasant anticipation—I would be spending a few days in Rome with an old friend before flying back to Philadelphia—and also sadness. I had come to feel at home in this out-of-the-way place, and I'd made a friend who interested me. I zipped the bigger suitcase and tugged it down the stairs to the kitchen. Then I took down the three-cup caffettiera from the shelf and set it up to make espresso. I had a similar small pot I'd purchased in Siena tucked into my luggage. I was now addicted to the morning espresso.

The previous day Ruggiero had left for Bologna to visit his mother before he returned to the States. Beatrice and I had agreed that she would go to the bar for our cornetti and bring them to my outdoor table under the roof, where it was cool and fragrant. When I took the plates and butter to the table, I saw that the Cinquecento was gone. The high, cool, secretive front of the villa glowered down at me, and I was struck again by the irony of its name. Villa Chiara. Chiaroscuro would be more accurate. The sun was already brightening the glass panes of the limonaia, which faced southeast, and I realized that my terrace was the only outdoor dining available on the property. As my fellow Americans never stop observing, Italians prefer to eat outside, a practice my countrymen insistently and mistakenly refer to as dining *al fresco,* to the befuddlement of Italians, as *al fresco* means "in the cooler," that is, jail. But here, at

Villa Chiara, no one was eating outside but me. When Sandro was young and the family visited in the summer, perhaps they had their lunch here. There might have been a larger table jutting into the drive, perhaps even an awning tacked onto the roofline or an umbrella. Beatrice's decision to preempt this space for her son and her potential tenants must have greatly outraged the cousins, who, after all, lived in the villa year-round.

I went back inside for the water bottle and returned to find the Cinquecento in its habitual post, the engine running. Beatrice engaged briefly in questing about the interior before she turned off the motor, threw open the driver's door, and stepped out into the fresh morning air, gripping the paper bag from the bar like a purse.

"Good morning," she said, taking a few quick strides to the table. "I hope you slept well. I can never sleep before a trip."

I took the bag and arranged the bread on a plate as she leaned across the table to pour out a glass of water. "I dreamed of your uncle," I said. "I'll just put on the coffee." In the kitchen I lit the burner and stood gazing at the pot. How quickly routine takes hold, I thought. In just a month my life in these few rooms had taken on substance, from waking until sleep, that held me like a charm or a spell, one I was reluctant to break. "I could stay here forever," I said softly, though this wasn't entirely true. I enjoyed the monotony and the heat, but I truly missed a few close friends, the excellent library at my college, and my cat, Stella, who was being cared for by my neighbor.

The pot seethed and spat white steam. After a few moments I slid it from the burner and carried it to the terrace. Beatrice was gazing wistfully out at the garden. "I wish you were staying," she said. "These plums are ripe and will have to be picked next week. It takes all day."

"Do you do it yourself?" I asked.

"Oh no. Anna and her family all come, and we make a *festa* of it. Then she makes jam for days."

"I would like to do that," I said.

"It's the last task of summer," she said. "As soon as that's done, I'm off to Munich to see my grandson, and then back to Pough-keepsie in time for the first class."

I took up a cornetto and tore it in half. Beatrice in Munich. I couldn't picture it. "Do you drive?" I asked.

This idea made her laugh. "Picture me on the autobahn in the Cinquecento," she said. "No. I fly out of Firenze. Then from Munich to New York."

"How old is your grandson?"

"He's just turned three. His mother is pregnant again."

"That's great," I said.

"Is it?" she said. "I don't think so. I hope she stops at two."

"Do you like her?"

"Do I like Greta?" she said, posing the question to herself. "She's very organized, very efficient."

I said nothing.

"Very German. Chilly. Crude, but not unkind. I do believe she loves David. They're happy together, full of plans for the future."

I chewed my bread.

"If he's happy, I'm happy," she concluded.

So she doesn't like her daughter-in-law, I thought. "What's your grandson's name?" I asked.

She smiled, raising her eyebrows in disbelief. "His name is Bern-hard Patrick Doyle."

"Wow," I said.

"Thereby eliminating entirely the pernicious Italian influence."

"Does he look Italian?"

"He looks like a little Teutonic lord. Blue eyes, blond hair, square jaw. He's a sweet child, very sunny and full of giggles."

"What does he call you?"

"He calls me Nonna. I insisted on that. I am not being Oma."

"Do they visit you in America?" I asked.

"Not often. David comes over once a year in the fall to see his father on the Cape." She sipped her espresso. "Then he visits me briefly in New York. Last summer they all came here for a few weeks. Recently he told me he was thinking of bringing the family to the Cape next July instead of coming here. Greta finds Tuscan country life dull, and they like the beaches there."

"Is your son close to his father?"

"His father is a pitiful wreck," she said, not censoriously, but rather as if she were describing some untoward, tragic result of lax oversight. "David feels sorry for him, and also I think he feels obligated to him, though why he would feel that way, I don't know."

"Do you see him?"

"I haven't seen Patrick in twenty years," she said. She took up a cornetto and tore off the end. I was carefully spreading butter over my own.

"You Americans and your butter!" she exclaimed, effectively changing the subject.

"You should try it," I said, sliding the butter dish toward her.

"Please, no." She waved the dish away. A small bird swooped down from the bougainvillea to investigate the crumbs we'd scattered on the stones.

"What is that bird?" I asked.

"A *pettirosso*," she said.

"Redbreast," I translated. "But it's not what we call a robin."

"No," Beatrice agreed. She dropped a larger morsel and the bird skittered away, then rushed back to toss the crumb about with its beak. "So what did my uncle have to say in your dream?" she asked.

The dream came back to me in ghostly black-and-white. "He didn't speak," I said. "He was tapping at the door, looking in. He had white hair, watery eyes, dressed all in white, very pale, perfectly ghostly."

"He was wearing a white hospital gown the night he arrived here," Beatrice said.

"Where was the asylum?"

"I'm not sure," she said. "It was a long drive. My mother left in the morning and came back after dark."

I imagined the scene. After forty years in a psychiatric institution, that wild night ride through a war zone must have been a nightmare for the luckless Sandro. "In my dream he seemed confused," I said. "I thought he was blind. Or in shock."

Beatrice nodded slowly, seriously. "I think it must have been him," she said. "Poor soul."

"I didn't know you believed in ghosts."

"I don't, actually," she said. "I think you dreamed up my uncle."

"That sounds like something Luca would say," I observed.

She lowered her chin, pulling away from this comparison. "My God," she said. "Don't tell me I'm like Luca!" In the next moment we heard the click and drag of the cousins' door, and as our eyes widened in wonderment, Luca emerged from the bower. We burst into simultaneous shouts of laughter.

He paused on the drive, patting his pockets, extracting his lighter and a cigarette.

"He's desperate," Beatrice said sotto voce. "Mimma won't let him smoke in the house." We watched him light a cigarette, take a deep drag, and slip the lighter back into his pants pocket. I knew him to be close in age to Beatrice, but his posture—hunched—and his complexion, pallid and wizened from smoking, made him look much older. After another drag and a flick of ash onto the drive, he fixed his gaze upon us and raised his free hand in a limp greeting.

"*Buongiorno,* Luca," Beatrice said pleasantly.

He approached, weirdly cautious, as if we might spring up at him. "Good morning," he said. "You are cheerful this morning."

Beatrice and I exchanged a furtive glance; we wouldn't let on that Luca was himself the source of our mirth. "Well," she said, "we are amusing ourselves. But really it is very sad, because Jan is leaving today."

His expressionless eyes rested on me. "I trust you have enjoyed your stay with us," he said.

"I have," I said, firm in my resolve to offer Luca nothing to gather about me.

"And you have concluded your research?"

"Research leads to more research," I said. "I don't see an end in sight."

"She's always asking questions," Beatrice put in. "She just asked me one I don't know the answer to, but you may remember. Do you know where Uncle Sandro was before my mother brought him here during the war?"

I watched Luca's face as this question activated the mechanism that dropped a portcullis across the portal to his high disdaining tower of self-regard. "How could this possibly be of interest to you?" he asked, tilting his head to look down on me from an indirect angle.

"I have a general strategy for understanding the past," I said. "The way a society treats children, dogs, and the mentally ill tells a lot about it."

"This is your idea of a strategy?"

"Don't you think it's true?"

"The Germans are mad for dogs," Beatrice observed. "Not so keen on children, I think."

Luca frowned at his cousin. "You are frivolous," he observed.

Beatrice shrugged. "So do you know where Sandro was?"

His gaze drifted to the staircase of the villa, up to the oppressive baronial door. He brought the cigarette to his lips, drawing in a quick puff of smoke, releasing it with a dry, shallow cough. *Those cigarettes are killing him,* I thought. A long moment passed in which we all attended on Luca's response.

"It was a psychiatric hospital near Milano," he said. "A vast old villa owned by the city. One of my teachers was there before the war, Dr. Ugo Cerletti. A brilliant mind. He later won the Nobel Prize."

I marveled at this detailed answer. "So the treatment was enlightened," I ventured.

This made Luca smile his weary, dismissive smile. "You might say so," he said.

The Interrupted Life
of Sandro Salviati

S andro Salviati was the oldest son of Giacomo Salviati, a man of property who had married Flavia Belli, the daughter of a Florentine banker, thereby enlarging the family coffers so vastly that the Villa Chiara was relegated to the status of a summer refuge from the heat in Firenze. The marriage produced five children: Sandro, the oldest, followed by two daughters, Celestia and Valeria, another son, Marco, and one more daughter, Maria. Marco, his mother's favorite, was spoiled and adored by his parents and destined to play a part in the undoing of his older brother, the rightful heir to the family estate.

Sandro, a dreamy child, immersed himself in tales of the Knights Templar and later in the works of Victor Hugo—he read French with ease—as well as those of Sir Walter Scott, translated into Italian. He was the darling of nuns and indulged by priests for his gentle disposition and exaggerated notions of valor. He exhibited musical ability at an early age, had a clear, mellow tenor voice, and could play both piano and violin creditably. He took a great interest in his sisters' education, which his parents did not, and it was thanks to his intervention that Celestia and Valeria were allowed to study with his tutor and became so independent in their thinking that they fostered hopes of pursuing studies at the University of Bologna, hopes that were summarily squashed by their father, who was more invested in their marriages than in their minds.

Sandro was at ease in the bustling, acquisitive, venal world of his large family. Art and music engaged his imagination. He had no interest in business, and so, as he came of age, he constituted a disappointment to his father and a mystery to his mother. This lady consoled her husband by recourse to conciliatory adjectives, such as *sensitive* and *artistic,* to excuse her gentle son. Sandro treated her with a courteous reserve, thereby keeping her at a manageable distance.

His brother, Marco, was his opposite in spirit and flesh, a thriving, hungry, obstreperous boy, quick to laughter as well as to anger and indifferent to his siblings and his adoring mother; his considerable energies were focused on surpassing—in wealth, power, and acumen—his vigorous father.

When Sandro turned twenty-five, his parents naturally looked about for an alliance that would bring profit and prestige to the family. Sandro had other ideas. No one knew how or where Silvia Rienzi, the lovely, simple daughter of a grocer who purveyed vegetables in the market near Santa Croce, captured his heart. A new century had dawned, business was good, change was in the air, but no one, including Silvia's father, seriously imagined that a grocer might marry his daughter into a family as rich and powerful as the Salviatis. Yet this was what Sandro proposed one morning after Mass as he walked with his father, his mother, his sisters, and Marco ranged behind, in the Sunday doldrums of Via Porta Rossa. Silvia, Sandro admitted to his father, would bring no dowry, but her beauty, gentleness, and kind heart were assets beyond price and recommended her as a wife and mother who would earn the respect of all who met her. So in his decorous, distant way Sandro offered a proposition he must have known would stop his father in his tracks, and this was exactly what happened. Giacomo pulled up short and gripped his oldest son hard by the elbow. Turning upon the astonished young man as the rest of his family jammed in close behind, Giacomo raised his free hand and, with enough force to send him staggering, slammed his open palm hard against Sandro's temple. His mother rushed to her son's aid, shouting a few outraged epithets after her departing husband, who moved off briskly in the direction of home.

That blow was Giacomo's only comment on his son's proposed marriage to a poor girl. When Sandro and the family arrived at the palazzo, the father was closed away in his library, where all understood no entry was permitted. Before the dinner hour, letters were dispatched in the hands of servants, but no one knew to whom they were addressed or what they contained. Letters left Palazzo Salviati at all hours, and though his mother fretted, Sandro didn't suspect that these messages might affect his fate. At noon the family gathered around the long table, where they stood behind their chairs for several minutes until they heard the click of the library key turning in the lock, then the creak of the heavy door, and then the brisk, sharp cracks of their father's boots slapping against the marble floor. He appeared, as he always did, distracted, but the sight of his waiting family brought, as it always did, a lift of his eyebrows, a turning up at the corners of his mouth, a softening of his eyes, an exhalation of breath that suggested the arrival of a relaxed and congenial frame of mind. *"Si prega di sedersi,"* he said courteously, and as his family commenced pulling out their chairs, taking their seats, the girls chattered among themselves about some shopping plans that concerned them. A signal from their mother brought two servants lingering near the sideboard to attention. Taking up the soup tureen and the two platters of meat, they approached the table.

No one spoke of the harsh incident on the street. Marco immediately brought up some business with his father, a legal detail he had consulted a professor at the law school about, which turned on a deed of property transfer. The sisters bantered with their mother, who recommended an eligible young banker from Milano recently transferred to the Banco di Santo Spirito in Firenze. Sandro couldn't meet his father's eyes and spent the soup course concentrating on his spoon. When the bowls were cleared away and the meat platters handed round, he glanced about the table at his family and had the sensation that he was invisible. He didn't mind, as it allowed him to entertain sweet thoughts of Silvia. His father's anger was certain to pass; he would be reconciled to his son's choice. He had only to meet Silvia, to observe her open, frank affection for her future husband. *Husband,* Sandro thought, a magical word. Where might they live to raise their children, their many children? At first his mother would want them to stay in the city, but perhaps they could settle at the Villa Chiara. Silvia would enjoy a country life. He pictured her in a straw hat and apron—she had no pretensions about dress— reaching into the branches of a plum tree to pull down a bough for her little boy and girl, who rushed forward to pluck the shiny, ripe fruit for their baskets.

"I have business in Siena in the morning," Giacomo announced at the end of the meal, while the servants filled their small cups with steaming coffee. "I'll leave this afternoon and stay over at Villa Chiara. Sandro, I want you to accompany me."

"Of course," Sandro agreed. He noted the curious smirk Marco gave him, as if he knew something unpleasant about what this trip held in store for his brother. But what could he know?

After the meal Sandro sent a message to his sweetheart, carried by a servant who knew the house. *Dearest,* he wrote. *I've spoken to my father. He will come around, I'm sure. I go to Siena with him very shortly and we will have leisure to talk over my proposal. I will persuade him, never fear. Dearest heart, I am all your own, Sandro.*

Giacomo was a great believer in progress, in engines and machines of all kinds. He was invested in a textile mill in Pistoia, as well as a farm machine factory near Prato that would, he assured his son, revolutionize agriculture. Soon one man riding a machine could hay a field in half the time it took six men to do the job. Plowing would not require animals at all. This was what he talked to his son about on the train and then in the carriage, drawn by two sturdy dray horses that met them at the Siena station. Sandro understood that his father was taking him into his confidence, as he had already done with Marco, who knew all the ins and outs of the family's many financial arrangements. Sadly, such talk made Sandro's head ache; he couldn't follow it, and his only thought, which he advanced timidly during a pause for breath on his father's part, was that the six men released from haying would have nothing to do.

"No?" His father laughed. "Nothing to do? What do you think they will do? Take up reading novels and playing the violin, like you?"

The thought of Vergilio di Pietro, a thick-necked bull of a man, tenant of fifty Salviati hectares just south of the Villa Chiara, taking up a novel from his kitchen table and settling into his old stuffed armchair for an afternoon of reading brought a snigger to Sandro's lips.

His father gave a snort of agreement. "No," he repeated. "There is always more work to do on the farm and never enough hands to do it. Machinery will free the workers to repair their wretched houses and clean up their chicken coops and their pigpens."

So Giacomo ran on, and Sandro despaired of introducing the subject dearest to his own interest, his forthcoming marriage to Silvia Rienzi. Yet he understood that Silvia was definitely in the air between them, and it calmed him to feel the presence of his beloved. Why else would his father have insisted on taking him away from the distraction of the family? It occurred to him that he had not been alone with his father for an extended period since he was a child, before Marco was born. He resolved to wait until dinner, when they would be in the comfortable, serene, walled privacy of Villa Chiara.

≈✿≈

At the villa, Lucia Falco opened the shutters, uncovered the furniture in the dining and sitting rooms, made up two bedrooms, and prepared a meal, all on short notice, as Flavia had called her after lunch to say that her husband and son were on the train from the city and would arrive before dark. Lucia was unruffled, confident, and especially pleased that Sandro would visit the villa. As a boy, he'd spent many a summer afternoon lounging in the shade of the ancient olive tree outside the kitchen door, book in hand, having assured her that her quiet presence was more agreeable to him than the constant chatter and bickering among his siblings at the villa. If her own son, Stefano, wasn't working in the vineyard, he passed the time playing cards with Sandro, or they kicked a ball up and down the drive that ran from the road to her bright, spotless little house. She observed that Sandro was indifferent to the advantages of his father's wealth and power. He took no pleasure in playing the heir to the estate. He preferred a passive role. If Stefano cheated at cards, Sandro pretended he didn't notice; if his father was out of temper, he appeared at Lucia's door, determined to avoid a confrontation.

Now he was grown, a willowy young man with heavy dark curls and liquid brown eyes, a diffident yet amiable fellow whom any smart young woman would identify as a desirable fish to catch. Lucia didn't guess that his father had brought him to the villa specifically to remove the first of what would doubtless be a succession of hooks lodged in his innocent jaws.

After supper was served, Lucia took a seat just inside the kitchen door to wait until the father and son finished eating and were ready for their coffee. From her perch she could hear snatches of their conversation, which was largely carried on by Giacomo with occasional murmurs from his son. The father spoke of problems at one of the olive presses; a hundred barrels of oil had been spoiled.

Then, after mumbling from Sandro, Giacomo spoke firmly of the necessity to guard against pilfering and waste among the tenants, though he admitted that for the most part, the Salviati retainers were reliable and honest, having been on the land since his grandfather's time. A passage of silver ringing against china signified the consumption of the meal. To her pleasure Lucia heard Sandro say clearly, "No one prepares *bietole* better than Lucia." Giacomo grunted in agreement. After another brief silence punctuated by the sawing of cutlery, the swish of wine refilling glasses, the barely audible smacking of lips and grinding of jaws, Giacomo directed his voice to the doorway and said, "Lucia, we are ready for coffee."

She stood up, entered quietly, her focus on the empty dishes.

"Lucia," Sandro said. "A delicious meal. Thank you."

She met his innocent eyes. "It's nothing," she demurred.

"How is Stefano?"

"Very well," she replied. "He is engaged to be married in the fall."

"Married!" Giacomo exclaimed. "And who is the fortunate bride?"

"Her name is Angela Ticio," Lucia replied. "She's a teacher at the middle school in Asciano."

"That's wonderful," Sandro said, keeping his eyes steadfastly fixed on Lucia. "Give him my warmest congratulations."

"A teacher," said Giacomo. "That will be good for the children."

Lucia had stacked the bowls and plates and lifted them from the table as she turned toward the kitchen. "I'll bring your coffee," she said. "I made an almond *torta* if you like. May I bring you a slice?"

"Yes, please," said Sandro.

She raised her eyes to Giacomo. "And you, sir?"

"No," said Giacomo. "Bring the grappa."

Then she went away and heard no more until she returned, carrying the tray of coffee, the torta, a silver dish filled with sugar cubes, and the crystal decanter of grappa. In that short time the air in the room had changed; it was vibrating with anger, and Sandro sat with his head down, his shoulders hunched as if to avoid a blow.

"I will say no more about it," Giacomo said. "It's impossible. You are a disgrace to our family."

Carefully Lucia laid out her offerings in the hostile silence. Giacomo took up the grappa bottle at once and filled his narrow glass. To Lucia's surprise, when his father set the bottle down, Sandro stretched out his arm and took it up. Without lifting his head, he splashed a good amount into his glass. "Thank you," he said softly to Lucia. Giacomo's burning gaze fixed her across the table, and the heat of it drove her from the room.

⟶✦⟵

By the time father and son returned to Firenze, Sandro had formed a firm resolve. He would defy his father and steal away with his beloved. They would escape to Milano and he would find work in a factory; they would live simply, save his earnings, and eventually his father would come round, as he surely must when his first grandchild breathed the murky city air. Then they would rejoin the family and move to Villa Chiara. At home it was clear the family knew nothing of the rift between father and son, though Marco, who always had a cold, calculating eye focused on his father, doubtless detected antagonism. Sandro wrote at once to Silvia, professing his intention to visit her the following day with plans for their bright future together. There was no reply; but this wasn't unusual, and on the second day Sandro slipped out of his father's palazzo and walked briskly through the thronging market streets to the Rienzi stand near Santa Croce. Silvia's father, Paolo Rienzi, was there, heralding the virtues of his zucchini and his *cicoria* to an attentive group of regular customers. When he spotted Sandro over their bowed heads, his expression darkened and his jaw clenched. He and his wife, Elena, who was carefully selecting plums from a mountain of fruit and dropping them into a shopper's basket, exchanged a fretful glance. Sandro, sensing hostility where he had always been welcomed, paused at the edge of the crowd. He captured Elena's attention with a wave of his hand, an inquiry in his innocent eyes. "Where is Silvia?" he asked.

"She's gone," said Elena, lifting her chin to indicate her husband, who motioned Sandro to step behind the display. His heart misgave him and seemed to sink in his chest as the grocer finished a transaction, saluted the health and good sense of his customer, and turned upon his daughter's wealthy and impossible suitor.

"She's gone," he said. "She left on Sunday. She's with my sister in Le Marche."

"Did she receive my letter?" Sandro asked helplessly, for of course she hadn't. "When will she return?"

"I'm sorry for you," Paolo said. "She's not coming back. She won't see you. Her mind is made up."

"I don't understand," Sandro said. He could feel his blood draining from his face, and a sharp pain leaped like a lightning bolt across his temples. "What are you talking about? What have you done?"

"I can't help you," Paolo replied. "You should have known better than to lead her on with empty promises. Now her heart is broken."

"Tell me where she is," Sandro pleaded. "Tell me what you've done to her."

"Don't ask me!" Paolo exclaimed. "Ask your father. It's all his doing." He turned to address a customer's question about the neatly arranged display of apricots. "In the front," he said brusquely. "The ripe ones are in the front."

Sandro stepped out from behind the stall and addressed Elena, who eyed him coldly across a crate of white onions. "Where in Le Marche?" he demanded.

She pushed out her lower lip, lifted her chin sharply in a gesture of dismissal. "Where you can't find her," she said.

Tears blinded Sandro on the walk back to his father's palazzo. The pain in his forehead spread and intensified until he could scarcely think and all he could hear was a monotonous thudding that he distantly recognized as the throb of blood seeping from his heart. He went straight to his room, pulled out his small valise from the *armadio,* and commenced packing it with clothes and books. His sister Valeria, passing in the hall, looked in to greet him. "Are you taking another trip with Father?" she inquired. Then, seeing his tearful, pale, agonized expression, she moved into the room. "Sandro," she said. "Dearest. What happened?"

"Ask my father," he said roughly, but Valeria reached out to caress his cheek, and at her touch he collapsed, sobbing in her arms. "She's gone," he wailed. "He's stolen her."

"Who?" asked Valeria, though she knew well enough, as Giacomo had told Marco of the outrageous proposal, and Marco had confided at once in his sister. "That girl?"

Sandro stiffened in her arms, gripping her shoulders as he pushed her away. "You know nothing about her," he said. "*He* knows nothing about her. Go and tell him he's wrong. Tell him I only ask that he agree to meet her."

"He won't," Valeria said kindly. "Sandro, you know he won't. She's unsuitable."

At this Sandro clutched his hair in both hands and uttered an uncharacteristic curse. Valeria backed away carefully, as if she expected this mildest of brothers to attack her. But he ignored her, turning back to his valise, taking up a pressed linen shirt and wadding it into a side pocket. Once she was outside the door, Valeria broke into a run, and Sandro heard the rap of her heels all the way along the marble hall and then down the staircase that led to her father's study.

⌘

Never in his life would Sandro Salviati visit the Regione Marche. Before he could close his suitcase, his father burst into his bedroom and turned his clothes and books out onto the floor. "You can't be trusted outside this house!" Giacomo exclaimed, to which his son replied, "I can be trusted to find Silvia. I can be trusted to keep my word to her." There was a good lock on the heavy door to the bedroom, and Giacomo, taking the key from the inside, slammed the door on his son's futile protests and thrust the key into the lock on the outside. Father and son listened to the sharp rap as the bolt shot into the plate. Sandro raised his eyes to the two narrow windows, three floors above the paving stones below. He was a prisoner.

⟬✤⟭

Sandro's mother and his brother and his sisters—all save Maria, who was very young and knew nothing about it—became his warders, bringing in food, taking out the chamber pot, bringing water and towels for washing. He refused to eat, he ignored the water and towels, he made himself ill, he lay upon his bed moaning incoherently or complaining of pain in his head. His sisters and his mother begged Giacomo to relent, but he was firm and refused even to look upon his miscreant son. At last, after two weeks, he was persuaded to call in the family physician, who was ushered into the bedroom by the patient's weeping mother. The doctor stayed an hour, then knocked to be let out. Flavia, who had drawn a chair up to the door, leaped to her feet. "How is my son?" she begged.

"I think he will take a little soup now," the doctor said.

Sandro's recovery was protracted; there were setbacks, bouts of high fever and delirium, but by the end of the month he was able to eat and speak sensibly again. He didn't ask about Silvia, and no one spoke of her until the day his father brought him a copy of an item published in the church record in Ascoli Piceno, announcing the marriage of Silvia Rienzi of Firenze to Franco Piselli at the Basil-ica di San Francesco. "Her husband is a distant cousin," Giacomo informed his son. "Now she will have a happy life among her own people." Sandro said nothing, but he picked at the coverlet of his bed as if he'd discovered an inexplicable stain. His father went out, taking the key from the lock outside the door and inserting it on the inside. Then, leaving the door ajar, he went back to his study.

Later, when Valeria brought his dinner, Sandro asked her, "How does Father know the man Silvia married is her cousin?"

"I'm not sure," she replied. Sotto voce she added, "Marco told me Father sent Signor Rienzi a generous wedding gift. Too gener-ous in Marco's view."

"A gift? What sort of gift?"

"Well," his sister said, "a gift she can deposit in the bank."

Sandro groaned, fell back on his pillow, and turned his face to the wall.

⸎

In the months that followed, Sandro returned to his ordinary pur-suits. He practiced violin and was invited to perform with a small chamber group. Encouraged by a fellow musician, he joined the choir at Chiesa di Ognissanti, raising his voice and his heart to the divine music of Allegri, Scarlatti, and Mozart. His father regarded him skeptically, as he distrusted priests and had no interest in spiri-tuality. Giacomo went to Mass because it was his duty, and when he prayed he asked God to bless his farms and his business enter-prises and his daughters with rich husbands.

One chilly evening in November during the choir's final rehearsal of Allegri's *Miserere,* as Sandro thrilled to the flight of the soprano's voice rising effortlessly, weightlessly above the staff, then omi-nously down again, as a leaf will spiral upward in a swirling autumn breeze, then as gently flutter to the earth, passing the very branch from which it once sprouted, he thought of Silvia, of her gentleness and childish piety, her heart open to all the world. Animals, flowers, even frost or a chill wind delighted her. Her laughter had no irony but was rich with innocence and delight. He watched the soprano, her mouth opening and closing over the angelic sounds, and for a moment he managed to replace her more stolid features with Silvia's wide dark eyes, her full lips and golden hair. "*Ossa humiliata . . .*" she sang. My humble bones will rejoice, she promised the Lord, who would deliver her from despair.

A sudden stab of pain shot across Sandro's forehead and a flash of white light blinded him so that he stumbled into the narrow aisle, where he fell to his knees. His fellow choristers rushed to his aid and guided him from the platform to the chancel, where he collapsed in a heap on the cold marble steps, his eyes wide and frightened, his breath coming in desperate gasps. The choirmaster called for water, which was produced from somewhere in a brass chalice. Sandro drank hesitantly and submitted to being dabbed about the temples with a handkerchief dipped into the holy water font. "God spoke to me," he said at last.

"Take him home," the choirmaster charged the two singers bending over him.

The walk through the damp, windy streets sobered Sandro, and on arriving at his father's door, he thanked his companions graciously, saying nothing more about his condition but that he was himself now. He begged them to proffer his apologies to the choirmaster and to assure him that he would be present for the performance in two days' time. He let himself in at the door, crossed the entrance hall to the stairs, took off his shoes, and slipped up the steps in his stocking feet, then along the hall to his bedroom. Once inside he dropped the shoes, wrestled off his coat, and fell to his knees next to his bed, holding his head between his hands. "God spoke to me," he said.

"It's one mania after another," Giacomo complained. "First he makes himself sick over a grocer's daughter, and now he wants to close himself up with those crazed monks at Galluzzo because God told him to be cheerful."

"He seems very determined," Valeria said. "Very sure of himself."

"I hear him singing in his room," Marco said. "It's crazy."

"He's practicing," Valeria, her brother's advocate, insisted. "The performance is tomorrow. We should all attend and encourage him."

"If he wants to make music, why can't he compose operas, like Puccini?" Giacomo observed.

"He acts like he's in an opera now," Marco observed.

"He says he wants to renounce the world," Valeria said. "He wants to serve God."

"He's completely out of his head," Giacomo said, but softly, as if he too heard a voice in the air.

Marco looked up, meeting his father's eyes with grim affirmation. "He's completely out of his head," he agreed.

The concert was well received and God kept quiet throughout. The Salviati women all attended dutifully, but Giacomo and Marco stayed away. Sandro lingered in the church; there was a reception in the vestry hall for the choir. Among his fellow choristers, he made light of his collapse at the final rehearsal. "I shouldn't sing on an empty stomach," he said.

"Even birds have more sense than to do that," said the choirmaster.

Sandro arrived home in time to sit down at the table, where his sisters praised the sublimity of the music and the beauty of the soprano's voice. His father and brother made no excuses for failing to attend and quickly changed the subject to a problem of replacing a manager at the farm machinery plant who had been charged with embezzling money from the syndicate funds. Sandro kept his eyes on his plate. A dull pain spread across his skull and down to the top of his spine. When he looked up, there was an aura of light around every object on the table. He stretched his hand across his brow, pressing his temples between his thumb and forefinger.

"Are you well?" Valeria, who sat next to him, asked.

For answer he forced a quick, soft puff of air from his nose, his mouth stretched in a thin smile.

"Are you ill?" asked his father.

Sandro looked up. Yes, there around his father's head was a halo of sparkling light.

"You're a saint, Father," he said. "I see that now."

The Ospedale Psichiatrico
Giuseppe Antonini at Mombello

In 1879, when the municipality of Milano purchased the long-abandoned estate at Mombello, the locals still called it Villa Napoleone, because it was said that Bonaparte himself had stayed there during his Italian campaigns. Several buildings and spacious grounds made up the property. The main villa, built in the seventeenth century, was a magnificent stone edifice of three wings surrounding a court. An elegant columned portico sequestered the fourth side from a mowed field that ran downhill to a dirt road shaded on both sides by ancient plane trees, presumably the same road Napoleon had arrived on with his entourage, weary from battle and eager for a night's rest inside the impregnable stone walls.

The city bought the property with the intention of renovating and converting it into a hospital for mental patients then lodged in a crowded and crumbling facility at Senavra. To that end, Dr. Giuseppe Antonini, an idealist with enlightened views concerning the treatment of the mentally ill, was appointed to serve as the director, a post he filled for nearly two decades with such distinction that the facility ever after bore his name. Dr. Antonini believed mental health was best fostered by returning the patient to a proper relationship with nature. A combination of rest and work was his simple prescription. He aspired to create a veritable self-sufficient village. The patients transferred to his jurisdiction would become both the residents and the keepers of the asylum.

The incapacitated were assigned to a progressive routine of rest and a reenergizing diet; then, as their condition improved, music, exercise, and art classes could be introduced. Those who recovered both strength and some measure of reason were integrated into the community, building roads, growing crops, working in a carpentry, textile, or machine shop as suited their abilities. Patients who possessed a particular skill—and there were many such, for carpenters and tailors go mad as readily as artists and musicians—could offer classes or form groups to provide entertainment and enlightenment. A spacious and well-stocked library was available to both doctors and patients, with a sunny reading room looking out over a well-kept herb garden that perfumed the air with the scents of rosemary, thyme, and oregano.

In 1906, when Sandro Salviati entered the gates, a uniformed nurse escorted him across the yard, through the portico and the large interior court, where a row of pollarded lindens created a shaded central walkway, and along a tiled corridor lined with arched windows. He believed he had come for a rest cure. As he suffered from crippling headaches that left him sleepless and delusional, he was content to seek treatment. At the end of a second wide, windowed hall, the nurse opened a set of paneled double doors, and the director rose from behind his polished desk to greet his new patient.

He was a small man with thick curling hair, heavy brows over dark, penetrating eyes, a neat mustache, and a soft, feminine mouth. The thick lenses of his glasses magnified the inquisitiveness in his eyes, and he wagged his chin as genially as a goat. "Ah, Signor Salviati," he said, opening his hands as if he had produced Sandro by some magical incantation. "You are welcome among us. I understand you are an extraordinary musician. We are in hopes that you will join our fledgling orchestra." The doctor motioned

Sandro into a wooden armchair facing the desk and resumed his own seat behind it.

Sandro slumped miserably, feeling the impress of hot pincers on his temples, the familiar buzzing chatter in his ears. "May I have a glass of water?" he mumbled helplessly.

The doctor leaped to his feet and crossed the room to a table with a silver pitcher and several glass tumblers ranged on a tray. "Of course, of course," he said. "It's all very overwhelming, and you are ill." He brought the glass to Sandro and stood looking down at him while he drank deeply.

When the glass was empty, Sandro handed it back, smiling weakly. "Thank you," he said.

The doctor nodded, exuding concern. "Now let us talk about these headaches," he said, returning to his perch behind the desk. "Do you associate their commencement with any event?"

At the end of this initial interview, the nurse reappeared to escort Sandro back down the hall and across the courtyard to his room. A number of patients were relaxing on benches in the shade of the trees or wandering aimlessly along the paved walkway, where thick tufts of grass sprouted between the flags. Two older men, facing each other in wheelchairs, argued wearily, their voices harsh and dry, as if they'd been having the same disagreement for many years. Seeing the new patient, a young man crouched on a wooden stool near the door leaped to his feet and ran up to the nurse, who smiled at him kindly. "Who is he?" he asked anxiously. "Why is he here? Does he know who I am?"

"His name is Sandro," said the nurse. "I'll introduce you. Signor Salviati, this is Generalissimo Garibaldi." Sandro held out his hand, which the young man grasped earnestly. He was dressed in a long linen coat over a white silk shirt, with a gay bright-green cravat tied loosely at the collar.

"A pleasure to meet you," said the general. "You must be one of the new officers arriving from the Veneto. Though you are out of uniform, I can tell by your bearing. Your legion has been eagerly awaiting your arrival."

"I came as quickly as I could," Sandro replied.

The nurse put herself between them and laid a hand on the general's arm, which caused him to start as if she had struck him. "He's very tired now," said the nurse. "I'll take him to rest, and you can discuss the maneuvers after dinner."

"Of course, of course," the general said, backing away cautiously.

"He's quite mad," Sandro observed as they left the courtyard and turned in to a hall lined with iron and glass windows. A greenish light streamed in from the upper panels. Wooden shutters covered the lower panes. Most of the shutters were closed, but as they approached the dormitory hall, he noticed one that stood open. That was when he saw the bars.

A Brother Recovered

Maria Salviati, born at the turn of the twentieth century, was the youngest of five children, a late-life baby entirely unexpected by her parents. Marco, her closest sibling, was twelve at her birth; her nearest sister, Valeria, fifteen. The new baby was so spoiled and petted by her indulgent family, and so accustomed to having her whims gratified immediately and attentively, that she had no opportunity to develop a bad temper. There were always ready hands and smiling faces to ease her way from dawn to dark. She grew to be a high-spirited child, confident of her own importance, talkative, thoughtless, and vain.

Maria was closest to Valeria, an openhearted teenager who kept her little sister as a mascot and was amused when, on their adventures about the city, in the market or the park, she was mistaken for Maria's mother. Valeria was also Maria's connection to her oldest brother, Sandro, twenty years her senior, a distant, benign figure in her life, who unlike her brother Marco never teased. Sandro spoke to her as to an equal. His room was in a separate wing of the palazzo, and visits there with Valeria had a magical, transgressive quality that delighted Maria. As they approached, the wistful music of a violin drew them along the marble hall, ceasing abruptly when Valeria rapped her knuckles against the door. Once, when Valeria had some urgent necessity to consult her brother and there was no music vibrating the air, she pushed the door open without knocking. Maria, looking in past her sister's skirt, saw Sandro on his knees, facing the high window, where the afternoon sun trained a narrow beam of rosy light directly down upon his bowed head.

"Oh," said Valeria. "Please forgive me."

Sandro rose and turned to face his sisters, his eyes unfocused and his lips parted in a smile of serene contentment. "I was just praying that you two would come and see me," he said.

This was one of the few memories Maria would have of her oldest brother.

He was Valeria's confidant, her ally against the vituperative Marco, who could not be trusted. Sandro was out in the world, a man, not a boy, arriving occasionally late for dinner, often with some little present for Maria—a picture book, a music box, a silk fan painted with flowers. She was too young to understand or even to feel much interest in the long conversations he had with Valeria, but they never made her uncomfortable or fearful, as happened when her parents disagreed or Marco was party to any family assemblage. Sometimes Sandro took down books from his shelves and instructed Valeria, slowly turning the pages, finding a paragraph or a poem and reading it to her in his high, clear voice. Often they laughed together. Once Valeria wept and Sandro put his arm around her, crooning softly into her ear until she smiled, accepted his handkerchief, and wiped her eyes.

For a time, when Maria was five, he was closed in his room and no one but the doctor was allowed to see him. Valeria said he was ill; perhaps it was contagious. Celestia had been confined for several weeks with some fever and spots that had left red marks on her face. Would Sandro come out of his room with red marks?

And then one day the door to his room was open, the bed was stripped, the armadio stood open and empty. Sandro was gone.

Valeria said he was in a place where he could rest, and Maria concluded he would return when he had slept enough. Her parents no longer spoke of him. The days, months, years, passed; her world filled steadily with wonders, and the memory of her older brother faded to a few impressions: a young man on his knees in a bright ray of sun, the surpassing beauty of violin music echoing eerily along a marble hall.

⚜

Giacomo Salviati was not a music lover, but he made an exception for the operas of Puccini. His business interests often took him to Milano, and if there was a production of a Puccini opera at La Scala, he had a standing invitation from an associate to join his family in their box.

When Maria was fourteen, her father announced that this excellent associate had offered the entire Salviati family this box for a performance of *Madama Butterfly*. They would stay at a grand hotel, where they could also dine after the opera, and in the morning the sisters would be free to do some shopping at the famous Galleria, returning to Firenze on the evening train. Marco, unsurprisingly, elected to stay at home. He declared he had no interest in music or in witnessing the unedifying sight of Italians wearing kimonos and pretending to be Japanese. At the last minute, Celestia came down with a virulent cold and was not inclined to sneeze and cough her way from Firenze to Milano and back again.

This meant Maria had her favorite sister to herself, which suited her perfectly. The trip was a welcome change of scenery. She was enchanted by everything: the train ride, the luxurious hotel room she shared with Valeria, the chaos of horse carriages and automobiles on the bustling streets, so much wider than Firenze's narrow byways, the opulence of the opera house, the sublimity of the music—she and Valeria wept openly through the last scene—the chilly ride in an open carriage back to the hotel, where the dining room filled steadily with operagoers, elegant women dressed in daring, stylish gowns and men pocketing tickets for the top hats they checked at the door.

In the morning a car was waiting to transport Maria and her sister to that magnificent temple to consumption, the Galleria Vittorio Emanuele II. It was a cold winter morning, and Maria could see her breath as she descended from the car and stood gazing through the great stone arch to the glittering glass and iron dome, like a barrel made of ice balanced across a double arcade of shops. On the smooth mosaic-tiled interior streets below, a genial press of shoppers passed in and out of the shops or gathered at white-linen-draped tables in voluble groups, sipping their cups of hot chocolate and espresso. But she had scarcely set foot in the fantastical arcade when Valeria caught her by the elbow and turned her back to the street. At the same moment, a powerful touring car pulled up to the curb and the driver, raising his goggles over his brow and leaping out of his seat, greeted her sister, hat in hand. "You are Signorina Salviati," he said.

"I am," said Valeria. He opened the passenger door and ushered the sisters into the deeply padded green leather interior. "What's going on?" Maria exclaimed as she followed her sister inside.

Valeria adjusted her skirts and patted her hat, which had shifted to one side in the passage from the street. "We're not going shopping," she said.

"Then where are we going?" Maria asked.

The driver climbed back behind the steering wheel and sat staring distractedly into the passing traffic, gauging the best moment for entering the flow.

"We're going for a drive in the country," Valeria said.

"But why?" Maria protested. "I wanted to go shopping."

"You'll see soon enough," Valeria said. "And you won't regret it."

They drove right out of the sprawling city and into a shabby neighborhood populated by factory workers crowded into cheap boardinghouses. The ragged, dirty children, who spent their days in the street, raced alongside the car, shouting insults, laughing, taking up clods of dirt to smash against the windshield. Then they passed bare fields scattered with two-room stone houses where somnolent chickens squatted on the roofs of their pens and truculant dogs chained to makeshift pergolas strained at their collars, howling as the unfamiliar vehicle roared by. At last the car turned onto a wide, potholed road between fields of grain that stretched before them without end. The driver swerved back and forth, navigating the holes. As they were flung together and apart, Maria and Valeria laughed, clinging to the door handles to keep from pitching onto the floor. A sharp turn brought them onto smoother terrain, the fields ended, giving way to two lines of ancient plane trees, and they drove on beneath a canopy of bare branches obscuring the pale, wintry sky. Valeria occupied herself with her disobedient hat while Maria looked ahead through the driver's windshield. The road appeared to end in a curtain of brambles, like the entrance to a castle in a children's story, and the driver slowed to a crawl. At last he pulled up alongside an ironwork gate set in a whitewashed wall. Through this gate Maria could see two modern outbuildings, evidently under construction, a series of garden patches, neatly pruned and mulched for the winter, and beyond, shrouded in a silvery mist, an elegant columned portico connecting two wings of a grand villa, such as, she thought, only a noble and powerful family might require.

"What is this place?" she whispered to Valeria, though there was no one but the driver to hear her.

"You'll see," said Valeria, looking out beside her. "It's beautiful. I had no idea it was so big."

The driver dismounted and threw the door open even as a man in a military uniform appeared from behind the wall and set to unlocking the heavy chain on the gate. "Signorina Salviati," he said, and Valeria nodded, extending her gloved hand to the driver, who reached up to help her descend. Maria jumped down behind, her brain buzzing with excitement and curiosity. Later she would wonder why she hadn't guessed where they were and why it was a secret, but at that moment, stepping through the gate to the worn footpath that led to the colonnaded court of the villa, she only imagined that Valeria had at last found a mate of whom her father would approve.

As they drew closer, they could hear the sound of voices, some raised, others calm and conversational, drifting out from the upper windows. A stout woman wearing a pale blue uniform with an apron and a nurse's hat came out from a door they couldn't see and stood just inside the colonnade waiting for them. "How do they know who you are?" Maria asked her sister.

"We have an appointment," Valeria replied.

"Signorina Salviati," the nurse said. She had a quizzical expression, as if she suspected the answer might be no. "Dr. Antonini is expecting you." She led them through the court, where two men sat side by side on an iron bench, staring blankly in opposite directions. They were dressed in identical knee-length white gowns over baggy gray-and-white-striped trousers and appeared not to notice the visitors. The court was lined with arched glass French doors. Stubby grass failed to thrive among the benches and chairs.

They entered a wide hall with a vaulted ceiling, scarcely warmer than the chilly courtyard. A few wooden chairs arranged in groupings of two or three were dwarfed by the proportions of the space. Two women in the same blue uniforms stood talking quietly between long metal tables. On the wall behind them, Maria noticed a case filled with bottles, jars, and folded linens. The soft voices echoed pleasantly in the still air, and one of the women met Maria's eyes as she passed with an expression of mild surprise.

They turned a corner and arrived at a pair of inlaid wooden doors, one of which was slightly ajar. When their guide rapped on the door, a cheerful voice called out, "Come in, come in."

It was a hospital, Maria concluded. Why had her sister whisked her away to visit a hospital? Was she in love with a wounded soldier?

A movement in the shadows beyond the door attracted her attention, and she paused while her eyes adjusted to the light. A woman was walking toward her. She was barefoot, her hair unkempt, thick and matted; she moved jerkily, and there was something odd about her dress. Maria took in the ravaged face, the crazed, staring eyes, and then the impossible garment, a tightly laced canvas jacket with long sleeves that bound the woman's arms across her waist, ending in straps tied at her back. *She can't move her arms,* Maria thought. The woman was very close, working her mouth as if she were chewing something sinewy, fixing Maria with a look combined of desperation and rage. "Stay away from me," she shouted. Maria darted inside the half-open door and pulled it closed behind her.

Dr. Antonini greeted the sisters warmly; he had clearly been in correspondence with Valeria for some time. He rang a bell on his desk as he expatiated on the subject of his achievements: a new pavilion, currently under construction; the women's ward, overcrowded now, but the plans for a new building with separate sleeping quarters and a modern water treatment facility were already drawn up. The hospital laboratory served doctors from all over Europe, and brilliant new cures were being developed and tested successfully. Patients who had been incapacitated for years were now able to enter into the life of the community.

Maria scarcely listened. Her eyes wandered over the details of the spacious office: the mahogany desk piled with papers, the tufted silk chairs, the walls of books, a table with a pitcher of water and two glasses, a bowl of apples on a low shelf. All the while her confounded brain repeated a bald refrain: *It's a madhouse, it's a madhouse.* The door opened and another nurse peered in, a small, round, and rosy person with a quick smile and merry eyes whom the doctor introduced as Signora Aldo. Valeria exchanged parting remarks with the doctor and, gesturing to Maria to stay close, followed the nurse out the door. She led them back along the wide hall where the winter sun splashed patches of creamy light across the tiles, and past a glass door that framed a view of a steam-filled room lined with odd wooden boxes, from the open lids of which protruded, like flowers from a pot, the heads of wild-eyed men, babbling or shouting as the spirit moved them. Another turn led to a set of metal doors with triangular glass insets at eye level. Here Signora Aldo stopped and unhooked a set of keys attached to the band of her apron. "We'll find him here," she said to Valeria.

Find who? Maria thought. With every step her mystification deepened. What business could the sound and sensible Valeria have in this place? When Signora Aldo pulled the door open, a riot of voices, pleading, angry, laughing, shouting, singing, mumbling, drove Maria back a step, but Valeria and the nurse entered briskly, so she followed. Signora Aldo pulled the door closed behind her and shot the bolt into place.

The room was as high and wide as a ballroom, which indeed it once had been. Now it was furnished with chairs, tables, and hard benches. Perhaps two dozen men, all dressed alike in white gowns and striped cotton pantaloons, moved about in small groups or sat alone; an old white-bearded fellow on his hands and knees crawled slowly around the perimeter of the room. Several nurses moved among them, but to what end, Maria couldn't fathom. Signora Aldo approached a colleague, and they exchanged a few words. A young man with thick unwashed hair hanging to his shoulders and an expression of intense anxiety got up from a chair near the window and sidled up to Valeria, his index finger extended as if to point her out for some misbehavior. Signora Aldo returned, warning the young man away. "Sergio," she said, "don't accost this lady. Go and sit in your chair." To Valeria she said, "He's in the courtyard. It's too cold to take the others out, but he insists. He says he likes the cold." The sisters followed their guide, threading her way through the chaos of men raving in their pajamas and out the glass doors to a walled courtyard, bare of decoration save a single leafless linden planted so long ago in a narrow bare space that it had cracked and lifted the surrounding flagstones. Maria noticed only that the tree blocked her view of what she wanted to see, the source of the wondrous singing that warmed the chilly air like a coat of velvet. Signora Aldo stepped to one side, and as Maria followed, she saw him.

He was standing with his back to the women, facing the wall. His arms were raised in a wide V, his long fingers splayed wide, his face lifted to the fading sunlight. He was singing with all his voice, his powerful, well-trained voice, an ancient sacred song, entreating God's mercy on mankind. The three women were stilled, unable to speak; Maria held her breath, exalted, as in a vision of the divine. Yet he sensed their presence, for he stopped singing midphrase, dropped his arms, and turned to see them there, clutched in a little trinity of femaleness beneath the bare branches of the linden tree. For a moment he didn't speak. Who he was, where he was, why he was there, all came crashing down on Maria with such force that she rocked back on her heels.

"Valeria?" Sandro said. "Is it really you?"

For answer Valeria ran to her brother and was enfolded in his embrace. Tears overflowed his eyes as he laid his cheek against her hair. Though Valeria was sobbing, the phrase she repeated was triumphant. "I found you," she said. "Oh, my dearest, I found you."

A Meeting in America

When I left Villa Chiara that August, Beatrice and I agreed to stay in touch, and we both expressed confidence that I would spend another month, perhaps an entire summer, at the villa in the near future; but time, as it does, slipped away. There was no Internet and we had busy lives, so our communication consisted mostly of postcards sent while traveling on college breaks. Beatrice went to more interesting places than I did: Munich, of course, but also Paris, Lisbon, and London. In 1986 there was a brief flurry of cards from Central America, San Miguel in El Salvador and Granada on the Lago de Nicaragua. She liked islands for winter breaks; I received green-and-blue aerial views of Malta, Elba, and Réunion.

In 1988 I attended a professional convention in Manhattan. It was as geographically close as I'd gotten to Beatrice in five years, and I was curious to see my friend. Before I left home, I sent her a postcard announcing my arrival. When I got to the hotel, there was a message waiting at the desk. She invited me to extend my stay with a train trip to her home upstate. Her son would be there, she said, stopping off on his way to Cape Cod to visit his father and returning thence to Germany from Boston. She had ample room and hoped I would stay overnight. She left a phone number, which I called at once.

Two days later, my brain fairly addled from the tedium of the convention, up the misty, partially frozen Hudson River I went in a clattering commuter train that stopped a dozen times before arriving at Poughkeepsie station. Beatrice stood waiting on the platform, elegant and straight-backed, with that intensity of manner that made her seem more severe than I knew her to be. She took charge of guests as she took charge of everything in her life, by ambush. "Here you are," she said. "I hope the train wasn't horrific. It can be a nightmare if there are too many students on board. At night they are mostly drunk, which is disgusting."

"It was fine," I said. We exchanged the requisite cheek kisses. She attempted to relieve me of my bag. "It's not heavy," I insisted, and she gave in.

"The car is here," she said, leading me to the curb.

The car was a red Ford Escort, not new but brighter than the Cinquecento, serviceable and as ordinary as a can opener. I shoved my bag into the back seat; we took our places in the front, and we were off. The road was a highway running straight through the town, which appeared to have been built at some expense at the turn of the twentieth century and abandoned shortly thereafter. Occasional blocks of neglected yet still stately Victorian houses gave way to cheap storefronts, gas stations, chain drugstores, and fast-food emporiums. Beatrice told me what I guessed. "This town is a sad place," she said. "It must have been rather pretty once, but in the sixties they built the big shopping malls on the highway, the businesses moved there, and the town died. Now it is *bruttissima*, and full of criminals. No one wants to live here."

"That's a shame," I said. "It's right on the river."

"The river is lovely," Beatrice agreed. "But the water is so polluted you can't eat the fish or swim in it."

At last we came to a wide cross street that served as a borderline. On one side dereliction, on the other shops, restaurants, a bookstore, trees planted to shade the road, and in the near distance the solid dusty-rose stone walls and towers of the college. Beatrice turned onto a wide road lined with large, attractive old houses of diverse styles set up and back from the street on rising land so that they appeared to brood upon their gleaming white lawns. "It has been snowing here for two days," she said.

"It was snowing in the city," I said. "Very hard to get around."

"Fortunately, my driveway was plowed this morning," she said, turning abruptly in to a short, steep driveway that led to a neat two-story Dutch Colonial house, cedar shingles above and dove-gray wood siding below, with a covered carriageway on one side wide enough for two cars. "Welcome to my house," Beatrice announced, pulling up inside this shelter.

"I'm curious to see it," I said.

She turned to me, giving me that amused, confident smile that reminded me I was something of a hobby to her. "Yes," she said. "I know."

"You must spend more time here than you do in Italy," I observed. We exited the car and I pulled my bag from the seat. "Do you feel more at home here or there?"

"I spend as little time as possible here," she said. "Does that answer your question?"

I followed her to the side entry, which led to a neat mudroom with a slate floor, the walls lined with hooks and shelves. On the other side of the glass-paned door I could see the kitchen—decidedly unrenovated. We shed our boots and went in. It was a comforting, spacious, old-fashioned space with wood floors and painted glass-fronted cabinets and countertops. A ponderous wood table similar to the one in the villa, the surface scattered with bowls and cutting boards, occupied the center of the room. The appliances were newer, bulky and out of place, but the stove looked original, a gas behemoth with curved iron feet, six burners, and a griddle. "When was this house built?" I asked.

"Nineteen twenty," she said. "It is a very solid house."

I peeked through a doorway beyond the refrigerator—a narrow room lined with shelves, some stacked with dishes, others empty. "A butler's pantry," I said.

"Sadly, the butler didn't come with the house." As Beatrice spoke, a man appeared in the doorway opposite her. "Ah, David," she said. "Here is my friend Jan, a wonderful writer."

He was tall and spare like his mother, and had her straight dark hair and dark eyes. But his complexion was all pink and cream, his nose a bit fleshy at the nostrils, and his thickish lips were unnaturally red. His eyes rested briefly upon me, distant and chilly, as if a glance sufficed to tell him everything he might want to know about me.

"Hello," I said.

He nodded, then gave his full attention to his mother. "Is there no aspirin in this house?" he complained. "My head is splitting."

"In the downstairs bath," Beatrice said. "Under the sink."

"Why would you put aspirin under the sink?" he retorted, stomping off to the bathroom.

"He's very angry with me," Beatrice explained.

"Because of the aspirin?"

"Because I won't give his father money, and so he has to do it."

"His father is unemployed," I concluded.

"Oh, he may have some little job. And his needs are small. But he left a message on David's service saying there was a problem with the house, which means he needs money. I told him his father's house isn't my problem. What can I give you? Would you like a caffè? A cup of tea?"

"Coffee would be great," I said.

When it was ready, we took our cups to a pretty sunroom where everything that wasn't bookshelves was windows and on every window ledge a large tropical plant was bathed in light. "I can never grow aralia," I said, examining a healthy specimen in a pot near the door.

"You probably give it too much attention," she said. "They like to be wet, that's basically it."

We heard footsteps from the hall, and in the next moment David stood looking in at us. He appeared highly agitated. "I just talked to Dad," he said. "The pipes froze two days ago. He's drinking bottled water and can't flush the toilet."

"He should call a plumber," Beatrice suggested.

"That's the problem. He owes the plumber for his last job and he won't come back unless he gets paid."

"Then you must go and write him a check. You can afford it."

David grimaced. "It's five hundred dollars. Money is tight for us now."

"I'm not writing a check," Beatrice insisted. "Why not give him your credit card numbers? The pipes will be fixed by the time you get there, and you will be able to flush the toilet."

David took a step forward, but just one. His hands had migrated to his hips, giving him an air of belligerence. "Why are you so uncooperative?" he said.

"I'm not actually related to your father," Beatrice reminded him. "My family paid for your expensive education, to which he contributed not one cent. Why should I pay his plumbing bill?"

"You're impossible," he replied. "You know how helpless Dad is."

Throughout this mildly heated exchange, I sat next to the aralia, pretending interest in the pot.

"You're just showing off in front of your friend," he said. His eyes settled on me. "Look, you've shocked her." Then they both scrutinized me for signs of shock, and all I could do was look back hopefully. David's mouth was set in a babyish pout.

"Are you shocked?" Beatrice asked.

"A little," I confessed.

"You think I'm being difficult?"

"I don't know about that," I said. "I just can't believe you keep the aspirin under the sink."

A pleasing moment of silence allowed each of us to consider the absurdity of this scene. Beatrice chuckled softly. To my surprise, David pulled in his chin, raised his eyebrows, and focused closely on me, as if he'd just noticed the existence of a talking cat. "Right," he said. "No one does that." Then, mumbling darkly to himself, he turned and left the room.

"Poor David," Beatrice said. "His father is a burden he has chosen to bear. I'm not sure why."

"How old was he when you divorced?" I asked.

"We didn't divorce all at once," she said. "When David was born we were in Boston. I'd just finished my master's degree and Patrick had completed the BA. He had no interest in graduate studies. I suppose these days he would want to attend one of these MFA programs that are everywhere, but then there weren't many options for young people who wanted to write. And that was all Patrick wanted to do. Actually he didn't so much want to do it, he wanted to be it, to be a writer. But as you know, it's not that easy."

"That's true," I agreed.

Beatrice nodded. "I didn't know that then," she continued. "I was naive. I worked hard myself and I assumed everyone did. I loved my studies. The college was my escape from everything I couldn't control in my life; I see that now. Patrick had a winning manner, and he was very respectful of me until he came to resent me.

"Before David was born we spent a few weeks in Italy. I assumed that, like most Americans, he would fall in love with my country and I'd have to disillusion him gradually, because Italy is not so wonderful in some ways, but he instantly disliked everything about it. He's something of a puritan, as it turns out. He's like Hawthorne. The Old World has no appeal for him; all he sees is corruption and tedium. Which is astonishing when you consider how deeply boring and depressing Cape Cod is. And of course, like his father, who was truly a dear man, Patrick is an alcoholic.

"So of course what he did for a living was work in a bar, though that helped in a way, because he wasn't allowed to drink when the owner was there. When he got home, he went straight for the cold beer. I'd been stuck with the baby all day and I was happy enough to join him with a glass of wine. We got on like that for a bit. Sometimes we argued, but then we made up. We were passionate about everything, but to no end. I continued to write essays; I didn't know what else to do, and Patrick sat at the typewriter sometimes. It took him months to produce a few pages.

"When David was a year old, we moved to Cape Cod because Patrick's father had gotten him a job on a fishing charter. We rented a shabby little house near the ocean. It was fine during the summer, but the winters there are brutal. I got through one and vowed to go home for the next. I was miserable, at odds with everything. I had a part-time job teaching Italian at a new community college; it was all I could get, and I realized I would need a PhD if I ever wanted to work full-time in America.

"I persuaded Patrick to take a second trip home with me in December. His charter-boat job was seasonal, and the idea had been that he would write in the winter. He claimed he couldn't write in Italy. Finally he agreed to go, but he held it against me. He lasted a month in Firenze at my mother's apartment. I suppose Patrick thought she would want to spend time with her grandchild, but my mother never liked children and showed no interest in David. This hurt Patrick's feelings.

"I was so relieved to be in the city. I was ecstatic, actually. I took David everywhere with me, to the gardens and art shows, to the movies. He saw *Peter Pan* dubbed into Italian. He was quick to pick up the language, and sometimes we carried on childish conversations in Italian in front of his father. This didn't go over well, as you can imagine. I knew that if I could keep David in Italy for six months he would be fluent, and that was important to me. I told Patrick I didn't want our son to be one of those Italo-Americans who only know the Italian words for food.

"A session for babies was starting at the Montessori school in January. It was near the apartment and the teachers were excellent. I enrolled David for the term. Patrick and I had a huge row about that. His theme was that I wanted our son to be like me and not like him, that I cared more for the baby than I did for him, that in fact I despised him, that I knew he was miserable in Italy—he had no friends and couldn't make any—and most importantly that I knew he couldn't write in Italy and this was fine with me as I had no confidence in him as a writer and assumed he would fail.

"I denied all these charges strongly and accused him of despising me because I was an independent Italian woman and not a clingy American with no goals beyond marriage. I said that he had no right to keep me locked up in a frigid hovel on the beach with nothing to do but look after a two-year-old.

"Later I saw that everything Patrick accused me of was true. I had no confidence in him as a father, a husband, or a writer. And with good cause, as he proved a failure on all those fronts. After a week of raging arguments by day and tragic, passionate lovemaking at night, we were both so exhausted we agreed that he should go back to America and I would stay on with David until spring. Patrick wept frankly and openly at this development. My mother saw him and told me she had lived through a war and never seen such a *manifestazione* as my young husband put on for us all.

"Travel back and forth wasn't so easy in those days. Airfares were astronomical and the boat took a week, so the decision to stay or go was complicated. Winter crossings can be rough. We'd had a hard one going over. David was so sick he got seriously dehydrated, and we had the ship's doctor in and out the entire passage. We'd bought one-way tickets because we weren't sure when we would be returning. I realized that it had not occurred to Patrick that he might go back without me, and also that this possibility had been in my mind from the start."

Beatrice paused. "This hurt me. We had been so close. It had all seemed so natural, our finding each other, the marriage, the baby. We tried to tell ourselves, we told each other, that the separation would do us good. He would go back and write. In the spring, David and I would go home, because home was where he was for me now. I didn't deny that."

"And did you go back?"

"I did. Even though David was happy in his little school and we spoke to each other only in Italian, one of the things he said repeatedly was that he missed his *babbo*. Everyone at school had a *babbo* but him. He'd picked up that word. I had feared he would forget who his father was, but when we came down the gangway in New York and he saw Patrick waiting there—he was holding a pathetic, oversized teddy bear—David broke into a run, shouting '*Babbo, babbo,*' and threw himself into his father's arms. Patrick started weeping, of course. I thought Italians were supposed to be the emotional ones."

"Italians are excitable," I said. "The Irish traffic in bathos. It's not the same thing."

Beatrice gazed at me wide-eyed, faux stunned. "What a politically incorrect observation!" she exclaimed.

"I'm not running for office," I said.

She laughed. "Well, it's true," she said.

"So how long did you last on the Cape?"

"Until David was five," she said. "I took him to Italy in the winter every year and we came back in March. He was perfectly bilingual by that time, with no accent in either language. Interestingly, he speaks German with an Italian accent."

"What happened when he was five?"

She touched her fingertips to her lips, turning her head slowly from side to side as what were clearly painful recollections clicked into place. "Everything happened when David was five. In the summer, Patrick's father, Davey, got a very late diagnosis of pancreatic cancer and lasted only two months. Patrick was truly heroic during that time. He nursed his father as tenderly as a mother and kept him home until the end. But after the funeral he went on what I think is called a bender for two weeks. He was an orphan; the world was required to bear witness to his grief. He lost his job. David was to start school in Wellfleet and I was told I couldn't pull him out from December until March—he would fall behind. It was a miserable school; I didn't like it, and David hated it. He cried every day, begging me not to leave him.

"Then Patrick's brother and sister descended like a pair of vultures to divide the spoils, and they insisted on selling the house. This enraged Patrick, but legally there was nothing to be done about it. We moved his father's beloved books to our rented cottage, and Davey's house sat on the market for a few months. When it sold, Patrick got a small check—that was his total inheritance.

"Shortly after that, out of the blue, one of his stories was accepted by a small journal, and he was paid the princely sum of fifty dollars. That was all he needed to declare himself an up-and-coming voice that must be heard. I was pleased for him, of course, but I didn't see why this meant he didn't need at least some seasonal work. We argued about that interminably.

"In November my mother wrote to tell me my aunt Valeria was very ill and not expected to live long. I wanted to go at once. I couldn't bear watching Patrick's decline. He was thoughtless and indifferent to my feelings. I had loved his father, in a way—he was the father I wished I'd had—and I couldn't understand how Davey Doyle could have produced such a helpless and conflicted son. I loved my aunt as well—she had always been my shield against my mother. Patrick was absolutely against my leaving. I think we both knew if I did, I wasn't coming back. We had terrible fights in which we said many cruel things to each other. David was caught in the middle of the misery and began to show the stress. He couldn't sleep, wet the bed, talked back to his ignorant teacher. Finally I booked a passage for the day after my last class at the community college, and when the time came, I packed two small suitcases and we left.

"Everyone was angry with me. Patrick accused me of deserting him, of stealing his son. My mother thought I deserved everything I got for being so stupid as to marry a poor American. She feared Patrick would sue me for desertion and the divorce would be expensive. I was past caring. My aunt's illness preoccupied me. I went to Villa Chiara to supervise her care. I found a good school for David in the little town there, the same one Anna Falco's son, Leonardo, went to. David was a happy child again, with friends and family. Like his great-uncle Sandro, he loved the villa and roamed about the woods and fields with Leonardo, who is a few years older. He came home with leaves and sticks in his hair, his shoes and his face streaked with mud, like a boy gone native.

"I wasn't happy, but I knew I'd made the right decision. I wrote a conciliatory letter to Patrick, begging him to understand why I couldn't make myself fit into the constricted role of the American housewife. To my astonishment—truly, I could hardly believe my eyes when I read the words on the page—he wrote to say he did understand. He assured me that he was not a 'gold-digger' and wanted nothing from me but that I make an effort to have David spend time with him in the future, so that he knew who his father was and that he was himself half American. 'I want him to have a choice about where he belongs, and if I can, I will teach him to love this place as much as I do.'"

As Beatrice spoke, the thought of her husband's eloquence touched her anew and tears clouded her eyes. "That sentence stuck in my brain, as you see," she said, forging on. "In a way it was a kind of challenge."

"That you continue your connection with a country," I said, "if not with a husband."

"Yes," she agreed. "And I wasn't against that. I wrote back to him at once and promised that I would find a way to do as he asked. I knew the best plan would be to get a doctorate in America so that I could find a permanent university position. I contacted a former professor at BC, and he suggested a new Italian studies program at UCLA. The program director was an old friend of his, and he would write to him on my behalf.

"It was the perfect solution. I had always wanted to live in Los Angeles; it was an old dream of mine from when I was a teenager and gorged myself on Raymond Chandler and Nathanael West during the summers at Villa Chiara. As David got older, he could visit his father on holidays and spend summers with him. Once I had my degree I would find a job on the East Coast within driving distance of Cape Cod. And that is exactly what I did."

"How long were you in Los Angeles?" I asked.

"Just three years. It was paradise. I loved everything about Los Angeles—even the smog struck me as romantic. I had a little apartment downtown in one of those Spanish-style U-shaped buildings with the patio and the palm trees at the front. David went to public school, a good school then, with lots of Latinos, so he learned some Spanish. In the summers his father drove coast-to-coast to pick him up and take him back to the Cape. They both loved those horrid road trips across the desert. When I got the job here, it was easier on all of us."

"But now David lives in Germany," I observed.

She smiled. "That is a good joke on his parents, isn't it?" she observed.

We heard footsteps approaching. "I hope he isn't going to badger me anymore about his father's plumbing bill."

David looked in at the door. His sour expression was gone, though there was a hint of peevishness about his mouth that I took to be a permanent feature of his character. "You two have been gabbing for a long time," he said.

"I've been telling Jan the story of your life," Beatrice said genially.

"Yes? Well, there are several versions of that. I wouldn't think yours is the most reliable."

"I don't see why not," Beatrice replied.

David looked at me. "Don't believe a word she says," he said, his tone ironic, more cautionary than prescriptive. "I wonder if you've given any thought to dinner?" he said to his mother.

"I'm making your favorite risotto," she said. "The artichokes are soaking in lemon water as we speak. Is your headache better?"

He smiled. The news about the menu clearly softened his feelings toward his mother. "It is," he said. "The aspirin helped."

❧

By the time I came downstairs in the morning, David was gone. The sky was heavy and white, with another snowstorm predicted, coming from the south, so he had made an early start in the hopes of beating the storm to Cape Cod. Beatrice and I had toast and coffee at the kitchen table. She never ate sliced bread in Italy, she said, because toasted sliced bread was so quintessentially American she never felt comfortable eating it anywhere else. But always, on her return to New York at the end of the summer, she made sure to stop and buy a bag of sliced wheat bread at the grocery on the edge of town.

After we left the subject of toast, I broached the possibility that I might stay again in the limonaia during the coming summer. I had a contract for a novel, the research was under way, and I knew her little apartment would be a congenial workplace in which to complete a final draft. Beatrice was at once enthusiastic about this idea and declared that I must arrive whenever it suited me and forget about paying rent, but rather stay as her guest and her friend for as long as I liked. I insisted on paying the amount I had paid the first summer. "If you won't take it," I said, "I won't come, though not because I don't appreciate your generosity. I got a nice check when I signed the contract, and you may be sure I can deduct the rent from my taxes. There is no better way to spend that money."

Beatrice frowned deeply and said, "All right. I can see why you might not want to feel indebted when you are concentrating on a deadline."

"You understand me perfectly," I said.

On the train heading back to Manhattan, I considered this conversation, as well as the story Beatrice had told me about her marriage and what I had seen of her relations with her son. It struck me that she had made a few rash decisions as a young woman, and as far as she was concerned, her options had thenceforth been both limited and clear. In her view, she had forcefully taken the helm and steered the little ship of her interests safely to shore. She was strong-minded and clearheaded, whereas her family, especially her ex-husband and her son, was recalcitrant and ungrateful. When she considered her situation, she never spoke of it in terms of class or wealth. Even as a girl, rushing through the streets of a war zone, where Germans battled Allies over territory neither side would ever claim, she had wanted to be independent, to remake her life on her own terms in a new world, beyond family, nationality, and class.

That was the appeal of American literature for her. The persistent theme of the reinvention of the self, free of the ravages of the past and the catastrophe of the family, resonated for her in a way most Americans couldn't understand. I recalled that evening in Villa Chiara when her tyrannical little mother stamped out of the dark hall, her black eyes fixed on her daughter with complete disapprobation, and Beatrice's deep frown as she set the espresso cup before this woman who would evidently sooner die than say, "Thank you." How old was Beatrice, I wondered, when she realized that she could never please her mother? And how soon after that had she made up her mind to please herself?

The Abandoned Farmhouse

On my second visit to Villa Chiara, Beatrice arrived two days before I did, having stopped off to visit her grandchildren in Munich. I had spent a week in Rome and took the train to Siena, where I picked up a rental car. I was in high spirits as I sped along the familiar highway, then crossed the narrow bridge and turned onto the two-lane road that led to the gate of Villa Chiara. The weather was pleasantly warm and dry, the scenery appeared exactly as I remembered it, not a sunflower out of place, and I had the agreeable sense of returning to a place where I was both welcome and expected. I had shipped a box of books before I left Pennsylvania, so even my reference library would be in place.

I parked the car in the drive, pulled out my two cases, and rolled them directly to the glass door of the limonaia. There was a large wooden trestle table with cushioned wicker chairs drawn up to it on the covered terrace. I found, as Beatrice had promised I would, the key lodged in the lock. I let myself in, rolling the cases behind me across the cool tiles of the kitchen floor. I noted small changes everywhere. In the kitchen, the rachitic table had been replaced with a solid farm table twice the size; there was a glass-fronted cabinet filled with good ceramic dishes; the refrigerator was a newer model; a red leather loveseat occupied a corner of the sitting room, across from a small, empty bookcase with the box I had sent myself on top, ready for shelving. Upstairs the creaky iron bedstead had been replaced with a solid frame of smooth golden wood and a matching bedside table. The walls, once putty-colored, were now a fresh pale yellow, and a valuable-looking carpet was on the floor. Pressed up against the window, a plain writing desk and a woven rattan chair invited the writer to stare past the blank page into a riotous maze of bougainvillea.

I lifted my suitcase onto the bed and unzipped the soft lid. As I took out the stack of summer blouses, I heard a sharp rapping against the kitchen door. I hurried down the steps to find Beatrice holding a basket in one hand; the other was raised in a fist that transformed into a salute when she saw me. She pulled open the door and greeted me with her preferred greeting, "Here you are." We exchanged firm cheek kisses.

"Let me help you with that," I said, taking the basket. It was heaped with supplies: bread, espresso, those odd orange sponge cookies Italians eat for breakfast, two bottles of wine, some packages wrapped in butcher paper that I took to be cheese, butter, and a carton of long-life milk. She followed me as I set the basket on the kitchen table. "You've changed things," I said.

"Did you prefer the spartan style?"

"No," I said. "Not at all. It's more comfortable. The refrigerator is definitely a plus."

"Yes," she said. "The time had come. I have a new one in the villa as well." She gestured toward the sitting room. "Your books have arrived."

"I see that. And a case to put them in."

She made no reply, and we stood for a moment smiling at each other. She was dressed, as always, in elegant, expensive clothes, linen and silk with strappy sandals that showcased a perfect pedicure. The heels, I noted, were not so perilously high and narrow as others I'd seen her wear. I took this to be the current fashion rather than any accommodation on my friend's part to the requirements of steady walking. I had the thought that she must be nearly sixty, a number no one who looked at her would ever guess. "You look great," I said.

She ignored the compliment. "How was Rome?" she asked.

"Eternal," I said. "How was Munich?"

"Very clean," she said. "Very orderly. Easy to get around; everything runs on time. You really have to hand it to these Germans."

"And the grandchildren?"

"Two wild animals. But affectionate animals."

"So, a good visit."

"Not entirely," she said. "David is furious with me, and I wasn't able to calm him down. I think we are not speaking for the time being."

"That's terrible," I said.

She shrugged. "He'll get over it."

"What was your crime?"

"It's a long story," she said. "I'll tell you about it at dinner. Now I'll leave you to unpack and arrange your work space."

"I'll have more than one," I said. "In the bedroom and on the terrace."

"That was the idea," she replied. "Come over for dinner at eight. And you don't need to bring anything, please."

"*Volentieri,*" I said, earning one of her encouraging smiles.

"*Prego,*" she said, leaving me to my own devices.

⌒☙⌒

There were changes in the villa as well, especially in the kitchen, where a wall of shelves and cabinets now surrounded the window and the sink and new appliances, bigger and incongruously bright, lined one wall. Overhead the institutional fluorescent tubes had been replaced with carefully spaced track lighting that shed an even silvery glow over the counters. "This is a big improvement," I observed.

"It is," Beatrice agreed. "It was a nightmare getting it done. All the wire, all the pipes, everything had to be redone. The electrician was a genius, but he was reduced to tears."

At dinner she told me what she had done to enrage her son.

Sometime after my first visit, Anna Falco had come to the villa for the express purpose of arranging a meeting between Beatrice and her son, Leonardo, to discuss a proposition he had in mind. "It was all very mysterious and pompous. I've known Leonardo all his life," Beatrice said, "but suddenly there was *una proposta* he must make to me at a private meeting. I told Anna to have him come by the house in the afternoon. She insisted on a time, so I said two thirty.

"He arrived exactly on time, dressed in his banker's suit, though it was a Sunday. I offered him coffee, tea; no, he would only have a glass of water. We sat across the table from each other and he folded his hands, his eyes down, looking for all the world like a nervous boy about to propose marriage. I said, 'So, Leonardo, what is it you want to talk to me about?'

" 'Signora Doyle,' he said, 'I would like to buy from you the old farmhouse at the back of the vineyard.' "

"There's a farmhouse?" I said.

"It's part of the villa property, very rundown. No one has lived in it since the war. It was closed up properly some years ago. Before that, water came in through some broken roof tiles, so there was mold; a small animal got in and chewed electrical wires; two shutters came loose and two windows were broken; a sink pipe burst and the entire first floor was flooded. It's a ruin, actually. When I remodeled the limonaia, David wanted me to fix up that house instead; he used to play in it as a child and has some attachment to it. I had a builder give me an estimate for repairs and it was an astronomical number. That's when I had the house closed up."

"And now Leonardo wants to buy it?"

"Yes. He's done quite well at the bank, and of course he knows all about financing. He lives at home with his parents and his grand-father, but their house, as you saw, is small. I assume he is planning to marry and have a family, and this house is so close to his parents, he can walk there. It struck me as a good plan, and when he told me the price he was willing to pay, I was pleasantly surprised. I knew it would mean I could finally get a real plumber here to fix all the pipes—that's expensive work you can't see, but it's done now and I can sleep at night."

"That's great," I said.

"It has worked out well, I think. But David is furious about it. The work is nearly done, and I didn't tell him about it until this trip. Leonardo has proved to be an excellent builder and supervisor. He gutted the house entirely and everything in it is new, though he's kept to the integrity of the structure. The walls are all replas-tered, the fine old brick floor cleaned and polished, there's new tile everywhere. Perhaps a little too much tile. He's very pleased with himself and eager to show it off. I told him I'd bring you by tomor-row afternoon; he's very keen on that. I'm not sure why."

"Is David angry because he wanted the house for himself?"

"Why would he want it?" Beatrice exclaimed. "He works all the time, he takes perhaps three weeks vacation a year, and he's made it clear the family prefers Cape Cod, because of the beaches, I sup-pose, and because his father is there. But now he says they go there because Greta hates the limonaia and is miserable if they stay in this house, which is certainly large enough, because she's terrified of my mother and the house is cold and gloomy. He says if I had fixed the farmhouse for them instead of trying to cram them into a broiling outbuilding designed for potted trees, they would have room to spread out; they would have some privacy and the chil-dren wouldn't have to be quiet to avoid disturbing my mother—"

"I thought your mother liked noise," I interrupted.

Beatrice gave me a thoughtful look. "She likes city noise, the bustle of humanity, not the whining of children."

"It sounds like David was digging up some deep resentment," I said.

"Yes," she agreed. "That is what he was doing. I had no idea how deep that well of resentment is nor how long he has been excavating it, evidently with the help of his wife. She thinks I spend all the money on myself, on my house in Poughkeepsie, and let everything else go to hell. I said, should I live in a shack for nine months a year so that your family can have a house to visit for three weeks? David has plenty of money. Was he willing to cough up some money to renovate the farmhouse? Not a chance. And then, of course, the true reason for his hysterical reaction was revealed. What he's really angry about is that I sold the house to Leonardo."

"But weren't they childhood friends?"

"So I thought; so I said. 'I thought you would be pleased to have your old friend rescuing this derelict eyesore of a house,' I said, 'and paying, I might say, a very good price for the opportunity to do it.' David wasn't persuaded by this argument, and I know why. The Falcos are *contadini*. I had sold Salviati family property to peasants. My mother raised the same issue, but she understood that we would be using the proceeds to do much-needed repairs in the villa and in her apartment in Firenze, which has many problems, and she gave in. My mother is practical, above all, and she knows just how much everything is worth. She said, 'In the end, they will have it all.'

"I thought that was a bit dramatic. 'It's a farmhouse,' I told her. 'It has never been lived in by anyone in this family.' She said, 'It's the first step. You'll see.' But still, she agreed to the sale."

Ah, I thought. *The ancient, hoary goblin of class struggle rears its contentious head in sunny Tuscany.* Here was the rank terror that lurks in every corner of the big house all over the world. The artlessness of the landed gentry against the native cunning of the peasantry. I pictured Scarlett O'Hara, on fire with indignation, bending down to claw up a clod of earth and taking aim at her father's former overseer, who has come to make an offer on the ruins of her mansion. "That's all of Tara you'll ever get," she snaps, as the famous red dirt of Georgia splatters across his astounded face.

"I'd love to see the farmhouse," I said.

⋆⋆⋆

After lunch the next day, Beatrice and I set off across the vineyard to meet Leonardo Falco at his nearly completed house. The walk was uphill, along the leafy rows of grapevines stretched between lines of wooden posts on wire that sagged beneath the weight of branches and heavy clusters of cloudy dark-blue grapes. "When is the harvest?" I asked.

"In October," Beatrice said. "I'm never here for it anymore, though I loved it when I was a girl."

"Did you tread barefoot on grapes in barrels?" I asked.

She smiled. "No, even then we had a press." We came to the end of a row and turned onto a path that ran along a field of wavy golden grain.

"What is this grain?" I asked.

"It's wheat," she said. "It's doing well enough this year, but last year there was a fungus and the entire crop was lost."

"How dreadful," I said.

"The sad truth is that farming is not very profitable in Tuscany these days."

"Yet it all looks so perfect and well managed."

We had come to the end of the field. The path forked in two directions, and Beatrice took the uphill route, where wide stone slabs set into the earth created convenient steps. The house came into view from the ground up, the beige stone wall rising before us, shedding waves of heat and light, for the sun was still high and beating down prodigiously upon the scene. "It's big," I said as we cleared the last step and came out between a pair of strategically placed cypresses on either side of a covered terrace. A man holding a briefcase in one hand stood there with his back to us, looking toward an oversized brick oven like a shrine attached to the far end of the house.

"*Ciao,* Leonardo," Beatrice called out.

He turned; his face brightened; he set the briefcase down on the stones and advanced upon us, emanating that curious, genial serenity I had noticed at our first meeting.

"*Buongiorno, signora,*" he said to Beatrice. He extended his hand to me and I responded by putting out my own, which he held gently, momentarily, saying, "*Bentornata, signora.* Welcome in Italy."

That was the extent of his English, so the rest of the visit consisted of long, rapid exchanges between Beatrice and our guide, interspersed with brief summaries translated for my benefit. I understood more than they probably guessed and I was free to study the tenor of their communications, which is often more revealing than the actual content of what people say to each other. Leonardo's manner evidenced no traces of deference or servility; in fact, it was confident and mildly aloof. Beatrice veered between indulgence and, as we passed from room to room of the now light-filled and glowing house, frank amazement. She had seen the renovation at a much earlier stage. Leonardo pointed out to her various appealing features as we went: the dark beams in the newly plastered ceiling; the cornices and door trims, all sanded, stained, oiled; the new casement windows throughout, with clever latches that allowed them to open from the side or the top; the small but highly functional kitchen, with the raised hearth fireplace so dear to Italians—which, I thought, the villa didn't have—the new gas stove and double ovens built into the brick wall next to the sink. As Beatrice had warned, there was a lot of tile: the kitchen counters, a tiled built-in sideboard in the dining room, two entirely tiled bathrooms, every inch of the floors, walls, even a tiled trim around the ceiling, one in dark gold and yellow that made me feel I was entering the secret chambers of a sunflower (and indeed I heard the word *girasole* bandied back and forth between my guides), the other a tropical green as bright as an anole on the grass, trimmed with black lozenges arranged in diagonal lines.

I murmured my approval, admiration, surprise, as we moved from room to room. *"Buon lavoro,"* Beatrice observed again and again. Good work. Whenever she paused to share the details of Leonardo's remarks with me, he stood very still, giving me his close, courteous attention. Upstairs some furnishings were in place: iron bedsteads, heavy wooden dressers, wicker chairs in the bedrooms, one of which opened onto a charming balcony with potted geraniums cascading over the wall. Beatrice and I mewed with delight.

At last we had seen every room and we descended the wide stone steps to the terrace, where Leonardo called our attention to the outdoor oven. Beatrice said, "When Leonardo bought the house, this was just a pile of bricks. Now he has made it useful again."

"It's a beautiful house," I said.

"Veramente è una bellissima casetta," she said to Leonardo.

I noted that she had called the house a *casetta*—a little house.

Leonardo nodded, taking a few steps to his briefcase, which he'd left behind on our tour. He bent over it, popped it open, and withdrew a white envelope. Beatrice watched him with an expression of deep perplexity. He returned to us, holding the envelope between his hands tentatively, for once not entirely sure of himself. He addressed me, drawing his spine up as if to enforce a resolution. "I have something for you, signora," he said. It was clear that he had rehearsed this phrase. He opened the envelope, pulling out a printed sheet. A photo of the farmhouse was featured at the top.

"What is it?" Beatrice asked, drawing close to me to examine Leonardo's offering.

"It's an advertisement," I said. The photo showed the house to great advantage: the terrace doors wide open, the stone walls burnished gold by the sun, the windows glittering, and the banner of sky above it so intensely blue it dazzled the eye. Beneath it, in bold print, the copy read: BEAUTIFUL VACATION HOUSE IN TUSCANY.

Now Leonardo spoke to Beatrice, who translated with a tone of barely contained impatience. "He says this is an ad that will run in an agency book. It's an international agency with offices in New York. The address is at the bottom. He's thinking your colleagues at the college might be interested in renting the house for short terms, and that you might put up this advertisement on a board, or perhaps your office door. Now that you've seen the house you can assure your friends it will be suitable for professors and their families."

I scanned the smaller print briefly as Beatrice spoke: "Lovely terrace, two bedrooms, two elegant baths, fully equipped kitchen, private balcony, view of the vineyard, children welcome."

Beatrice paused, and I looked up to see Leonardo regarding me with that quiet confidence that made his company so steadying. He must be great with loan applicants at the bank, I thought. *"Volentieri,"* I said. And to Beatrice, "Tell him I will make copies and post them on various department boards."

Beatrice translated and Leonardo gave me a smile of such genuine goodwill that I smiled back. I was *molto gentile,* he assured me. Beatrice continued as he spun off into Italian. "He is very hopeful that Americans will come to stay in his house," she said.

Ever so slight emphasis on the word *his* in that phrase. I didn't have to look at Beatrice to know something of her state of mind, but curiously Leonardo, who had known her all his life, appeared blithely unaware that she would not be delighted at the idea that he planned to use the old house she had sold him as an investment property. She made some final remarks, congratulating him again on the renovation, while I stood by, studying the offensive flyer, mentally preparing an appropriate parting remark. *"Mille grazie per avermi invitato a vedere la tua bella casa,"* I said. Was I correct to use the informal address?

"Prego, signora," Leonardo replied, grasping my hand. Then followed some politesse that Beatrice translated flatly. "He hopes your

stay in Italy will be a pleasant one and that you will visit him and his family once again before you go."

One more *"Volentieri, grazie"* from me, and we were out. Beatrice presented her back to her tenant's son and stepped down from the terrace, striding briskly across her wheat field to her vineyard. I followed, rolling up the printed sheet as I went. We didn't speak until we rounded the bend to the vineyard path. It was wider there and I drew up alongside my friend. "I am very disappointed in Leonardo," she said.

I made no reply, and we walked along in silence. Now that the motive for Leonardo's eagerness to show me the house was revealed, we both fell prey to the flattening effect of a reproof. The sun struck us at an angle, making us squint as we ambled down-hill now, with the farmhouse rising steadily behind us. Perhaps, I thought, Leonardo could see us from the terrace.

"Why didn't he give you a flyer?" I asked. "Surely he knows you're an American professor as well."

"He thinks I'm the competition," she said.

I puzzled over this; then I realized that she meant the limonaia. "But you don't advertise," I said.

"I would never do that," she said coldly. We walked on, both following our own thoughts on the subject. I was thinking that Leonardo stood to make a nice profit on his farmhouse, as it wasn't far from several popular hill towns, yet private and spacious, with new plumbing and a modern kitchen. We entered the villa garden, flushing out an enormous rabbit that shot across our path, causing us both to cry out sharply.

"That's the biggest rabbit I've ever seen," I remarked.

"They are hares. Very destructive and strong. Even the foxes are careful of them."

"The fox and the hare," I said. "What happens in that fable? I can't remember."

"The fox invites the hare to dinner," Beatrice reminded me. "But the table is set for one and there's no other food."

"Does the hare escape?"

"In some versions," she said.

We were silent again until we came out at the front of the garden. "So," Beatrice said. "Now I understand. The farmhouse is to be no more than a hotel."

"And Leonardo will continue to live with his parents," I added.

"Yes," she said.

We had reached the parking area, where we would part. "Shall we go out for a pizza this evening?" she said. "I don't feel like staying in the villa tonight."

As it turned out, Leonardo was in the vanguard of a trend. The Italian government had sanctioned his entrepreneurial adventure a few years earlier and given it a name, *agriturismo*. The Falco family owned just enough land and had a going agricultural concern—they grew sunflowers and olives—which made them eligible for subsidies to renovate "historic" buildings. "I should have known," Beatrice said over a slice of pizza margherita at her favorite trattoria on the outskirts of Castelnuovo Berardenga. "This is happening all over Toscana. The *contadino* who owns a rundown cowshed or a stone gristmill is turning it into an apartment with a covered terrace, because there's no place to eat inside, and renting it out to Germans or to Americans, if he can get them. Some even build swimming pools. Then they put on airs and have parties with their neighbors where they serve Coca-Cola and shrimp."

"Do you think Leonardo will build a pool?"

"If he does, it will be a small one. He doesn't have enough land, and I'm certainly not going to sell another inch to him."

We concentrated on our pizza. I was thinking of Beatrice's remark about the shrimp. This crustacean evidently represented a delicacy so pretentious that aristocrats scorned serving it to guests. What did it mean in Italy when peasants served shrimp to their neighbors? Again I was put in mind of the painting I'd seen in Milan, by Giuseppe Pellizza da Volpedo, with its massed humanity striding determinedly toward the viewer and the stalwart trio at the front, two men and a woman holding a baby; doubtless these were the leaders, the ones who would speak, the ones who could read, assailing a future they could contemplate only with misgivings. They sought to better their lot by refusing to work.

It was painted in 1901. Two world wars and a twenty-year dictatorial regime that would leave the country bankrupt and in ruins—that was what those disenfranchised workers could neither see nor imagine.

And beyond that, in the here and now, an even stranger consequence of history—peasants renovating farmhouses to rent to their former enemies, and giving parties for their neighbors where they served Coca-Cola and shrimp.

"Have you ever seen that painting by Pellizza da Volpedo in Milan?" I asked Beatrice as the waitress took our plates away.

"*Il Quarto Stato?*" she said. "Everyone in Italy has seen it. What makes you think of that?"

⌇⌇⌇

Beatrice's mother, Maria Salviati Bartolo, enjoyed enviable health and lived by invariable routines. She spent the winter and spring in Firenze and the summer and fall at Villa Chiara. When she was younger, she took the train to Siena, but now that Beatrice had a more commodious car and Maria's vision was not as sharp as was necessary to defend herself from the thieves who made train travel an adventure, she consented to being driven from her city apartment to her country estate. On the first weekend of my visit, Beatrice drove out from the villa to effect this transfer. She would stay two nights in Firenze, taking advantage of the opportunity to visit friends, enjoy some entertainment: music, an art opening, a favorite restaurant, and especially the revitalizing walk along the narrow streets of the *centro,* gazing idly in the shop windows as she artfully consumed, without so much as a drip, a scoop of pistachio gelato nestled in a crisp cone.

I had unpacked my materials in the limonaia and supplied the refrigerator with good things from the market. The best place to work was at the new table on the terrace, where I could lay out my pile of books, my pens and paper, my stacks of folders containing reprints of articles, and my journal notebooks with a key at the front to various topics of interest. As I worked, the occasional bird joined me to pick at the bread crumbs on my plate or to perch boldly on the edge of my coffee cup, peering into the depths just long enough to ascertain that the distorted reflection on the oily surface of the liquid was not another bird.

It sounds serene, a writer's dream, but I was anxious because my novel had become something of a loose, baggy monster. I had signed a contract on the strength of a proposal and several opening chapters that made the project appear a much more straightforward enterprise than I now knew it was likely to be. And though I had a pretty clear idea how it would end—it was a historical novel, after all—as I'd told Luca, research leads to research. I had allowed myself to stray far afield and reached at last the unenviable, possibly inevitable condition in which I couldn't stop seeing thematic connections between the past and the present. My imagination lurched from the rise of fascism and the tumultuous career of Benito Mussolini to the youthful Beatrice setting out from Firenze on her American adventure, from the painting of a workers' strike at the dawn of the century to the sale of an abandoned farmhouse to an upwardly mobile clerk. Relentlessly I circled what was for me the primal event of my story: the violent death of Beatrice's uncle Sandro in the driveway of Villa Chiara shortly after his deliverance from a psychiatric institution where he had been incarcerated for forty years.

Beatrice had described her uncle as confused and so weak he was scarcely able to walk. What was he doing alone in the driveway? Was it during the day or at night? Who was in the villa besides Maria? Beatrice had speculated that the murderers might have been partisans who thought her uncle was his brother, Marco. Was Marco there as well? I looked out at the dusty car park, once again trying to picture the scene. At that time the house wasn't divided, so Sandro could have come out under the wisteria arbor. This would make sense, as a confused, sick, possibly drugged elderly man wouldn't be able to get down the staircase from the main doors of the villa. The door itself was heavy and might constitute too great an obstacle.

Where did Sandro think he was going?

I stood up and stepped out into the drive, noting the various angles and obstacles to a clear view. It had been nearly fifty years ago, but I doubted there had been much change in the configuration of the scene. Beatrice had suggested that her uncle's death might have been the result of crossfire between Germans and partisans, and I could see that this was certainly possible. A person standing where I stood would be in a direct line between groups of intruders who came through the gate and from the garden. I raised my hands over my head, turning slowly in place.

"I wonder what on earth you are doing," a voice I recognized inquired. Luca stepped out from beneath the arbor, his brow furrowed skeptically.

Luca, but how changed, how shrunken, how sallow, how clearly diminished. Yet his regard was the same chilly, distant, lightless business I remembered from my last visit. I dropped my arms to my sides. "Luca," I said sharply. "You startled me."

"I can see you didn't expect anyone to be watching," he said. He was, as usual, neatly suited, one hand hovering about the jacket pocket containing the packet of cigarettes, but the jacket hung loosely on him now, the collar too high and the shoulders too wide. It stood a little apart from him, as if in the process of swallowing him one day at a time. His cheeks were sunken and the sclera of his eyes threaded with blood.

When I was confronted with such a physical alteration, my natural response might have been to ask after his health, but there was something about Luca's presence that made me skirt engagement and rush straight to the defensive. "I was just stretching," I said. "I've been sitting at the table too long."

He glanced past me at the table, laden with my books and papers. "Surely you're not still chasing after Mussolini," he said.

"I'm still interested in the period," I replied. As I spoke we heard the crunch of gravel from the road; then a tan Chevy van swerved into view and came to a halt alongside my latest Panda.

"Here is Beppe," Luca said. "Coming to our rescue."

"Is something wrong in your house?"

"This is often the case," he observed.

Beppe switched off the engine and got out of the van. He hadn't changed, I noted, except perhaps he looked more solid, more vital next to the emaciated Luca, who fumbled in his pocket for his cigarettes and lighter, coughing all the while. He tapped a white cylinder out into his palm as Beppe cleared the back of the truck. Seeing me, Beppe smiled wearily. *"Buongiorno, signora,"* he said. *"Bentornata."*

"Buongiorno," I said, stifling the impulse to offer my hand.

Luca lit his cigarette and took a long puff, breathing smoke out through his nose as he launched into a barrage of Italian. Beppe took it all in without speaking, nodding his head to confirm his apprehension of the complaint. Behind Luca, the door opened and Mimma stepped out beneath the arbor. She too appeared altered, a little heavier, her white hair pulled back from her face with two girlish plastic barrettes, her cheeks rouged, her lips garishly red. Beppe saw her at the same moment I did. At once he spoke soothingly, interrupting Luca, who turned to his sister with a scowl.

It struck me that Luca and Beppe were both out and about in the world in their different capacities, one a man of the earth, the *terra,* who knew exactly when the sun would rise and set and how to fill the hours in between with animal pleasure and physical labor, and the other routinely engaged in his pseudoscience, his brain stuffed with the neuroses of his patients, his sense of his own superiority ever inflated by the abysmal failures of others, but Mimma, to my knowledge, had no life beyond the walls of the villa. She didn't drive; everything she needed was brought to her. Beatrice said she had been selfish and mean as a child and had not changed. On the few occasions I had seen her, she had steadfastly refused to acknowledge my existence. Now she cried out to Beppe in a rapid, high-pitched, babyfied whine. I caught the word *tubi.*

"I thought Beatrice replaced the pipes," I said to Luca, who stood beside me assiduously smoking his cigarette.

"My cousin keeps you informed of the state of her plumbing," he said. "I find that strange."

"I was admiring the renovation of her kitchen," I explained.

"Our kitchen has not been renovated," he said. "And the faucets are very old. One of them is now leaking."

I smiled. "I appreciate your sharing this intimate detail of your household arrangements," I said.

To my surprise, as he blew out a puff of smoke, Luca made a strangling sound which I took to be a laugh. His eyes skated past mine, but their expression approached amusement. Mimma had come to the end of her oration, and Beppe, murmuring confidentially, followed her back into the villa. On an impulse I said to Luca, "I was about to have a caffè on the terrace. Would you care to join me?"

He looked off into the air wonderingly, then sharply back at me. "Yes," he said. "I would like that, and I know Mimma will be pleased, as it gives her time alone with Beppe."

We crossed the drive to my table, where I busied myself clearing away a stack of books and notes to make room for my guest. "This big table really makes my work easier," I chattered, as Luca stood by watching me indifferently. "Have a seat," I said. "I'll go put on the caffettiera."

From the kitchen, as I packed the espresso into the steel cup, tamping it down with the base of the scoop, I could see Luca perusing my books. He picked up one, turned it over, read the copy, opened it at random and read from a page, then closed it and considered another. I set the cups and saucers on the tray, added the sugar bowl, the tiny spoons. I could put out a plate of orange sponges, I thought, but I knew Luca wouldn't touch them. In general Italians don't approve of eating anything with coffee. Dunking in general horrifies them, though it is approved for biscotti and vin santo. I reconsidered my invitation. Did I really want to have a friendly chat with Luca Salviati? I'd invited him because he had laughed at my teasing remark, which suggested he actually had a sense of humor lurking beneath the relentless self-regard. Also, I couldn't deny, it was pleasurable to speak English. I suspected this was a draw for him too, a chance to practice a language he knew but rarely used.

The caffettiera bubbled, and when the steam abated, I poured the hot black liquid into the little cups and carried the tray out through the open door. Luca was still standing, absorbed in reading a book I recognized without having to see the cover. It was an extended interview that Mussolini's widow, Rachele, had given to a French journalist in 1973. As I set the tray on the table, Luca snapped the book closed and laid it facedown on a stack of legal pads. "How did you even find such a book as this?" he asked.

"Please," I said, "have a seat." I placed a cup, saucer, and spoon before the chair I wanted him to take. He dropped into it and leaned forward to rest his forearms on the table.

"We have a system of interlibrary loans at my college," I said. "I can get books from all over the state, and as a professor, unless someone else requests a book, I can keep it for a year."

"There can't be many requests for such a volume in America,"

Luca observed. He lifted his cup and moistened his lips, a preliminary to actual drinking.

"It does seem unlikely," I said. "Especially in the summer, when the faculty is away. So I took the chance of bringing it with me."

"Have you read it?" he asked.

"I have," I said. "I found it extremely interesting."

"Doubtless she is making up stories to vindicate her husband."

"That goes without saying," I agreed. "And the journalist may be encouraging her to exaggerate. And it's translated into English, so I can't exactly hear her voice. Still, she was in a position to know a lot. She's quite full of herself. In her version the Duce never made a decision without consulting her. Even the queen sought her counsel."

"That's unlikely," Luca observed.

"Is it?" I asked.

He shrugged. It was clear that he had no desire to talk about Rachele Mussolini; for some reason the subject made him uncomfortable. I resolved to pursue it.

"She's very frank as well. She talks about her husband's mistresses. She forgives Claretta Petacci because she was willing to die for Mussolini and in fact did die for him."

"This is widely known," he said.

"That's true," I agreed. "I knew about Claretta, but I didn't know about Ida Dalser and the Duce's son who died during the war."

Luca's brows lifted slightly and he shifted his gaze to the inside of his cup, as if he had found something of particular interest there.

"She's arch about it," I continued. "She says Ida Dalser came to see her and made a scene. And she says, 'She was no beauty,' which I thought unkind. She calls her *la matta* and says she died in an asylum. I wonder where."

There was a pause. Luca allowed it to open meaningfully, a trick he had no doubt perfected in his professional capacity. I declined the opportunity to stumble into the silence, and this seemed to please him. He nodded his head, focusing his tired eyes on the middle distance. "It was in Venice," he said. "The hospital was on San Clemente."

I actually had this information—Rachele named the hospital—but I pretended gratified surprise, pulled in a legal pad and pen, and wrote the name in the margin of a page of notes. *He knows all about this,* I thought.

"Do you know what happened to the son?" I asked.

He gave me his bemused look, as if I were some new species of insect he'd heard about but never seen. "This is just an old woman's gossip," he said, fluttering his fingers at the book. Then, noticing that his hand was empty, he dropped it over the open pack on the table and began working a single cigarette free from the others.

"Maybe so," I said. "But the son was real, and he knew who his father was. Rachele says Mussolini acknowledged him; he even provided him with a small income."

Luca had liberated his cigarette and now produced the lighter from his jacket pocket. The air was still and hot, and the silence that fell between us had that lazy, amiable quality that summer produces, when time stretches out like a cat anticipating a nap. Luca felt it too, I thought. He lit his cigarette and took a long drag, leaning back in his chair, his eyes unfocused and dreamy. Again I had the impression that he was ill; even his smallest movements suggested a convalescent weariness. He didn't think much of me. My enthusiasms and curiosity vexed him, but he didn't feel like moving either. Smoke drifted out through his nostrils. I removed the saucer from under my cup and pushed it toward him for an ashtray. This provoked a complicit nod. He tapped the cigarette ash into the saucer. I lifted my cup and drank off half the coffee.

"I persist in wondering why the recent history of a country you know so little about occupies your imagination in this way," he observed.

"In what way?" I asked. He brought the cup to his lips and allowed himself another teaspoon of a sip. "In a salacious way?"

"Are there no American scandals to investigate?" he suggested.

"Is it because I'm an American?" I said. "If I were French, would my interest bother you so much?"

"It would make more sense to me," he admitted. "France was engaged in the war and damaged by it, not just its soldiers but everyone, civilians, women, children. Whole towns were destroyed, children were shipped away to safety, neighbors no longer trusted neighbors. They shaved the heads of women who took German lovers and forced them to walk naked through the streets. Every detail of daily life was disturbed, sometimes significantly, sometimes irrevocably, as it was here in Italy, and all over Europe, even in Britain."

"But not in America," I said meekly.

He smiled wanly at my naïveté. "The Americans revved up their war machine, shipped it to Europe, and when the war was over and Europe was in ruins, they shipped it home again. Then they became rich and decided to visit Italy as tourists. Or to dig up war stories that prove to them they were heroes."

It was my turn to look away. His charge, so thick with contempt, stung me. I stifled my first response, which was to remind him that if the Americans hadn't arrived where they did and when they did, he would be speaking German. I studied the photo on the back of the book that had provoked this display of bitterness. Rachele Mussolini, a lively-looking old lady—she was eighty-four when it was published—is seated at a table next to an amiable young Frenchman, who is pointing out something on a page to her. She's smiling confidently, doling out her version of a calamitous history with the cunning of a fox. She was never outwitted. She died peacefully in the fall of 1979 at Predappio, the town where she was born.

Luca was silent, drawing languidly on the most recent cigarette, coughing as the smoke left what was left of his lungs. I kept my eyes on Mussolini's wife as I spoke. "Still," I said. "A lot of Americans died in Italy."

He blew out the smoke in a huff, opening his hands in a gesture that suggested I had stated, once again, the obvious. "Was someone in your family killed here?" he asked.

"An uncle," I said. "My father's brother. He was a pilot and got shot down somewhere in the south. I never knew him. It was before I was born."

He said nothing.

I returned to my subject. "The thing I find odd is that Rachele says Ida Dalser had a son, but she doesn't say his name, and then she says he was studying radiotelegraphy in La Spezia and he died near Milano, and then she gives the exact date of his death. Month, day, year."

"What's odd about it?"

"Why would she know the specific date but not his name? Or exactly where he was?"

Luca picked up the book and scowled at the cheerful old lady rummaging in her memory for the benefit of the French journalist.

"Rachele says it was common knowledge in the family that she was a secret agent. The archsleuth," I added.

"Donna Rachele," he said. "A very dangerous old bird."

"And a secretive old bird. She's not telling a lot of what she knows."

Luca nodded. He set the book back on the table and stubbed out his cigarette in the tiny saucer. "The boy's name was Benito Albino Mussolini," he said. "He was in the navy briefly. Like his mother, a very unstable young man. Eventually the Duce disowned him entirely. There was some incident, I don't know exactly what happened, near the start of the war. He was evacuated from a ship and sent to a psychiatric asylum. He died there a few years later."

"How do you know this?"

"I knew a doctor who treated him. He insisted that he was the

Duce's son. Sadly, there were others who made the same claim. In his case, it turned out to be true."

"He must have been young."

"I don't think he was thirty," Luca agreed.

"And where was the asylum?"

Luca reached for the sugar bowl, measured a careful spoon into his cup, and stirred it idly before answering me. Then he tossed back the contents in one swallow. *He works on his timing,* I thought.

"It was the Giuseppe Antonini Hospital," he said. "At Mombello, near Milano."

I felt my eyes widen. "The same hospital where your uncle Sandro was," I said.

"Yes," he said. "My uncle was there as well. It was very crowded at that time. They may never have crossed paths."

How did he know it was crowded? "Did you go there?" I asked.

Luca put his cigarette down in the dish and folded his hands on the table, his distrustful eyes fixed firmly on my face. For a long moment he said nothing, and I knew he was deciding whether to tell me the truth or a lie. It was going to be a one-word answer, that I was sure of. I met his gaze steadily, though I could feel the pressure of a smile at the corners of my mouth, which would become more pronounced as another moment went by. *Tell me, I was thinking. Tell me the truth,* and that thought caused me to turn my hands palms up in a gesture of supplication I knew to be clearer than speech to an Italian. He looked down at my hands, unfolded his own, and brought one palm to his chin, stroking his jawline, visibly making up his mind. At last he sat back in his chair, resting his fingertips on the edge of the table.

"Yes," he said.

PART 5

The Runaway

Luca Salviati wiped the sweat from his forehead as he rounded the last corner on his walk home from the training center. He'd passed a miserable morning doing group calisthenics beneath the blazing sun on the parade yard. When he fell behind the pace, the Gioventù leader berated him cruelly, calling him a disgrace to the country and to the Duce. All he wanted to do was go straight to the cool courtyard, pull off his shirt, and plunge his head and arms into the palazzo fountain. But there, blocking his way, what should he find but a shabby, derelict old man slouched on the pavement, his back pressed against the portone of the Palazzo Salviati, gazing out at the street with an expression of pleasure and ease. *The audacity,* thought Luca. *He looks like he thinks he belongs here.*

Luca was fifteen and very clear about who belonged where in his world. He approached the loiterer with a boldness he didn't really feel and announced, "Sir, you can't sit here."

The man shifted his gaze to the boy and offered him a gentle, sun-crazed smile. "I'm waiting for someone to let me in," he said.

Luca was incredulous. "Why would anyone do that?"

"I've forgotten my key," said the man. "Or lost it on the way."

"If you don't get away from this door, I shall call the police," Luca said.

"I'm very tired," said the man. "I've come a long way. You should at least offer me a glass of water, for charity's sake. I only want to rest in my own bed."

"And where is your own bed? It's not here."

"It was here. I'm sure of that."

Luca paused, considering the right response. Unconsciously he clasped his hands behind his back and stood with his legs apart. He was miserably uncomfortable in his camp uniform, a long-sleeved black shirt, azure scarf knotted at the neck, gray-green wool shorts, knee-high black socks, and tough laced-up boots that were all wrong for marching.

"You look like my brother," the man said. "Except for your chin."

"Get out of my way," Luca shouted, raising his boot to kick the fellow aside. Though he missed his mark and his boot struck the door next to the man's hip, it was enough to drive the fellow scrambling toward the street. Luca jammed his key in the lock and threw all his weight against the panel, which opened so abruptly he staggered against it. As he attempted to close it behind him, the man hurled himself into the gap and collapsed on the stones inside the door.

"Help!" Luca cried, rushing up the steps to the landing.

He heard an inner door open, footsteps, then another door. His father appeared above him, scowling and irritable. The sight that met his eyes, a beggar cowering on the floor and his son in hasty retreat, amused him. "What are you afraid of, you coward?" he exclaimed. "Are we now in danger from old beggars on the street?"

The beggar in question raised himself to his knees, lifting his face with an expression of wonder, his hands raised and pressed together in prayer. "Marco," he said. "May God have mercy on your immortal soul."

Marco's eyes widened. The face was unrecognizable, but the

voice, a little high, yet clear and sonorous, and the posture . . . "Sandro?" he said. "How is this possible?"

"Who is this man?" Luca demanded. "Why do you know his name?"

Marco frowned, keeping his eyes on the humble petitioner. "He's my brother," he said coldly.

"Why are you in a uniform?" the newfound brother asked. "This boy is in uniform. The whole city is in uniform. Are we at war?"

"Not yet," said Marco. "How did you get out of Mombello?"

"I climbed a tree and went over the wall. I don't want to stay in that place any longer. I'd like to go to my bed now, please."

"Oh, do you imagine we've kept the linens fresh for you all these years?"

Luca fanned the air as he put a few steps between himself and this creature he was now expected to believe was a near relation. "God, he stinks," he exclaimed.

At this Sandro brightened, pulling himself to his feet. "God makes stinks and sweet perfumes all alike." He trailed up the steps behind his outraged nephew.

"Your own mother despaired of you," Marco snapped as his brother approached him. To Luca he said, "Take him to the bath and let him wash. Then find him some clothes to put on. Where did you get those rags?"

"I found them in a wash basket," Sandro said cheerfully. He arrived at the landing and pushed determinedly past Marco. "I know where I'm going," he said.

"Follow him," Marco commanded his son. "Keep an eye on him."

"Where am I supposed to find clothes?" Luca complained.

Sandro paused, turning to face his brother. "Where is Valeria? Where is my dear sister?"

"They're all at Villa Chiara, the lot of them," Marco replied.

"Little Maria is there, and Celestia?"

"The lot of them," Marco repeated. "Three harpies."

Sandro turned away, speaking over his shoulder. "I want to go there," he said. "To Villa Chiara."

Luca followed his uncle along the hall toward his own bedroom. Sandro seemed to know where he was going, but when he shambled past the bathroom door, Luca ran up beside him and pointed it out. "The bath is here," he said.

Sandro halted, confronting the door, his brows knit in puzzlement. "When did this get here?" he asked.

"I don't know. It's always been here." Luca pushed the door open, revealing the sumptuous interior, the porcelain tub gleaming and opulent on its stubby legs, the marble counter and sink with chrome faucets, the tufted satin stool before a gold-encrusted mirror, a lacquered chest of drawers with a few spotless white towels folded on top. Sandro stepped in, wide-eyed. "They give us baths," he said, "but the tubs are wooden and have lids on them with holes for our heads so we can't move."

"I've never heard of such a thing," said Luca.

"I don't mind it. But these days it's so crowded we only get a bath every few weeks."

"What is this place?"

"It's a rest home of some kind. I was ill and needed a rest. Once it wasn't a bad place. I have friends there. We had a music group. But that's all gone now." He stepped into the room and sat down wearily on the pouf. "I'm very tired," he said.

"Can you manage a bath by yourself?" Luca asked.

"Oh yes," he said. "I'd like that very much."

"I'll go find you some clothes," Luca said.

"Will I be wearing one of these black shirts? I see them everywhere."

"No. Those are worn by *squadristi* and young people in training camps, like me."

"Training for what?"

Luca backed into the hall. His uncle had begun to unbutton the front of his shirt, and he wasn't keen to see what was underneath. "To serve our country and our Duce," he explained.

"Why not just serve God?" said Sandro.

⋅⟨❋⟩⋅

Where was he going to find clothes? His own would be too small, his father's too large. Sandro was tall and thin, like the cook, but how could he ask the cook for clothes? It was impossible. He slunk down the stairs and along the hall to his father's office. Two rough men in black shirts with leather cudgels depending from their belts stood arguing affably in the doorway. Beyond them Marco sat at his desk, bellowing into a phone. The men, seeing Luca, parted to let him pass. His father, as was his custom in concluding conversations, delivered a string of threats and commands. He slammed down the receiver and turned on his son. "What are you doing here? You're supposed to be watching that madman."

"He's in the bath," Luca said. "I can't find him any clothes unless I take some of yours, and they would fall off him."

Marco scowled. The two men looked on, their faces set in identical lines of attentive servility. "I'm not going to sit in the car with him in those stinking rags all the way to Milano," Marco said. "Giuseppe, you're the right size. I'm requisitioning your clothes."

The men exchanged startled glances.

"Right now," Marco said. "Your pants and your shirt. Don't worry, you can keep your *manganello*. Pietro, you go to his house and get him a change. I need those clothes now."

Luca stepped back, lingering in the doorway. His father's orders would be obeyed, he knew, without protest. What he didn't know was why. Giuseppe pulled his club free of his belt and laid it lovingly on a side table. Then he began unbuttoning his shirt. Marco looked on, amused, impatient. It was revealed that Giuseppe wore long woolen underwear.

"My God, Giù," Marco said. "In this heat! We should take *you* to the asylum."

Luca draped the shirt and trousers over his arm and trudged back up the stairs, his brain a turmoil of conflicting impressions. How was it possible that his father had kept this brother a secret for so many years? No one in the family had ever hinted at his existence, though surely Luca's aunts knew him. He had asked after Aunt Valeria and called his father's archenemy, Aunt Maria, who was forty and had a ten-year-old daughter, "little Maria." And why had this whimsical Sandro been confined in an asylum? He didn't appear to be insane. A bit simple perhaps, clearly a religious fanatic. Why had Marco told him, "Your own mother despaired of you?" Luca paused on the landing, gazing down the wide marble hall. Sandro had said he wanted to rest in his own bed and then headed straight for Luca's room. Had he been sleeping all his life in his uncle's bed?

He took a few steps into the cool marble gloom. His plan was to open the bathroom door just wide enough to shove the clothes inside. He was conscious of a sound as he approached; it was a voice he didn't recognize, a high, clear voice, and it was singing, rising and falling, melodious, continuous, gliding through a musical passage of sweet melancholy, then rising confidently higher and higher in a jubilant ascent to a single note, oh, impossibly high, and yet clear and full as a tolling bell.

Luca formed a mental picture of the scrawny, filthy beggar who was his uncle Sandro sitting up straight in the big tub of steaming water, his chin lifted, his eyes closed, transfixed and transformed, singing as joyfully and compulsively as a bird announcing the arrival of spring.

In fact, Luca reasoned, his uncle was insane, and this proved it. For in this cruel world, what could it be but madness to sing as joyfully as that?

Marco had ordered his biggest car, the black Ministeriale, an official vehicle with an interior as commodious and plush as a luxury train. When Sandro came out of the bathroom, he was dressed in the squadristi black shirt and the puffed-out trousers designed to be worn with knee-high boots. As he had only soft woven shoes such as farmers wore in the summer, the effect was ludicrous. Luca escorted his uncle, who appeared much refreshed by his bath, down the steps. "I'm ready to go to Villa Chiara," Sandro announced. "I'm longing to be there. It is the dearest place in the world to me."

Luca said nothing, reasoning that if his uncle thought that was where they were going, he was under no obligation to disabuse him. Marco was at the door, sweeping his swagger stick back and forth across his legs. "You look like an idiot," he observed as his brother approached.

"I haven't eaten since yesterday," Sandro said. "Will someone give me something for the trip?"

Luca was dispatched to the kitchen, where he said nothing about the return of his mysterious uncle. "My father wants a lunch packed for the road," he told the cook. His mind wandered as he watched the taciturn man laying out bread, cheese, ham, and salami on a sheet of white parchment paper. This uncle Sandro possessed a studied indifference to his brother's casual contempt. He seemed hardly to notice Marco, as if he were somehow unsightly or just mildly distracting, like a fly buzzing in an otherwise silent room. Yet they were brothers, had been children in this house. And though—surely Sandro knew this—he was completely in Marco's power, his first act upon seeing his brother at the top of the stairs was to entreat God's mercy on his soul. Luca smiled at this recollection. It must have disconcerted Marco to be reminded that he had a soul.

The cook folded the paper over the food, crimping the edges to make a neat package. This he tied up in a linen napkin and handed to Luca without comment. He was a brooding fellow; Marco said he was a socialist, probably a criminal, as likely to poison them as not. But his wife was a favorite of Aunt Maria's and so he was kept on in the palazzo. Luca nodded, turning away without speaking and heading briskly up the stairs to the foyer, where his father and his uncle waited for him. Marco pulled the portone door open and stepped out into the street, where the big car glowed like a burning coal in the sun. He looked up and down the street before turning back to his brother and his son. "Right," he said. "Sandro, you get in the middle. Luca, you sit on the outside." This was when Luca knew he was going along for the trip. Later he would wonder why his father chose to take him rather than one of his ever-ready, always willing henchmen. Was this perhaps, in Marco's eyes, a shameful mission? Sandro, clutching his lunch napkin and sending Luca a confidential look—lifted brows, upper lip pulled down—clambered into the padded elegance of the back seat. Luca followed, reaching out to pull the door in behind him. As he did he looked up at his father, who still gazed down the street as if he expected opposition, and noticed a pair of black steel handcuffs attached to his belt by the same loop that held the leather manganello he took off at dinner only when Aunt Maria was at home. She didn't allow weapons at the table, as the table, she maintained, was her only territory.

Marco crossed in front of the car, exchanged a few words with the driver, pulled open the passenger door, and dropped onto the seat next to Sandro. The engine woke with a roar and the driver steered the powerful machine into the traffic teeming along the Arno toward the medieval arches of the Ponte alle Grazie.

Sandro, blocked in between his brother and his nephew, occupied himself in unwrapping his lunch package and consuming the contents. Before he took a bite he offered to share it with Luca, who declined; the students were served an outdoor meal at the training center. The training center must be an excellent place, Sandro opined, breaking off a chunk of bread and chewing it reflectively. He kept his torso slightly turned away from Marco; indeed, it appeared that as far as Sandro was concerned, his brother wasn't there, with his club and his handcuffs and his pitiless gaze. Sandro ate steadily, doggedly, and Luca wondered when he'd last had a meal. Finally he had devoured every morsel. He folded the paper painstakingly, smoothing it and pleating it, evidently with an eye to future use. As he did this, he glanced out the window and saw a sign for Sesto Fiorentino. "We're going the wrong way," he said.

No one spoke.

"We're going the wrong way," he repeated. "This isn't the way to Villa Chiara."

Marco lowered his chin and raised his eyes, fixing his brother in an icy glare. Luca felt his stomach drop; it was a look he knew, and it never bode well for its object. Sandro dodged the look; perhaps it triggered some memory from long ago, of the last time he had dared to oppose his brother. He sat up straight and leaned forward, trying to see out the front windshield, then turned to look past Luca at the ugly industrial scenery flashing by. The car picked up speed as they turned onto the main highway heading north. Luca studied his uncle's face, where a procession of emotions played out: confusion, disbelief, then dawning understanding, and with it fear. After that he succumbed to a descending cloud of sadness, an unfathomable sadness such as Luca had never witnessed before. It settled deep in the lines around his eyes, his face seemed to lengthen, his lips parted as his head dropped forward until his chin touched his breastbone and his long body sagged against the seat. He was still holding the folded square of paper, which he turned slowly between his fingers. He began to mumble something. At first Luca couldn't make it out, then he recognized the refrain: "Holy Mary, mother of God, pray for us sinners now and at the hour of our death." Marco grimaced contemptuously and turned away. He wouldn't need the handcuffs. Luca too occupied himself in watching the passing scenery. Sandro sat quietly between them, calling on the intervention of the mother of God all the way to the psychiatric hospital at Mombello.

The courtyard of the asylum was crowded, noisy, and filthy. All manner of humanity milled about: men in uniforms, men in pajamas, men restrained in straitjackets, men with shoes and without, and moving among them, women in faded blue uniforms, administering medications, advice, and concern. On one bench, three men with matted white hair, their arms confined by dirty gray straitjackets, sat side by side, croaking and raving like wounded crows. Two men leaned against a wall, screaming abuse at each other, punctuated by jabs and slaps, given and returned as in some choreographed routine. In the dust beneath a linden tree, four men wearing pajamas squatted in a circle, throwing down playing cards and shouting as each one fell. The attendant led Sandro, Marco, and Luca past a row of rusting iron beds with thin, bare mattresses upon which men in long gowns lay still as death; perhaps they were dead, Luca thought, and no one had noticed. The family entered the domed hall, where more iron beds with the same stained, lumpy mattresses were lined three deep along the walls on both sides, leaving a passage just wide enough for the rolling metal carts piled with bandages, towels, and trays of medication and disinfectant that the nurses pushed back and forth according to some unintelligible plan. As they turned in to a passageway lined with shuttered windows, two men wearing a combination of hospital gown and ordinary trousers came toward them, deep in conversation. They passed a steel door with a small window where two unwashed men with long, uncombed, greasy hair stood peering in, laughing nervously.

Cries of terror and pain issued from inside the room, piercing the humid air. Sandro stopped praying.

"This way," the nurse they were following encouraged them. "Here we are." They had arrived at a paneled door with a small sign affixed to the frame. As the nurse raised her hand to knock, Sandro laid a hand on his brother's arm and spoke, his voice soft and earnest. "Marco," he said, "if you ask him, he can release me. You can take me to Villa Chiara. I'll stay with my sisters; you'll never hear from me again. I beg you to do this." The knock sounded and a voice called out, "Come in." Marco batted his brother's hand from his sleeve. "This is where you belong," he said coldly. Then all three filed past the nurse into the director's office.

It was more than an office; it was a sanctuary of peace, a book-lined, well-appointed study with windows that opened upon a greensward and an oak desk piled with papers, behind which sat a small, bald man wearing thick spectacles that magnified his reddish, rabbity eyes. Marco approached the desk; Sandro hung back, his hands clutched at his waist. Luca stood with his back to the door.

Luca would remember little of the conversation that took place between his father and the director of the asylum at Mombello. One sentence, uttered by the director in self-defense, did stick in his brain: "This facility was designed to serve at most three thousand patients; we have more than six thousand." And another, again from the embattled director, in response to Marco's suggestion that the Duce should be informed of the hospital's failure to keep insane people off the streets.

"The Duce!" exclaimed the director. "Any poor fool who dares to criticize him winds up here. This is his own personal dumping ground."

In the car on the way back to Firenze, Luca ventured an observation. This was not something he was in the habit of doing, as his father looked on all requests for clarification as insolence. "Your brother doesn't seem that crazy to me," Luca said carefully. "He's a religious fanatic, I see that, but he seems harmless enough."

"Harmless!" Marco exclaimed. "I'll tell you how harmless he is. First he seduced the grocer's daughter and my father had to pay a bundle to get him out of it, then he started praying all the time and wanted to join a monastery, which probably would have been the best place for him, but my father begged him to think it over before throwing his life away. He sent him to Milano to work in one of our factories there, to learn what the world is about, what the family business is about, and what did this mild-mannered religious fanatic do there? He got himself mixed up with a bunch of idiot socialists and he organized *our* workers in a strike against *our* company. He supervised the whole thing. They all walked off the job at the same time and marched around in the yard demanding more pay and less work and every sort of benefit, enough to bankrupt the factory. It went on for weeks. And Sandro, this saint, was at the head of it; he was out there with them all day every day, betraying his own family. It almost killed your grandfather."

Luca said nothing. His father's face was flushed with blood, a dangerous sign.

"And now he just wants to go live with his sister at Villa Chiara. He just wants to be with his dear Valeria and rusticate in the country. Do you believe that?"

Luca kept his face free of expression.

"He wants to join the partisans in the hills above Castelnuovo Berardenga and hatch plots against the Duce. He wants to use the villa to hide a bunch of socialist, antifascist criminals. They'll be manufacturing bombs in the cantina. The Duce is right. He should be put away; they should all be put away, and Mombello is as good a place as any. This country can't stay out of the war much longer, everyone knows it, and when it happens, whining, useless cowards like my brother, who just want to get in the way and gum up the works, should be locked up. And they *will* be locked up!"

Shock Therapy

Sandro opened his eyes to find the dawn light gilding the slats of the shutters and no sound save the rustling of leaves and the *rat-a-tat* of a woodpecker drilling for his breakfast in the cypress tree outside the window. He closed his eyes. *Where am I?* he thought, and then, *Who am I?*

The answer to the first question eluded him, but the second provoked a not entirely satisfactory reply: *I am a man in pain.* Possibly a man who had been beaten. He raised one hand and laid his palm gently alongside his face. Surely his jaw was broken. The slightest movement of his lips sent lightning bolts of pain into his ears. His fingers stretched upward to his temple. The flesh there was swollen, bruised; he flinched from his own touch.

His feet beneath the linen sheet were tangled somehow, bone scraping bone. Cautiously he eased them apart. He was thirsty, but so nauseous he knew that if he were offered a glass of water he wouldn't take the risk of drinking it. His heart thumped painfully against his ribs, too strong, too fast. He closed his eyes and eased himself down into a deep well of unconsciousness, a place he knew how to find without even trying. It was deeper and darker than sleep, and he could stay there until such time as it was safe to come out.

The question of who he was could wait until then.

When next he opened his eyes, a woman was standing at his bedside, smiling kindly down at him. Too old to be an angel, he thought, so evidently he was still alive.

"Who are you?" he asked. His voice was a harsh croak, unrecognizable to him.

"I'm your sister," she said. "Don't you remember me, Sandro?"

"Is my name Sandro?"

Her brow furrowed in gentle puzzlement. "Yes, dear, it is. Don't you remember?"

"No," he said. "What is this place?"

"You're at Villa Chiara," she said.

Somewhere in the cacophony of his brain a single note rang out, pure and clean as the mysteriously audible chime of the triangle over the full blast of an orchestra. Unconsciously his fingertips sought his jaw, where the vicious throbbing pain captured his attention. "I think my jaw is broken," he said.

"The doctor will be here soon," she said. "Will you try to drink a little water?"

The thought of swallowing made him wince. "Not just yet," he said.

"I'll sit with you until he comes." She turned to the window, where a wicker chair and a side table curiously stranded in the vast, high-ceilinged room caught the strong morning light now streaming through opened shutters.

"Villa Chiara," Sandro said. They had strapped him to a table and shorted out his brain with cruel clamps attached to his temples, braces on his legs, and a hard rubber bar thrust between his teeth to keep him from breaking them when the shock was administered. *My name is Sandro,* he thought. *And I'm at Villa Chiara.*

The day passed in confused patches of waking and sleeping. Each time he woke he knew there was a woman in the room, sitting in the chair, watching him, but not, he thought, the same woman.

Each time she offered water, and at last in the afternoon he was able to drink a little. In the evening, a man came in, the doctor, who examined him, asking him questions. Did he know where he was? Did he know who he was? Did he know who the leader of the country was? Did he know what year it was? He wasn't able to answer any of these questions with confidence. The doctor said his jaw was fractured and he should take only liquid food. While he was there, a woman and a girl—she appeared to be in her teens—came in, and the woman, who said her name was Maria, spoke to the doctor while the girl stood gazing wide-eyed at Sandro as if she'd never seen a sick person before. "This is Beatrice," Maria said when the doctor had gone. "She's my daughter."

"Do I know you?" he asked Maria.

"I'm your sister. I brought you here. Don't you remember?"

He closed his eyes. "I don't remember anything very well," he said. But then, in the darkness, he could see a car with its lights on, a woman standing at the open door, handing him a blanket. He was inside the car.

Bit by bit pieces fell into place.

In the morning, after a long and dreamless sleep, he woke to find Valeria sitting in the chair, knitting a long scarf of pink wool.

"How do you feel?" she asked.

He almost smiled, but it was too painful and he grimaced instead. The thought that had provoked the smile sounded in his head. *I'm at Villa Chiara.*

Later that day he was able to sit on the edge of the bed while Valeria fed him, spoon by spoon, half a bowl of chickpea soup.

⤳✿⤶

Beatrice argued with her mother about her return to Firenze. The world was in an uproar. Hitler had rescued Mussolini, and no one knew what would happen next. Travel was dangerous, school might not even open. Maria had been stopped twice on her trip to

Mombello, once by partisans and once by Germans. Beatrice was determined to go. The trains were safe enough, or as safe as they had ever been. She would phone from the palazzo as soon as she arrived. She should leave at once, before things got worse. At last her aunt Valeria offered to drive her to the station in Siena and see her all the way to the train. Maria agreed. "Say goodbye to your uncle," she instructed Beatrice. Dutifully the girl returned to the sickroom where Sandro, with the assistance of Celestia and a chair, was trying to stand on his feet.

"Goodbye, Uncle," Beatrice said, standing in the doorway. "I'm going to school."

Her uncle sank back onto the mattress, turning his lifeless eyes upon her. "That's a lovely child," he said to Celestia. "Who is she?"

The train from Siena to Firenze was delayed by weary pedestrians pushing and pulling all manner of carts. They thought they were in less danger on the tracks than on the open road, where retreating Germans, advancing partisans, and deserting soldiers from both sides collided in violent encounters that were occasionally resolved with rifle fire or exploding hand grenades. The train crept along; it was crowded, and Beatrice had to stand all the way. When at last she descended at Santa Maria Novella station, she pushed through the crowd on the platform, her eyes down, gripping her suitcase to her chest with both arms. On the street she scarcely looked up until she had reached the palazzo door. Glancing furtively left and right, she turned the key in the lock, slipped inside, and pulled the door firmly closed behind her.

The cool marble serenity of the foyer enfolded her and she sighed, setting her suitcase on the middle step. She was safe, and she was home.

Upstairs she found her cousin Luca bent over a book at the dining table. He allowed her to stand in the doorway a few moments before raising his eyes from the page.

"I'm back," she said.

"I see that," he replied.

"It took forever," she said. "The train kept stopping. It's a nightmare out there."

He smiled indulgently. "It's going to get worse," he said.

Beatrice nodded. He returned his attention to his book, but as she made no move from the doorway, he looked up again. "Is something bothering you?" he asked.

"What do you know about an uncle named Sandro?" she said.

"Why do you ask?"

"He's at the villa. My mother went to Milano a few days ago and brought him back. He was in some kind of hospital. He seems really sick. In the head sick. He doesn't know who he is."

Luca closed the book and pushed his chair back from the table. "I have to inform my father," he said. "He'll want to know."

⁊⁊⁊

Luca stood at his father's side, waiting at the curb for the car. This time Marco had ordered the spyder, a sporty, wine-red two-seater that was his favorite car for jaunts outside the city. The driver pulled up, leaped out, and held the door open wide while Marco took his place at the wheel. Luca yanked the low passenger door open and slid onto the seat beside his father.

Marco pulled his driving goggles down over his eyes and revved the engine, once, twice, spurting a cloud of hot dust from the exhaust pipe so that passing pedestrians stepped away, the women pulling in their skirts and bending their necks down to see who the driver of this rude and powerful machine might be. Then Marco shifted the gears and the car shot out into the traffic. Luca sank down against the black leather upholstery. He disliked the sensation of warm air rushing at him over the windshield.

At nineteen, Luca was still entirely in his father's sway, though he had begun to imagine a time when that might not be the case and to examine alternatives that could lead him to an independent life.

He was secretive by nature as well as by necessity, and adept at a presentation that offered neither assent nor defiance. For the most part he was a confident youth and acted in his own interest whenever possible, but because of his inexperience, it was not always clear how that interest might best be served. He seldom had second thoughts, yet as Marco steered the car skillfully through the city streets, left, then right, then left again, Luca admitted to himself that it might not have been the best idea to tell his father that his uncle Sandro had once again escaped the asylum at Mombello. For the past two days Marco had been glued to the radio, waiting to learn the fate of the Duce, who had been rescued from the hotel-prison in the Gran Sasso and was now safely with his disciple in Berlin. Luca's announcement of the equally unexpected rescue of Sandro by his sister infuriated Marco, and he cursed Maria and Valeria forcefully. But for a day he did nothing, and Luca thought Sandro's presence at the villa might simply be allowed. In the evening Marco went out to one of the endless secret meetings with his fellow fascists and various German counterparts who controlled daily life in the occupied city. Luca imagined that there too all ears were tuned to the radio.

The next morning his father commanded his presence for the trip to Villa Chiara. "Those hills are crawling with partisans," he observed. "Your aunts are stupid women and have no idea what they're doing. When Mussolini returns—Hitler loves the Duce, he won't desert him; I am convinced the Duce will return—he will call up his loyal forces, and those mad dogs and communists will be on the run."

Luca thought it unlikely that his uncle Sandro, described by Beatrice as mortally ill, was in more danger at Villa Chiara than he had been at the asylum, but he said nothing. He was curious to see his strange uncle again, that mild-mannered, unwashed, quirky wanderer who had called down God's mercy on his incorrigible brother's soul.

Marco took back roads, skirting Siena and coming down just west of Castelnuovo Berardenga. They passed an abandoned tank, toppled on its side in a ditch, the gun turret aimed pointlessly at the sky. Further on, at the edge of a field of trampled sunflowers, a burned-out stone barn with windows like blackened eyes smoldered silently in the sun.

"That's the Falcos' barn," Luca observed.

Marco glanced past his son. "They'll be lucky if that's all they lose," he said.

When they turned in at the villa gate, Luca felt a swell of relief; everything was as it had always been. There were lemons still pendant among the dark leaves of the potted bushes on the limonaia terrace; his aunt's car was parked near the foot of the staircase; the villa shutters were open, inviting in the warm midday air. The retired, almost inviolable quality of the world inside the wall vibrated a peaceful chord from his childhood. He recollected himself as a boy, lounging on a couch in his grandfather's study, watching a small red-breasted bird picking at a stack of papers on the vast green leather-topped desk in the center of the room.

Marco braked the roadster and turned off the engine. The door to the landing opened and Maria, Luca's tiny yet fierce aunt, who possessed an obdurate willfulness that knew no bounds and who capably intimidated large men, including her brother Marco, stepped out and stood looking sullenly down on them.

Marco got out of the car and Luca followed, leaving a few steps between as his father, armed in every possible way for a fight, marched up the stairs.

~❦~

"They wouldn't have him back if you took him," Maria informed her brother. They were seated in the *salone,* Maria, Marco, Luca, Celestia, Valeria, and "him," the mysterious uncle Sandro. He was obviously ill, alarmingly thin and frail, but he was dressed in ordinary clothes, a plain white shirt and khaki pants, socks and soft house slippers. His hair was combed, his hands and face looked scrubbed, but his eyes were cloudy, unfocused, and he sat slumped forward in his chair, his long arms hanging at his sides. "Half the staff has gone," Maria continued, "and they're farming patients out to military hospitals. They haven't got enough food, they're running out of drugs. I don't know what they did to him, but they had him strapped to a bed—he was hardly conscious. They couldn't wait to get him into my car."

Marco studied his brother. "Do you know who I am?" he asked coldly.

Sandro lifted his face, vacantly taking in the scowling presence before him. "No," he said, and then, widening his eyes as if he were trying to see his own thoughts, he added, "Should I?" His gaze shifted to Luca, rested upon him. *Does he remember me?* Luca wondered, staring back anxiously. To his amazement, Sandro lowered his chin and winked one eye, the other brow rising as if in punctuation. Was he inviting his nephew into his confidence, or was the broad wink just an involuntary muscle spasm, caused by exhaustion or radical medical treatments?

He's pretending, Luca thought. *He knows exactly who my father is.*

Sandro remained silent, slumped, throughout the discussion of his fate. It was revealed that Luca's silly old aunt Valeria had been instrumental in the decision to liberate him from the hospital, that she had in fact been in touch with the administration there for years. When Mussolini's government fell, she was unable to get any message through at all, and there were rumors that the Germans would burn or bomb or requisition the place and turn all the inmates loose on the countryside. "He's safe here," Valeria said. "There are three of us to look after him. He's already much improved."

Marco moved his head slowly from side to side. "No one is safe anywhere," he said.

Sandro shifted in his chair. "I have to use the toilet," he said.

"I'll help you, dear," Valeria said. They all watched as she pulled and lifted the invalid to his feet. Maria brought him a cane that Luca recognized as having belonged to his grandfather, or so legend had it, and with halting steps the three went down the hall to the room where Sandro was staying. Celestia, whom Luca had always believed to be the strangest of his aunts, rose ghostlike from her chair and announced softly, "I'm going to the chapel." Luca and Marco watched as she glided soundlessly into the hall on the opposite side.

"Yes, go pray," Marco called after her. "Pray for the Duce."

Father and son sat alone. "Valeria is a traitor," Marco asserted. He stood up, stamped to the sideboard, and poured a glass of grappa. "I should take him back to Firenze and put him in a prison cell." He lifted the glass and shot back the clear liquid.

Without thinking, Luca observed, "There isn't room in the car."

Marco huffed, setting the glass back roughly in the tray. "You really are an idiot," he said.

From the hall they could hear soft footsteps approaching, then they stopped. There were two steps down to that wing of the house and before them a window with a view toward the garden. Luca pictured his aunt—which one?—stopping there, looking out. They lived so peacefully here, he thought, though Aunt Maria and her daughter, Beatrice, quarreled endlessly. Marco disliked the villa because it was too dull, he said, and the peasants were all lazy socialists and anarchists who let their property go to hell while they sat around in their clubs plotting treason.

The footsteps recommenced, and in a moment Valeria stood in the doorway, her eyes wide and her upper teeth digging into her lower lip anxiously. "There are three men coming through the garden," she said. "I don't recognize them."

Marco strode to the door, pulling his pistol from the leather pouch attached to his belt. "Where's Sandro?" he asked.

More footsteps, quick this time, and Maria appeared. "They're partisans," she said. "They're wearing bandoliers. They're probably just looking for food."

Marco charged to the door.

"Don't start a fight with them," Maria called after him. "The war is over."

"The war is not over," Marco snapped at her. "The Duce will return, and these are his sworn enemies." He pulled the door open, and Luca followed him onto the landing, where they stood together gazing down at the yard. Two men hovered at the edge of the garden. Marco snorted at their outlandish attire. One wore a loose gray cotton sweater, puffy yellow riding breeches, black stockings, and sandals; the other had on a brown suit jacket, no shirt, short khaki pants, and leather brogues. Both carried rifles loosely at their sides, and the bandoliers, belts studded with bullets, crisscrossed their narrow chests. They were joking with a third comrade who had advanced into the parking lot, where he was examining, with evident amusement, Marco's expensive car. "You can take your girlfriend for a spin," the one in shorts advised him. "She might give you the time of day for a change."

Luca could smell the sweat soaking into his father's black shirt. Marco cleared his throat, calling the men's attention to him. Their good-humored expressions evaporated, and they exchanged looks of caution and warning. The man in shorts lifted the barrel of his rifle so that it was level with his waist.

"What do you think you're doing here?" Marco said. He strode forcefully down the steps, gripping the pistol in his hand but with his arm relaxed so that it pointed at the ground.

Luca felt the tension in the scene dilating like the pupil of an eye abruptly blocked from all light. He had no desire to get any closer to the steadily rising hostility. Nor could he take his eyes away from the men confronting each other on the dusty drive. Marco paused at the foot of the stairs, taking the measure of his position, which he must realize, Luca thought, wasn't at all favorable, as he stood surrounded by armed and irascible men who answered to no one. He turned to the man leaning on the door of his car. "Step away from the car," he said calmly.

That was when they all heard a voice no one recognized, not speaking but softly humming a dirgelike tune. In the next moment Sandro, staggering so that he gripped a loop of the wisteria vine as he stepped out from the arbor, came into view.

"Oh for God's sake," Marco exclaimed. "Will you go back in the house?"

Sandro glanced dazedly at his brother, then turned to the three men, but he was distracted by a riotous display of late-blooming roses at the edge of the garden. "I know this place," he said, taking a shaky step toward the bushes.

The man nearest the car lifted his rifle, pointing the barrel at Marco.

Luca, frozen on the landing, felt his breath stop in his throat.

Brazenly Marco turned his back on the threatening man and raised his pistol at his two comrades. Sandro, now squarely in the line of fire between four raised weapons, turned to the two men and raised his hands high, palms open and flat in a gesture of submission. Or was it, Luca would wonder later, an attempt at pacification? Was he begging for death or for the end of hostilities? Was he a peacemaker or a martyr?

As gunshots shattered the enveloping silence of the yard, Luca didn't move. He felt no fear and his eyes strained to take it all in, but he would never be entirely sure what he had seen that day. His father dropped to his knees on the ground and fired his pistol at the man near the car, who crumpled slowly forward, clutching his rifle to his chest as if it were his last friend in the world. Luca saw one of the men near the garden backing away as Sandro approached him. The second man raised his rifle and fired a shot at Marco, who leaped up and rushed at him, pistol raised. Sandro turned slowly, his hands raised, his expression solemn, and faced his brother. There were two shots. The partisan's rifle clattered to the ground as he fell sideways, clutching his neck. Sandro sank to his knees in the dirt. A bright spot of red materialized on his chest, blooming through the white linen of his shirt.

The last partisan turned and fled into the garden. Marco fired two more shots after him but missed both times. Sandro crossed his hands over his chest, dropping forward. When his head hit the ground there was a sickening thump. Then the world fell silent.

Luca backed up against the door and slid to a squat, rubbing his knuckles into his eyes as if to erase what he had just witnessed. He heard the women rushing out through the arbor, shouting and weeping, and Marco protesting, ordering them about. It was determined that all three of the men lying on the ground were dead. Luca waited until his father and his aunts, moaning and arguing, had all gone back into the villa before he stood up and advanced to the rail.

Blood was pooling around the bodies. Blood from the dead partisan near the car had splattered onto the front tire and even on the driver's door. Blood spread steadily from beneath Sandro's prostrate corpse. One of his slippers had somehow wound up near his face, and his open, dead eyes appeared to be staring at it. He must have turned his face aside just before his head hit the ground.

He had raised his hands in supplication, first to the two partisans and then to his brother.

With a stab of awe and terror, Luca recalled that hot afternoon in Firenze when he had returned from his training exercises to find his uncle Sandro collapsed on the pavement outside the palazzo door. Sandro's first words upon seeing his brother Marco glowering down at him from the dark staircase repeated in Luca's brain so clearly it was as if his uncle were speaking into his ear. "Marco," he said, "may God have mercy on your immortal soul."

PART 6

Beatrice Takes Charge

Six years had passed since my last visit to Villa Chiara, and though little had changed in my own life, I knew I would find the world of my aristocratic friend fundamentally altered. The previous winter Beatrice and I had attended a professional conference—our college departments were both hiring and we were on interview committees—in a perfectly bland hotel in Chicago. It was bitterly cold, and as windy as that great midwestern metropolis can famously be, so we agreed to meet for dinner in the smaller of the two hotel dining rooms on the street level. This was an expensive yet pleasantly understated venue renowned for its steak, a specialty I knew my friend would disdain, as she maintained that the best American beef was so uniformly inferior to its Florentine equivalent it was fit only for "grinding up into hamburgers."

I arrived early, as is my habit, ordered a glass of wine and studied the menu. The room was dimly lit, the tablecloths dark; even the china was indigo blue, and my fellow diners looked both familiar and weary, all having spent the day interrogating aspiring academics who had one foot on the bottom rung of a ladder they imagined would lift them up, to freedom, to tenure, to the respect of their colleagues, their friends, and, at long last, their parents. It was an exhausting process. I studied the menu—what was shrimp doing in Chicago?—and when I looked up, Beatrice was approaching the table.

My first glance reassured me; she was elegantly dressed, perfectly coiffed, and her smile was as always tinged with irony. Time was bearing lightly on her, and I had the thought that Beatrice would go straight-backed to her grave. But in the two hours we spent together that night over mediocre wine and passable food, I perceived that she was in fact changed. Something had provoked her, had tested her, and though she was still prodigiously armored, there was a quality of indifference in her manner; it was as though she no longer cared how little she appeared to care.

We discussed the menu and the conference, both disheartening and easily summarized. Then I asked about her life since our last meeting. The postcards we'd exchanged during that interval had been largely confined to greetings and brief descriptions of travel experiences. Beatrice took a sip of red wine, set the glass down, and studied its ruby depths briefly. "There have been some changes," she said. "Especially at the villa."

I was saddened though not surprised to learn that Luca had died, not, as I'd predicted, of lung cancer, but of pancreatic cancer. Mimma, Beatrice reported, had spent the last months of her long cohabitation with her brother in complete denial, insisting that indigestion was the cause of his steady decline. Now she was a sad figure, and so stupid and without resources that Beatrice feared leaving her at the villa without some professional oversight. Yet she was also haughty and dismissive of her cousin's concern. "She told me Luca had never trusted me," Beatrice said. "He said I didn't want to be an Italian, that I'd become an American and only cared about money."

In addition to this crisis, Beatrice had spent two summers coming to difficult terms with her mother, who was determined that nothing should change in her daily routine though she was nearly blind, had fallen twice, once fracturing an ankle, and had been briefly hospitalized during a bout of severe gastritis. Her recovery had been slow, and she now required such constant attention that she strained even the limitless energy and devotion of Anna Falco.

"The doctors are telling me she can't be left alone in a big house or even a small one. I've made the rounds of the care facilities in the area. Really, there are some beautiful places with excellent care, not like the dreary rest homes old people are shut up in here, where the windows can't be opened and the television is always on. These are grand villas with terraces and frescoed ceilings. The one I like best is near Firenze. The staff is excellent, the rooms are large and comfortable. I took Mother to see it and she covered her eyes as if I was showing her a prison. I said, 'Look at this place—the air is fresh, the views are stunning, the nurses are professional. There's a beautiful old chapel and two big saloni where you can meet and chat with friends.'

"Mother was absolutely silent for the entire visit; even the delightful director couldn't get a word out of her. She told me Mother's reaction was not uncommon. In the car, on the way back to Villa Chiara, Mother remained silent. As I was helping her out of the car, she pushed me away. I followed her up the stairs, enthusing about the facility all the way. Once we were inside she turned to me with such a glare that I said, 'Why are you angry with me? I'm only trying to help you. You look at me as if you hate me.' And she said, 'I have always hated you.'"

Here Beatrice paused and, taking up her fork, pierced a limp asparagus spear pushed up against the roasted chicken breast on her plate.

"This is awful," I said. "Your cousin never trusted you and your mother always hated you. That's a lot to process."

She chewed the vegetable, nodding agreement. When she had swallowed, she said, "It made me very sad, but I wasn't shocked. Mimma may be lying about Luca; she has a very hypothetical relationship with the truth. Saying Luca didn't trust me may be her way of saying she doesn't trust me. As for my mother, I suppose I knew she resented me, and it has sometimes seemed to me that she hated me, but I didn't think she knew it, that she had ever put it to herself that bluntly. Does that make sense?"

"It does," I said.

"David insists I must persuade Mother to sign a power of attorney, and then we can force her into the Casa di Riposo. He says once she's there, she'll calm down and see how much better it is for her. She'll be grateful."

"Would you do that?"

"Force her to go? I'd rather not, though now that I know she's always hated me I feel more inclined to play out my hand. I'll talk with a lawyer this summer."

"What happens until then?" I asked.

"They'll muddle along. Anna looks after my mother, and Beppe is very attentive to Mimma. He brings her a cornetto and caffè every morning, and he takes care of any problems with the house. I'll go over as soon as my classes are done in May. Hopefully this will all be settled before you arrive and you'll not be disturbed by this ordeal of my family."

"I won't be disturbed," I said. "I'm interested. And if I can help in some way, I will."

"Well," Beatrice said, "I'll be relieved to have you there. We desperately need a rational head on the property."

"Is Ruggiero coming?" I asked.

"No." She sipped her wine, her expression rueful. "Ruggiero has found a lady younger than I am and with a bigger villa. Last summer he met me for lunch in Perugia; that was all the time he could find for me. Perugia is a lovely town with an excellent museum. His new friend is very well connected there."

As Beatrice had predicted, the transfer of her mother to the nursing facility near Florence was complete by the time I arrived at the villa that summer. David had come down from Munich, consulted the lawyer, persuaded his grandmother to designate her daughter the administrator of the property, loaded her and her luggage into his car, and driven her to her new abode. "She gave in at the end," Beatrice told me. "What could she do? She's nearly ninety and very frail. She refused to help me pack or even to answer any questions about what she might want to take. Anna came, and I went out; she's still talking to Anna. Then she wouldn't let me help her down the stairs, so I stood on the landing and waved. She never looked back at me. I felt like a criminal."

"Obviously you did the right thing," I said. "Old people can be very stubborn, but this change will give you both some peace of mind."

"The idea of my mother having peace of mind is entertaining," Beatrice said. "And even if she had it, she wouldn't let me know."

"At least," I said, "she's in a beautiful, safe place with good care round the clock. You've done what you can do."

"It is a truly lovely place. She has a large room with lots of light and a modern bath designed to keep her from falling down. The meals are served in a dining room with frescoed ceilings and views of the Florentine hills. Of course, the expense is staggering. David is complaining that it's exorbitant and we can't afford it."

"Oh," I said. "David is here?"

We heard the sound of tires on gravel, and as we looked toward the gate an ostentatious hunter-green Mercedes-Benz turned in to the drive. "He is now," Beatrice said. The car passed us and came to a halt in the space between my Panda and Beatrice's Punto.

"That's quite a car," I observed.

"Don't mention it to him unless you are longing for a lecture on the superiority of German auto engineering over all others."

David stepped onto the drive, straightening his spine with his palms pressed against his lower back, a gesture that suggested chronic pain, or a very long drive. After delivering his grandmother, he had stayed over in Florence to attend to family interests there. He was dressed for the weather in a white linen jacket, black T-shirt, and soft black jeans. Again I noted the combination of Italian and Irish features that made it difficult to guess his nationality. He greeted his mother and me coolly. "Hello," he said to me, and to his mother, "Why are you standing around in the driveway?"

"We're going to Siena for lunch," she said. "Will you join us?"

"No," he said. "I have to call Greta. And I have to measure the furniture for the movers."

"I can't think where you're going to put that huge armadio," Beatrice said.

"Greta wants it," he replied.

"All right," she said. "Do as you please."

I followed her without comment to the Fiat. Once we had left the driveway, I said, "He's taking the furniture?"

Beatrice shifted gears, gazing intently into the rearview mirror, though there were no other cars on the road. "Yes, can you believe it? It turns out Greta has long coveted my mother's bedroom set. No wonder Mother despised her."

⟨❦⟩

The morning after this conversation I was up early and at my table on the terrace with my books and notepads ranged around me. I had come to think of the driveway as a stage on which the drama of the Salviati family, for better or worse, was played out. It was there that Beatrice's uncle Sandro had met his untimely end, and as such, in my imagination, hallowed, possibly haunted ground. My chair at the table on the limonaia terrace gave me access to scenes no one else saw. David, I sensed, was conscious of this and not pleased.

Whenever he left in his car, he only raised a hand to me in greeting. I found myself missing the guardedly social Luca.

The first to arrive was Beppe Bottini, clattering to a halt in his antiquated van on the far side of the yard, near the wisteria arbor that shaded the entry to Beatrice's benighted cousin Mimma's private domain. Beppe shoved the van door open and hopped down, holding a white paper bag I knew contained Mimma's daily cornetto. With his free hand he rifled his thick, oiled hair, pulling down a curling forelock. Then he patted his mustache into place with two fingers. He had his side to me and didn't, I assumed, know I was there. He went quickly under the arbor, hitching up his pants on one side, and let himself in at the door. Did he have a key? I couldn't tell. Was the door unlocked because he was expected? A little time passed. I rummaged among my books and decided to read a chapter of *A Room with a View*. I had set my Mussolini book aside and determined to write a novel about a young American publicist who comes to Italy to assist a famous artist and winds up falling in love with a rogue and getting everything wrong. On the strength of forty pages I had a contract and a deadline. It was a lighthearted story, and my narrator, an earnest, ambitious young woman, was such an innocent I could only wish her well. Forster was the obvious model for this undertaking.

The villa door opened and David stepped out onto the landing, pushing on his sunglasses as he hurried down the steps. Though he couldn't fail to see me, he made straight for his car without acknowledging me. Just to irritate him, I called out, "*Buongiorno, David.*" He paused, his hand resting on the door handle, turned only his head, and raised one hand in a weak salute. Then he got in and sped away in his powerful machine, off to the bar to pick up the morning cornetti, I surmised. He might have offered to bring me one. His mother certainly would have.

Everything has changed, I thought gloomily.

Next on the scene was Beatrice. The villa door opened with its familiar creak and she stepped out, closing it carefully behind her. She was casually dressed in a checked cotton blouse, an A-line skirt that ended just below her knees, and red sandals. She advanced to the landing and stood looking down at me.

"*Buongiorno,*" I said, shading my eyes with my hand against the sun, which was up, high and bright, heating the tiles on the villa roof until they appeared to glow.

"Good morning," she said. "You are working."

"I'm not," I said. "I'm reading an old novel."

She started down the stairs. "I will come sit with you, then. The house is chilly." As she crossed the yard, I saw her notice Beppe's van. She joined me under the beams, pulling out one of the chairs.

"I'm watching the world go by," I said. "Beppe has gone in and David has gone out."

"It's just as well they don't cross," she said. "They're not getting along."

"Somehow," I said, "that doesn't surprise me."

"Mimma is enjoying herself," Beatrice continued. "She has Beppe dancing in attendance and telling her the family isn't worthy of her and has abandoned her. She told me the other day that David had better be nicer to her or he might lose a very good thing."

"Is Beppe courting her?"

Beatrice pressed her fingertips to her lips. "What an idea!" she said. "Beppe is married with three children and he's at least twenty years younger than Mimma. Maybe twenty-five."

"Does he imagine she might reward him in her will?"

"Ah," said Beatrice. "You don't think Beppe is just a kindly peasant devoted to an old aristocratic family he has faithfully served all his adult life?"

"I suppose that's possible."

"I don't know what he's up to," Beatrice said. "Or what he thinks he's up to. But neither of them knows a thing about the law. She could leave him something, I suppose, but Italy has forced heirship; it's not possible to disinherit one's family. Also Mimma thinks she's very ill; she's always exhausted, but she's actually quite healthy and will probably outlive us all."

"Neurasthenic," I said.

"That's what Luca called her. He took care of her, so he knew. Luca was a saint, actually, but he was a cold fish. Beppe's here every day with the cornetto and the chocolates. She's having a ball. Last week he brought her two kittens. That's what David is upset about."

"David doesn't want her to have kittens?" I said.

"They're brother and sister kittens," Beatrice explained. "Mimma has no idea how to take care of animals. She barely keeps herself clean. David thinks the kittens will have kittens and so on. Soon Mimma will be a crazy cat lady, as Americans say, with dozens of cats, and the house will be destroyed."

"I had a neighbor like that," I said. "It's no joke."

"I told David, if there are too many cats, Beppe will drown a litter or two; that's what the contadini do in the country. Or they let the kittens out at night and the wild cats or foxes get them."

"Why not just neuter the male?" I suggested.

"Obviously, that is the solution," Beatrice agreed. "Americans are very careful about things like that. Italians not so much."

We both looked up at the sound of tires on the gravel. David entered the drive, his engine so smooth the car seemed to glide into place. He climbed out, again a bit stiffly, and stood facing us, holding the white paper bag from the bar.

"Come and join us," Beatrice called. "It's pleasant to sit outside." I expected David to hesitate, but he didn't.

"I'll make coffee," I said.

"That would be very nice," Beatrice replied. I stood up to go inside as David arrived at the table. "Do you have enough for us all?" Beatrice asked him.

"I do," he said, taking the remaining chair. As I passed into the kitchen I heard him say, "Salvatore told me Americans have bought the old Petrocelli property."

I filled the caffettiera and set it on the burner, took out plates, cups, and saucers, little spoons, the sugar jar, and set them on a tray. I was puzzled by Beatrice's nonchalance, though of course she had been contemplating the necessary alterations in her family situation for some time. It must be, I considered, both a relief and an added anxiety to have moved her mother out of the villa. Now Beatrice's half would be empty most of the year and this left Mimma the sole full-time occupant of a large estate. Beatrice relied on Anna Falco and would probably continue the arrangements they had, whatever these were, to keep an eye on her interests, make sure the house was cleaned for her arrivals, and perhaps cook and clean for Mimma. It could be managed, I assumed, but now there was Beppe, circling the property with his nose quivering and his eyes alert, like a wolf who has come across some wounded sheep panting out its last breaths in a field.

I lifted the tray and carried it out the open door to the terrace.

"I was frank with him," David was assuring his mother. "I told him we were perfectly capable of looking after my aunt, especially in the summer, when you are here. And he said, 'Oh, really? You want to spend the day with Mimma? Take my word, it's not so easy.'"

Beatrice laughed at this remark. "Beppe has us by the horns," she said.

I set out the plates, poured out the coffee, and took my seat. David opened the bag and laid a roll on each plate. Immediately we began tearing off bits of the bread and stuffing them into our mouths.

"I told him kittens are not a good idea," David continued. "He said, 'Fine. Take them away from her. She's named them Risi and Bisi.'"

"That's a soup," I said, airing my culinary expertise.

"Rice and peas," said Beatrice. "How ridiculous."

We heard the door open, and a bubble of high-pitched laughter floated out from the arbor. Beppe appeared at the entrance, closely followed by Mimma. She was smaller and rounder than I remembered. Her hair was loose, wiry and white, framing her chubby face like a collapsing bird's nest. She had applied a blood-red lipstick to her mouth and blush to her cheeks. Her eyebrows were an unnatural mink brown. Beppe, half turned toward her as she clung to his elbow, delivered some soothing parting remarks, something silly that made her gush with laughter. *So,* I thought, *she's happy.*

Then they both saw us enjoying our breakfast in the shade of the limonaia. Beppe's lips compressed in an expression of wry amusement, but Mimma's smile vanished, and she backed away without a word. He stepped out onto the drive, passing across the front of his van.

"*Ciao,* Beppe," Beatrice called out.

He turned, inclining his head in a mock bow. "*Buongiorno a tutti,*" he said. Then he climbed into the van and revved the engine so that the exhaust pipe coughed out a plume of black smoke. As he drove past us, he raised his hand out the open window in something between a salute and a dismissal.

When he was gone, we continued our meal. "Mimma's looking well, don't you think?" Beatrice said, her eyes dancing with glee.

"What's with the makeup?" I said.

"It's actually frightening," David said.

"She looks like Bette Davis in *What Ever Happened to Baby Jane?*" Beatrice said.

Then we all laughed at Mimma's expense.

༺❦༻

The next morning I awoke to the roar of an engine and furious male voices bellowing in Italian. Dazed, I consulted the clock:

6:15. A screech of brakes, more shouting, the grinding of gears. I sat up in the bed and pulled on the T-shirt I'd thrown off in the night; the heat in my bedroom gathered under the tiles after the sun went down, and I often woke sweating in the dark. Outside the engine revved frenetically, then settled to a steady rumble. I crossed to the bathroom and unlatched the shutters, pushing one side open carefully, as if the soft creak of the hinges might be heard over the ongoing din below.

I was looking down upon several pallets stacked with flagstones in the back of a flatbed truck. The driver, a big, rough-looking fellow, thick-necked and wild-eyed, his thinning gray hair tied back in a ponytail, leaned out the window, muttering fiercely at his coworker, who stood inside the gates gesturing frantically and shouting two words I understood: *"Alla destra, alla destra."* To the right, to the right. The truck had halted halfway through the gates with what I estimated to be four inches of leeway on my side.

I ran a glass of water at the sink. My car might be in the way; I should move it. I threw on my pants and sandals and hurried down the stairs. By the time I got to the terrace, David had come out in his robe. He stood on the stair landing fulminating vociferously, one hand raised and open in a gesture between a threat and a prayer. Just like a real Italian, I thought.

"I'll move my car," I called to him as I dashed out into the drive.

He glanced down at me, briefly mystified, then paused, switching to English only long enough to issue an order: "You, go back inside."

Right, I thought. Veering like a rabbit pursued by hounds, I scurried to the shelter of the terrace. What was going on?

Back to the bathroom window. The driver had pulled the truck into the road. Then, as David and his comrade continued shouting, he adjusted the angle of his wheels and backed straight through the gate, passing without a pause, though it was so close on my side he pulled in his mirror at the last possible moment. I crept down the stairs and stationed myself just outside the door on the terrace. David, retying the sash on his white cotton robe, came down from his perch and stood barefoot in the dirt, remonstrating with his adversary while the truck backed past him and ground to a halt at the entrance to the wisteria arbor.

The engine died; the driver, ignoring the argument entirely, hopped down and went to the back of the truck, where he began unfastening a rope that served, in some obscure and impossible fashion, to keep the heavy pallets in place.

Mimma appeared at the entrance to her bower, her hair in wet ringlets clinging to her face. She was dressed in a voluminous multicolored caftan with an incongruous pink cotton cardigan buttoned tightly over her breasts. She stood there, wringing her hands and keening wordlessly. Something David said to the workman set the driver off; he dropped the rope and hurled an angry skein of language in the direction of his colleague. Then he strode over manfully to join the fray.

Everybody was yelling; nobody was listening. I felt safely removed from it all, my back to the door: the definition of the innocent bystander. The competing voices rose straight up in the still-mild morning air. *It's like an opera,* I thought. *Three men arguing and a woman wailing in the wings.*

Abruptly, as in an opera, the voices fell away, and all turned to face the open gate as the wheezing van made the turn and rattled into the open space in front of the truck. Beppe Bottini sat for a moment surveying the scene. First the truck, then Mimma, who now stepped out boldly from her shelter. When his eyes lit on David hunched gloomily in his robe, Beppe pursed his lips, moving his head slowly from side to side with an expression of amused dismay. *Would you believe it?* his dark, penetrating eyes seemed to say. He pushed open his door and slid down to the dirt, brushing the thighs of his pants with the flat of his hands.

Mimma, emboldened by his presence, came out into the sun, tottering toward him with outstretched arms as if she would surely fall if he didn't come to her rescue. He spoke to her soothingly, his expression a mockery of kind concern, and skillfully guided her back to the safety of the arbor. David quit the two laborers, waving them away with a sharp dismissal, and followed Beppe and Mimma, talking all the way. At the arbor, the three faced off, Mimma standing shakily behind Beppe, who contemplated David without speaking, the fingers of one hand resting lightly across his lips, his eyes narrowed, calculating his response. David ranted briefly. Beppe dropped his hand, raised his chin at the truck, and said a few words in his calmest manner. Then, to everyone's surprise, Mimma stepped out from behind him and launched into a long, dolorous, breathless complaint.

Fascinated by this sudden display of verbosity from the reclusive Mimma, I moved away from the door. Her Italian was impenetrable to me, but the word *sole,* combined with a lift of her eyes toward the bright sky above, was repeated with increasing frequency. Why was Mimma complaining to David about the sun? As I watched wonderingly, she pointed a trembling finger past David, right at me. She jabbed the finger repeatedly into the air between us, tears overflowing her eyes. Beppe spoke softly to her, taking her by the arm, gently turning her away, leading her back to her door. She let herself be guided, sobbing, evidently heartbroken, all the way.

David, left standing in the heat, whirled away from the workmen, who had been watching the scene with obvious pleasure, and stalked back across the drive. He saw me there but ignored me, climbing the stairs to the villa with his head lowered, his shoulders squared. "This fucking family!" he exclaimed as he reached the landing, pulled open the door, and disappeared inside.

༺๑༻

It took Beppe and the workmen an hour to unload the flagstones onto the drive. They stacked them efficiently against the wall of the cantina, hardly speaking, though Beppe said something at one point that caused all three to laugh. Then they climbed into their respective vehicles and drove away. All was silence, except for the birds. I settled at the kitchen table with my notebooks, not wanting to appear overeager for the revelations I longed to receive. But I couldn't concentrate and reverted to reading a story by Italo Svevo in a parallel text collection I'd brought with me from home. It began with a description of two houses.

After a while I heard the villa door open, steps on the stairs, and the sound of David's car—I could tell the difference between his engine and his mother's with no effort—going out the gate.

Beatrice and I had no plans to meet until the afternoon, when we had agreed to drive out to the Etruscan exhibition at the museum in Castiglion Fiorentino, which she described as "limited but well curated." We were both fascinated by these ancient peoples, whose culture, like so many in the ancient world, was ultimately absorbed by Rome. Once they were wealthy and powerful, profiting from a thriving trade in bronze with the Greeks. They spoke a language like no other. The myth of Romulus and Remus was their invention, the word *Toscana* derived from their designation in Latin. Remnants of their elaborate mausoleums and tombs, funerary statuary, often featuring couples or children with smiling, joyful faces—a welcome departure from the customary solemnity of the dead—various surpassingly strange statues of mythological beasts, scattered troves of jewelry stamped with the ancient swastika symbol, believed to elicit good luck, artifacts, bits and pieces of a vanished world: these are all that remains to us.

The museum opened at two. At 1:45, Beatrice arrived at my door, looking fresh and unruffled. I took up my purse and joined her on the terrace. "I hope you weren't alarmed by the ruckus this morning," she said.

"What's it all about?" I asked, gesturing to the flagstones. "Home improvement?"

"Ha," she said. "You might call it that. David is so angry he's gone to the provincial offices in Siena. They are very strict about these historical buildings; you can't change a doorknob without their permission." I followed her out to her car and we took our seats, fastening our seatbelts mindlessly. She turned the key and the Fiat came to life.

"Mimma spoke," I said. "I didn't know she could do that."

"She's in revolt," Beatrice said. "Poor old Mimma. It's all too late, but she'll have a bit of fun before it's over. Beppe is her knight in shining armor, wearing her sleeve into battle." She steered the car into a U-turn and we darted into the road as I considered the fantastic vision of Beppe Bottini in armor on a horse, leveling a lance at the onrushing offender of his sovereign lady's honor.

"In battle against what?" I said.

"Her cruel, neglectful family. That would be me."

"How does the flagstone fit into this story?" I asked.

"It seems she's in desperate need of a place of her own to sit outdoors and enjoy the sun and fresh air. Beppe has persuaded her that a covered terrace such as you have is absolutely necessary for her health."

"So that's why she was pointing at me," I observed.

"Of course," Beatrice said. "But it's not your fault. There was bad blood long ago because my mother insisted on our having the limonaia in the division of the property, but as long as it was in disrepair and only fit for trees, no one made a case of it. When I renovated it for David, Luca wasn't happy, but there was nothing he could do about it."

"So now Beppe is going to build a terrace for Mimma."

"Your future as a great detective is secure."

"Where will he put it?"

"That's what has David so agitated. Beppe's going to pull down the pretty arbor and lay the stone right up to their door. Then he'll attach one of those dreary iron-and-rush awnings the farmers are all sick for. It will cover the whole front of their house and take up part of the drive."

"Your part?"

"I wouldn't think so. Actually we have no grounds for complaint, and that's what I told David. I do agree it won't improve the look of the house. But it's Mimma's property now, and she can afford to do what she wants with it. She has a nice income from the farm, two apartments in Firenze, and an office in Siena that Luca owned. He managed all their money and never spent a penny if he could help it. He was always trying to cut corners and complaining that Beppe was robbing him. Beppe despised Luca, I've no doubt, and he doesn't like me much these days because I didn't hire him when I renovated the kitchen here."

"Why didn't you hire him?"

"He's a good plumber, I don't deny that, but not a great electrician, he works very slowly, and he has no design sense. He's like Leonardo: the answer to every problem is tile."

"So Beppe sees Mimma as his last shot for steady employment at the villa," I concluded.

"He's found the employer of his dreams. There's no end of work for him, and all he has to do is convince Mimma she deserves the best of everything. That's a new idea for her. She trusts him completely. I wouldn't be surprised if he knows exactly how much she takes in every month and has inflated his fees accordingly."

We had come to the exit from the highway, and Beatrice focused on the rearview mirror as she crossed a lane to get on the ramp. "I feel for Mimma," she continued. "I really do. Men who don't care for her have controlled her life since she was a girl. Her father and her brother made sure she remained stupid and helpless. My mother always had contempt for her; in fact, it was partly the spectacle of Mimma that inspired me to strike out on my own."

"And you were successful," I said.

Beatrice glanced at me, her expression mildly skeptical. Then she shifted her attention to the oncoming traffic. "Do you think so?" she said.

"You're the most independent woman I know," I said.

She took in this notion thoughtfully. "It is true," she said, "that I don't like anyone telling me what to do."

We spent a pleasant afternoon among the Etruscans. Shortly after we returned, David arrived from the *provincia* offices with the unsettling news that Beppe had applied for and been granted the requisite permits to proceed with the addition to the villa. "I don't know who he paid," he observed. "But it must have been expensive."

"And you may be sure Mimma wrote the checks," Beatrice concluded.

"God help us," David said. "Next she'll need a swimming pool."

By the time I left Villa Chiara that summer, the flagstones were in place. The wisteria vine, pruned to a stub, was already sending out shoots, its sights set on the new iron trellis that held up one corner of Mimma's covered terrazza. A glass-topped table and two cushioned wicker chairs provided all the comfort she required. A row of large clay pots overflowing with rosemary and geraniums created a border between the edge of her realm and the dusty territory of the drive. It actually didn't look that bad.

Now on sunny mornings Mimma would appear, her hair damp from the shower, arrayed in some voluminous, brightly colored garb that cascaded in folds over her breasts and hips so that her head peeped, small and vulnerable, from the top, like that of a woman buried to the neck in sand. Clutching a water bottle, she took her seat in the chair facing the drive, and there she sat, sipping hesitantly, waiting for Beppe to arrive with her simple breakfast of bread and coffee.

I had stopped sitting outside. First I was driven inside by the infernal racket and dust of the construction. By the time that was over, I had changed my routine. But it wasn't only that. In truth, on that day when Mimma enforced her complaint to David by jabbing her finger at me, it had dawned on me that my presence constituted an affront to her. Though I had occasionally seen her and Beatrice carry on conversations that could be characterized as civil, their relationship had been strained since childhood, and there was clearly no love lost between them. But Beatrice was family, a known quantity, and her right to be where she was and do there what she liked was incontestable. For Mimma, I was an interloper, a creature from an alien world, threatening and incomprehensible. We had no language in common, nothing comparable in our experience of life; I could have come from another planet. Beatrice said I frightened her. The notion of myself as scary was novel to me, and I didn't like it.

On my last morning at the villa, I looked out the kitchen window and there she sat, anxious and hopeful, waiting for the symbolic cornetto, deluding herself that at last, at long last, she had found someone who cared for her. She unscrewed the water bottle cap, took a tentative sip, screwed it back again. When she spotted the van pulling into the drive, her crudely painted lips parted in a smile of relief and anticipation. One hand rose involuntarily to anchor a stray curl behind her ear.

It was sad. And it couldn't come to a good end. Beatrice's view that Mimma was having a grand time, that she was stringing Beppe along, struck me as shallow. Anyone could see that she was a bundle of nerves, anxious to please, desperate for kindness. Her brother's death had left her adrift and unprotected, though not without resources. For the first time in her life, she held the purse strings.

As I watched from my post behind the window, I could see what Mimma could not see: Beppe's face. As he stepped down from the van, he wore the same expression of weary determination that glimmered in the eyes of the strike leader in the painting I'd seen in

Milan, and again I had the impression that Beppe was at the head of a powerful force, a mass of humanity that speaks in one voice and has but one message forever: *We are coming to take what's ours.*

She's so helpless, I thought. A lamb to slaughter. In fact Mimma's plight seemed to me so profoundly and abysmally sad that I felt tears pressing in my eyes. She rose to her feet, still clutching the water bottle, calling out to welcome her new master in her baby-fied voice, fluttering her eyelids flirtatiously, unable to disguise her delight.

No. The end would not be good, and it probably wasn't far off. And though Beatrice had said she felt for Mimma, I didn't think she would weep for her. Poor Mimma embodied the mindless bondage Beatrice despised and had refused. It occurred to me that no one in the world ever had wept or ever would weep for Mimma. As Beppe approached, she held out her hand to him, then shyly pulled it back and laid her palm against her flushed cheek.

Tears overflowed my eyes and I sniffed hard, struggling for control. *No one will weep for her,* I thought. *Only me.*

And that thought really made me cry.

A Final Act

I didn't hear from Beatrice until the New Year, when she sent me a seasonal greeting with a photo tucked inside. I laughed when I saw the picture, not so much at the scene—it was a family gathering posed for the camera—but at the expression on Beatrice's face. She was seated on a carved bench in front of a towering Christmas tree, richly decorated with all manner of ornaments: golden stars like sunbursts, shiny, metallic green pickles, long strings of silver beads, and a scattering of what looked like real candles in carefully secured wooden holders. On either side of her sat two pretty children, a boy and a girl of perhaps six and eight, dressed in traditional German costumes, leather lederhosen for the boy, a dirndl dress and apron over a blouse with puffy sleeves for the girl. They both grinned hard at the camera, showing all their white teeth. Their limpid blue eyes looked painted on beneath the slabs of bright yellow hair helmeting their foreheads. Behind them, perfectly centered and attentive, stood David, looking haggard, and a woman I presumed to be his wife, Greta. Her fair skin was lightly freckled, and she had pulled her heavy golden hair back in a braid. The tentative smile she offered the camera could have masked diffidence or contempt. She had the chilly yet engaging quality I associated with the actress Liv Ullmann.

Beatrice, flanked by her grandchildren, was sitting slightly forward, her hands resting on her knees, gazing at the viewer with an expression of total incredulity. She was like a warm gold Italian sun trapped in a snowy forest; her eyes were wide with the wonder of finding herself there.

The card was plain vellum with a design of holly and berries stenciled around the edges. On the blank interior Beatrice had written:

Auguri, Jan. Or should I say Gutes Neues Jahr? Here I am in Munich with David's family.

Next stop? Rio!! Con affetto, Beatrice

Beatrice in Rio? Well, I thought, why not? It was winter and the college break was long. After Christmas in Munich she would be ready for a warmer clime. I myself was headed for Key West in the next week. I glanced at the postmark. She might be in Rio already.

When I returned from my sojourn among palm trees, iguanas, and feral chickens, I found a postcard from Rio waiting for me. It was the famous image of Christ the Redeemer, his arms open wide to embrace the unrepentantly hedonistic city broiling and seething at his feet.

Ciao from Rio, Beatrice wrote. *A city of great beauty and contrasts: poverty, suffering, music, dance, and joy, all mixed in a stew. Here Christ the Redeemer must compete with Carnevale. Viva la Carnevale! Con caldi saluti, B.*

Messages from Beatrice were always brief, bright, engaged in observation and evaluation of the place where she happened to be. If she was tired, if the travel was difficult or dangerous, if she found herself in shabby lodgings or gazing anxiously at a plate of some unidentifiable or just inedible creatures, she never let on. I thought of her as adventurous and intrepid. At some point in the past she had come to terms with an entrenched solitude and made up her mind to embrace her condition and enjoy the freedom it allowed her. She made friends easily and her willingness to maintain a friendship, as evidenced by such tokens as this postcard, was sincere; I didn't doubt that. But Beatrice was now and had been for many years, in the routine dailiness of her life, determined to go it alone.

Determined? Or resigned?

She always appeared confident and competent, in charge and largely indifferent to criticism. I doubted that she ever stood before the mirror, as I sometimes did, and asked the questions *Who are you? How did you get here?* How much of it was choice and how much accident?

I didn't know how Beatrice understood the arc of her life—how could I? She had altered the expected trajectory as a young woman when she made up her mind to study in America. It must have seemed at the time that she was opening her options, freeing herself from the claustrophobic atmosphere of her family and her country, embracing the new, the possible. Her improvident marriage may have seemed that way too, an unexpected option that literally flew open before her, like an unseen door in a blank wall, but no sooner had she entered than it slammed behind her, and after that nothing was ever the same and there was simply no going back. She had effectively cut her world in half.

She would be sixty in the spring. Her family, once large, obstreperous, demanding, had steadily dwindled; her mother, whose coldness had driven her as far away as she could get, was now largely silenced. Her relationship with her son appeared fraught and combustible; how often, I thought, had I heard her say, "David is angry with me. David is not speaking to me," and always with an undercurrent of amusement, as if hostility and contradiction were the best one could expect from a son. David struck me as headstrong and defiant, as his mother had been, but not indifferent to his own interests. His mother had encouraged him in the notion that he deserved everything she could give him, and more. All that, and more.

In April, Beatrice responded to my birthday greeting with a card mailed from Italy; she was there seeing to family affairs, then going back to New York until summer. Her mother was very frail, still angry about the nursing home, though the nurses told Beatrice she was quite cheerful when Beatrice wasn't there. Beppe continued his devotion to Mimma. *He is constantly taking her from doctor to doctor,* Beatrice wrote, *in the hopes of finding something wrong with her. He has his sister cooking for her—Anna tells me she has practically moved into the house—and they feed her sweets and heavy cream so that she is as fat as a pig.*

Another year passed with only infrequent exchanges, postcards, another greeting from Munich, a photo of Beatrice standing at the foot of a giant sequoia in California. *This tree was old when Julius Caesar was born,* she wrote. *Sadly they never met.*

In the winter of 1996 I received an engraved card with the announcement in Italian that Maria Salviati Bartolo had passed away. Beatrice's note, scrawled across the back, read: *At last my poor mother has succumbed. She was ninety-six years old. I am going home to see to her burial. Hers was a sad life, I think, though she would probably disagree. Fondest thoughts to you. Beatrice.*

I sent my sympathy card to Villa Chiara; then, not certain that it would arrive before she returned, I sent a second message to Poughkeepsie.

That summer, when I returned from a month's sojourn in Montreal, I found a card with a welcome surprise inside, a photo of Beatrice and Ruggiero smiling into the sun on the deck of a boat I recognized as the ferry from Passignano to Isola Maggiore in Lago di Trasimeno. *Dopo il pranzo,* Beatrice wrote. *We missed you this year! Maybe next? Con affetto, B. and R.*

Some years earlier, after a particularly brutal winter, Ruggiero had vowed he couldn't bear another and determined to move back to California. After a season of applications and interviews, he obtained an excellent position at a small college east of Los Angeles, in a town he described as "perfectly bland, entirely civilized, and it never snows."

As I examined this photo, I wondered if Ruggiero was back in his old post as summer resident at Villa Chiara. They both looked older but well. Beatrice had given up dyeing the silver in her hair, and Ruggiero's remaining white thatch was cut close, which gave him an oddly piratical look. They both appeared sharp-eyed and energetic. I could imagine the bickering over the plate of perch at lunch.

A few weeks after this greeting, Beatrice sent a card embossed with a coat of arms I didn't recognize. Was it the Salviati family crest or something more generic, like the emblem of Florence? The message, as always, was succinct. I gasped as I read it.

Cara Jan, I received today an announcement from the provincia in Siena that legal documents have been filed naming Beppe Bottini as the adopted son of Caterina Maria Salviati (Mimma). Brava Mimma! She has finally become a mother!

I return to Poughkeepsie in August. Perhaps you will come for a visit and I will elaborate on this commedia. I know you are following the story. A presto? B.

⳥⳥

Brava Mimma! How could Beatrice be so complacent? Mimma had put her head in the wolf's mouth. And surely Beatrice realized that David would be effectively disinherited of half the villa by this triumph of the former handyman. Her conviction that both Beppe and Mimma were ignorant of the law was now revealed to have been sanguine to the point of naïveté. If Italian law favored direct heirs, on Mimma's death Beppe would inherit two-thirds of the entire Salviati estate. Until then Mimma would clearly be ruled by her new son; he was for all practical purposes the manager of her property, though presumably she would still be writing the checks.

I found myself imagining the celebration around the Bottini family table at the conclusion of the adoption process. Leonardo Falco, the quiet, courteous banker, had managed to pry an old farmhouse from the estate and by dint of hard work and careful investment turned it into a going concern. But Beppe Bottini, a crude bumpkin who repaired pipes and car engines, whose prized possession was an old, beat-up American van, having nothing to offer but a lubricious manner and a daily cornetto, was now sole heir to the largest property in the area. Shrimp and Coca-Cola! They probably served caviar and American whiskey!

I took out my calendar and checked the dates near the end of August. Then I studied the Amtrak schedule. I would have to change trains at Penn Station.

Good God, I thought. David Sandro Doyle must be fit to be tied.

⌒☙⌒

"David has consulted a lawyer who thinks Mimma could be declared mentally incompetent," Beatrice said. We were sitting in the bright sunroom of her Poughkeepsie house, drinking tea from ceramic mugs stamped with the emblem of her college.

"So would you have to sue her?"

"Not necessarily. The lawyer thinks it might be better to wait until Beppe actually claims the estate."

"Until Mimma dies."

"Yes. But David is convinced there's a way to declare the adoption null and void before that. It should never have been allowed in the first place."

"Does Mimma know you plan to lodge a protest?"

"I don't think so, but surely Beppe expects it. Mimma has a line he must have fed her. I couldn't get her past it. She says her family abandoned her and only Beppe really cares for her; he is always concerned for her health. He takes her to doctors and makes sure she eats properly. He is in every way a son to her."

"What did you say?"

"I told her I was happy she had such a good friend and that Beppe is a fine fellow and should certainly be remembered in her will, but that she is in control of a large patrimony—house, lands, bank holdings—that has been in our family for generations, and our grandparents would not look kindly on the transfer of her share out of the family."

"What did she say to that?"

Beatrice sipped her tea, her eyes drifting past me to the flourishing aralia near the window. It was twice the size it had been on my first visit. She set the mug on the side table. "She said that David was hardly an Italian, and that his wife was a bad woman who had tried to seduce Luca. I said I was entirely Italian and her closest relative, and that David was half Italian and also the rightful heir to the family property. We all agreed to that when we did the original division, and she knows that. Then she said I was threatening her."

"Wow," I said.

Beatrice smiled. "That's where we are. But there are laws and judges who must understand the gravity of the situation. It's going to be expensive, but David thinks the adoption can be reversed. There's a process, as I understand it."

Not for the first time, it occurred to me that the ones who didn't know much about Italian law were David and his mother. Beppe had outfoxed them once before, on the matter of the terrace, having obtained the necessary permits by applications of cash in the right offices. Surely he had investigated all the possible legal recourses available to Beatrice and David and done whatever he needed to do to block their access.

"Have you seen the adoption papers?" I asked.

"No. David's lawyer has requested them."

"Is Beppe staying at the villa a lot?"

Beatrice sighed. "It's very aggravating," she said. "He is always there, and some members of his family are often about, his sister and his wife. They're all clownish, loud people with no manners. I can hear them shouting through the wall in the dining room. Luca had the same excellent farm manager for twenty years; now Beppe has replaced him with a brash young man who thinks there are better ways than the old ways to get olives off a tree and oil out of the olives; everything must be modern. They're both in for a surprise when they figure out how little return we get from the investments in the vineyard and the orchards. Beppe and this fellow stand around in the drive prattling at each other for hours at a time. I can't go in or out without passing them. If he spots me, Beppe always makes a big show of greeting me with elaborate and totally fake courtesy."

"This is a nightmare," I observed.

Beatrice nodded. "It is," she agreed.

During my visit, Beatrice and I had several long conversations, over dinner, breakfast, and lunch, not always entirely devoted to the subject of Villa Chiara but never straying far afield. Even the topic of her pending retirement from teaching led straight to the possibility that she would have no peaceful place to live should she decide to spend half the year in Italy, as she had always planned to do. "I could do what Leonardo did and rent my half of the villa out to Germans—that would serve Beppe right—but I don't have the energy for that," she said. Then she reiterated her faith that legal procedures, somehow evolved from the ancient principle of primogeniture, would inevitably result in the designation of David Doyle as the rightful and only possible heir.

Neither of us mentioned the dark thought that was in both our minds: now that Beppe had secured his inheritance, Mimma Salviati might not live very long.

❦

Nor did she. In the spring Beatrice decided to spend the short school break at Villa Chiara. She arrived unannounced and prepared for a serious legal battle. Beppe, taken by surprise, appeared reluctant to have her visit her cousin. He said that Mimma was feeling unwell and that Beatrice's visits always left her unsettled and anxious. Beatrice insisted. She took Anna Falco with her to witness the meeting.

"The house was a mess," Beatrice told me when she returned. "Beppe's sister was bustling about, pretending to be busy cleaning. She was pushing a mop around on the kitchen floor; it was ridiculous. The whole place smelled of cabbage. Mimma was shut up in the back bedroom. The shutters were closed, it was hot as an oven in there, yet she was buried under a pile of blankets, sweating and nearly delirious. She was confused at first; she begged for a glass of water, which Anna went to the kitchen to get for her. Then she recognized me. Her hand—it was icy cold—shot out from under the covers and gripped me hard by the wrist. 'Oh, Beatrice,' she said. 'Beppe doesn't love me anymore.' I didn't know what to tell her; she was clearly very ill. Anna came in and said she thought Mimma should be in the hospital. Mimma cried out, 'No. I'm afraid of the hospital.'

"Beppe had been hovering around the door. At this cry, he pushed in and said we were upsetting his poor mother and must go at once. Mimma started sobbing. I tried to comfort her, but we had no choice but to leave. Mimma kept repeating that she was frightened. As we went out the door, she called out in such a panicked, childish voice it went through me like a sword. 'Beatrice, Beatrice, I'm afraid.' And then, two days later, she was dead."

"My God," I said. "Do you think Beppe murdered her?"

"The autopsy said she died of natural causes. Evidently she had chronic coronary disease and her heart just gave out. So no, I don't think it was murder. I think it was neglect."

"It's so awful," I said.

"David's lawyer says neglect of this kind, if we can prove it, is a crime and could be used to reverse the adoption decree."

"I thought he was going for mental incompetence."

Beatrice blew out a puff of air. "Beppe was ahead of us there. During the adoption business he insisted that two psychiatrists examine Mimma and declare in writing that they found her to be in her right mind and competent to make decisions about her future. God knows what Beppe paid them, because Mimma was clearly crazy, as anyone who talked to her for five minutes could see."

"This is an incredible story," I said.

"It is," she agreed.

"You couldn't make it up," I observed.

Beatrice tilted her head toward me, giving me a slow, indulgent smile. "You like it?" she said. "I give it to you."

Epilogue

That conversation took place nearly ten years ago, and it was the last time I saw Beatrice Doyle. I had a message from her later that year, saying that the legal case was still unresolved and the lawyers were steadily draining David's coffers. She had no plans to visit Villa Chiara until she knew the outcome of the lawsuit. Another year passed. In the summer she sent a card from Munich. She had a knee problem that made it difficult for her to travel, and David had persuaded her to have replacement surgery there. She made no mention of the villa.

I wrote back, wishing her a good recovery. Several months passed before I received a card from Rio. She had returned for the winter break; her knee was as good as new, but now she was having problems with her hips. She would retire from teaching in the summer.

I sent her a card, congratulating her on her retirement.

Then I heard nothing from her.

A few years passed. I received a postcard from Munich with no return address, saying she was spending more time there, as her grandchildren had become interesting and active young people. No mention of the villa.

I continued my teaching and writing and published the novel about the American publicist in Italy. I put together a collection of short stories and then began another novel about an American history professor who is obsessed with Mussolini, thereby unburdening myself of the research I'd done during that first summer I spent at Villa Chiara. At dinner parties, my friends listened tirelessly to my stories about fascist Italy. In fact, I was surprised at how much interest they expressed in the odd details I'd turned up: that electroshock therapy was invented in Rome the same year the Jewish laws went into effect; that Benito Mussolini had a son by an Austrian hairdresser who wound up dead in an asylum, probably at his father's express command; that when Italy surrendered to the Allies, deserting Italian soldiers were showered with civilian clothes as they ran through the villages on their way to join the partisans. As I worked on that book, I often thought of the limonaia, of the odd conversations with Luca on the terrazza, and of the stories Beatrice told me about her family and her life during the war, her flight to America, and the division in her allegiances, echoed in the division of the villa between those who stayed and those who went away.

One day while clearing out my office, I discovered the stack of notebooks I'd filled during my visits to Villa Chiara: sketches of characters, records of conversations and the banal events of daily life. As I read, I was reminded that the limonaia had become both a refuge and a lookout post for me, and I recalled Beatrice's crisp way of telling a story, unearthing a complex world in a few sentences. I saw that my sense of security and contentment had been made possible by the precise and courteous distance she maintained, as well as by her natural openness to my questions, her impulsive generosity. Though she knew little about me, and in fact evidenced minimal interest in my personal history, she was always willing to engage in speculation about those subjects that interested us both: literature, academia, travel, history, and cooking. It was clear to me that there were subjects she preferred to skip; for example, despite many long conversations over wine, we never talked about sex, as most women are inclined to do when they have earned each other's trust.

In my notebooks I had recorded her family history as I received it, not in chronological order. As I read, I realized that though much of what happened was predictable, even inevitable, neither of us had anticipated the forfeiture of Villa Chiara. The devolution of the Salviati family's influence was not an unusual event; indeed the struggle of aristocrats to maintain their holdings and their status is a perennial subject for novelists. It all comes down to property, to the house, to who gets the house.

Beatrice had accepted her duties in the compulsory exercise of family responsibility reluctantly; she had run away, married away, she was restless and resentful, her family was a burden and the villa a financial vampire, gradually bleeding her dry.

And yet, I thought, Beatrice loved Villa Chiara.

I remembered one evening when we were sitting in the big salone; Ruggiero was with us, talking amiably about various subjects—politics, perhaps, or American movies, or the departmental imbroglios at our colleges. As we prattled on, the light in the room faded; it was high summer, and daylight lingered until very late. It crossed my mind that we would soon be sitting in complete darkness, but I didn't feel it was up to me to do anything about it. At last, when I could barely see my companions across the space between us, Beatrice said, "Ah, the evening has come and it's time to light the lamps." She stood up and crossed to an old chrome standing lamp with a painted shade. She switched it on. It cast a glow just wide enough to illuminate the patch of carpet she then crossed to the table lamp next to Ruggiero's chair. When she switched this one on, it bathed his shoulder and knees in a buttery sheen. We were quiet then, and the only sound was the comforting whir of the steadily oscillating fan that swirled the warm air over us like a tide. Beatrice returned to her chair, took up her wineglass, and sipped from it, glancing about the room with an expression of deep satisfaction. "This is my favorite time of day in this house," she said. "It reminds me of summers when I was a child and we stayed here with my aunts. It was paradise to me then."

I decided to begin a new novel with a description of Villa Chiara.

༺⁕༻

It takes me a few years to write a novel. Presumably the court cases Beatrice and David had brought against Beppe Bottini were settled during that time. Beatrice had not mentioned the villa in her last brief messages. Either their suit had failed and Beppe Bottini had inherited the two-thirds of the Salviati estate that had originally been settled on Luca and Mimma, or Beatrice had succeeded and the entire villa now belonged to her.

I thought the latter outcome less likely. If she had won and the adoption was reversed, she would have sent a triumphant message to that effect. Her silence suggested that their efforts had failed, that she was humiliated and defeated, in possession of only half the villa, the other part occupied, or possibly rented out for profit, by Beppe Bottini. What would she, what could she do then?

Not knowing suited me for the time being, and I worked steadily on my novel, expanding scenes I'd taken part in and imagining those I knew only from Beatrice's descriptions. It's a pleasurable business, creating a world. It's like gardening; I try to keep everything alive and thriving, but some characters prosper while others wither and die away. I tend to a novel, and when I'm not actually writing it, I think about it, especially when driving, in the shower, and before I fall asleep. I didn't particularly want Beatrice to know I was carefully fictionalizing the events of her life. I've certainly written books in which the central character was based on someone I know, or a combination of characters I've observed, and for the most part, when my models actually read my books they don't recognize themselves at all, which, as any novelist will tell you, is one of the great joys of writing fiction.

But when I had at last a draft of the novel about Beatrice, her family, and the disposition of her property, a pang of guilt at having lost touch with the friend whose stories had so occupied my imagination stopped me from sending the manuscript along to my agent. I had heard nothing from Beatrice in several years, and I knew that wherever she was, she was aware that I didn't have her address. I also knew that she had mine, so evidently for some reason Beatrice hadn't felt the desire to contact me.

I sent an email to Ruggiero at his university address in California, saying only that I had heard nothing from our mutual friend in so long, I had begun to worry that all was not well with her. Did he have an address where she could be reached?

He replied almost at once.

Dear Jan,

It's very good to hear from you. Your message is a timely one. As it happens I had an email from David Doyle a few weeks ago; I've known him since he was a child in California and have kept up with him and his mother over the years, as you know. Now, of course, the internet makes this easier. He wrote to tell me that Beatrice has been very ill. A bronchial infection turned into pneumonia and she was hospitalized in New York for some weeks. When she was released, she was too weak to stay on her own. David went to Poughkeepsie and persuaded her to sell her house there and move to a small apartment near his family in Munich, where she is now. She continues to suffer from various infirmities and is not able to walk any distance because of hip problems, but is unwilling to have replacement surgery as it might, in her view, be the end of her. David has hired part-time in-home care, but he's convinced that the best option for her now is a nursing home in Italy. In fact he is looking into the very institution near Firenze where his grandmother died. Beatrice is resisting this idea with some determination, though she is also adamant that she doesn't want to stay in Germany.

It's a sad case. Beatrice is a person of substance; intelligent, curious, fearless, and generous. I've admired her since she arrived in California so many years ago, with her small son in tow, determined to make a place for herself in academia, though her family disapproved and all the odds were against her. When I received your message, I recalled that pleasant day we three went out to Isola Maggiore and enjoyed a wide-ranging conversation over the plain but excellent fare at the restaurant there. We could not imagine what the future held for us; Beatrice, I think, least of all. She has a way of being completely present in the moment, and is often reckless or just indifferent to consequences. I'm sorry to hear you have lost touch with her, as I know she values your friendship. She doesn't use a computer herself, but if you send her a message through David, I'm sure he will pass it on to her. His address is Dsdoyle@heisspost.de.

I send you warmest wishes and the hope that we will meet again 'ere long—perhaps in la bel' Italia,

Ruggiero

This was terrible news. Beatrice stuck away in an apartment in Munich, unable to take care of herself. Was she in a wheelchair? Of course her family was near; her grandchildren were teenagers, so she wasn't all alone, but I couldn't picture her there. She was, I calculated, seventy-seven or perhaps seventy-eight. It seemed too soon to trundle her off to the Casa di Riposo in Florence.

Ruggiero was right; it was a sad case. His assessment of Beatrice's personality also struck me as acute; she was brave, fearless to the point of heedlessness. When I had received her cards from odd parts of the world, I had often had a moment of self-criticism. I compared her far-flung itineraries to my own timid jaunts to safe places; I was like a mouse, always in search of quiet, of a place to be tucked away, always anxious about my inability to speak the language or ask for help. I'd once spent three days in a hotel room in Paris eating takeout from the supermarket to avoid the humiliation of sitting alone at a bistro and being sneered at by a waiter for ordering poorly. My pleasure in Beatrice's company was partly that she told good stories and partly that she included me in her world without hesitation. Come to the bar, come to dinner, come to the neighbors, let's go to the museum, to the pizza restaurant, to the island.

I closed the computer and for some minutes stared blankly at the manuscript squared up neatly on the back of my desk. Wasn't my novel about the last thing Beatrice needed at this low point in her life? And when it was published, what was the likelihood that she would even know of its existence? Minimal at best, though Beatrice was an avid reader and followed book reviews in two languages. And what if the book was successful and she came across it in some bookstore window? Unlikely, unlikely, though not impossible.

I decided to do as Ruggiero had suggested: write to David and inquire after his mother. No more, no less. After several cups of coffee, I was satisfied with the following message.

Dear David,

Recently I had an email exchange with Ruggiero Vignorelli, who told me that your mother is now in Munich and in very poor health. I have been out of touch with her for too long, as I had no address for her since her retirement. Ruggiero suggested I write to you and ask you to convey my concern to her.

I was both shocked and saddened to hear of her illness. As I once told her, she is the most independent woman I've ever known, and I admire her immensely. I can only imagine how discouraging it must be for her to be unable to travel. Please give her my fondest regards and sympathy, as well as my hope to hear of some improvement in her condition.

And please accept my best wishes to you and your family,

Jan Vidor

A few days passed before I received the following reply.

Dear Jan,

Thanks for your message. I passed it along to my mother, who was pleased to hear from you. She is, as you imagined, despondent about her current condition; she is unable to walk more than a few steps and is in constant pain, even at rest. The doctors can do little for her. However, her mind is clear and she keeps herself occupied in reading. She asked me to tell you that she particularly enjoyed your last novel and felt you'd made the best possible use of your visits to Villa Chiara.

She is also able to enjoy the company of her grandchildren, who are both at home now for the summer and very attentive to her. For the present my wife and I think it best that she stay here in the hopes that a new therapy she will begin next month may alleviate some of her suffering.

Sincerely, David Doyle

My spirits sank as I read this parsimonious and guarded reply. Any communication I had with Beatrice would henceforth go through David, that much was clear. Also she had read my last novel, and it was therefore not unlikely that she would read this one as well, though it wouldn't be published for a year or so, and who knew what condition she would be in by then.

And, of course, David made no mention of the villa. What about the villa? I could hardly ask David about it—in fact, I thought, I'd be damned if I'd ask that snooty David. If they'd won their suit, David would at his mother's death own it entirely; if they'd lost, then he would inherit his mother's share. And what would he do with that? He'd been outraged by the fate of the farmhouse, bitter about his mother's selling it to an old friend. Could David bring himself to make a financial deal with Beppe Bottini?

How could I find out? I taxed my brain. Might Ruggiero know? He had, he'd told me, known David since he was a boy, and kept up with him now through email. I wrote to Ruggiero, asking if he knew anything about the fate of Villa Chiara. His reply, again, was immediate.

Dear Jan,

Yes, sadly, I do know the answer to your question. You'll find it here: https://vistatuscany.com/tuscany/villas/siena/villa-bottini-tuscany -vineyard-villa/

Best, Ruggiero

"Oh no!" I said as I read this url. And "Oh no!" again as I clicked on it. A highly professional photograph of Villa Chiara immediately filled the screen. An iridescent blue sky backed the wisteria-festooned terrace, now lined with pots of geraniums and furnished with comfortable cushioned lounge chairs and iron tables. An arrow at the side of the picture took me to the limonaia. A striped awning attached to the roof covered an extended flagstone terrace, also furnished in style for outdoor dining. Another click and I was inside the villa. A heavy brick arch divided the kitchen and the dining room. I felt sure the dark wood table, without a cloth as I'd never seen it, was the one Beatrice had inherited from her mother. Another click. The salone, replastered, painted white; all the furniture was new. The room-sized nineteenth-century Persian carpet I remembered was gone, revealing a newly polished terra-cotta floor. Another click: a bedroom, modern furnishings, garish paisley bedspreads; a click, a shot of the exterior staircase again, this time angled to take in a walkway beyond Mimma's terrace, leading us, leading us, I thought, to the garden, but no—another click—

leading us to where the garden used to be, the space now taken up entirely by a marble-lined swimming pool, sparkling invitingly beneath the blinding sun.

My eyes retreated down the screen to the copy:

Spacious, elegant property, seven bedrooms, including separate guesthouse, can sleep up to 15 people. Five baths, two sitting rooms, family-style kitchen with all new appliances, two large terraces for al fresco dining, swimming pool, surrounded by working vineyards (own production wine available for purchase), wifi and internet, Villa Bottini offers every comfort in a serene setting close to Siena and the delightful hill towns of Tuscany.

Villa Bottini, I thought. He could at least have called it Villa Mimma.

☙❧

I spent a few days putting the final touches on the book, stewing about whether to send it to Beatrice at once or wait until it was published. The villa and her family didn't really figure in the novel she had praised to David—the one about the professor obsessed with Mussolini. Much of it was set in Rome. What would she think when she discovered the use I'd made of her life, her family, and her home in this one? Of course I'd changed all the names and moved the villa, added a few salient plot points, deleted a character or two, compressed the time frame, etc., but the stories she had told me in her offhand, ironic way were largely intact, and anyone who knew her would recognize that she was the model for the tale—anyone, including Beatrice herself.

If I'd had to box up the manuscript and commit it to the United States and German postal services, knowing it would spend a week in transit and then constitute an unwieldy bundle of paper for my poor ill friend to page through, perhaps I would have made a different decision. But now I had the option of attaching the entire novel to an email and sending it, weightless and ephemeral, to David's computer instantaneously. I won't go on about the mental exertions, the chalking up of pros and cons, the late-night cogitation about the moral obligations of friendship, of trust, the back-and-forth about possible recriminations or accusations (in spite of Beatrice's repeated offer: *I give it to you, I give it to* you). What I knew was that it's easy to offer the gift of a story, sometimes difficult to accept what can be made of it.

I also knew (and I felt both sadness and guilt about this) that ultimately it didn't matter what Beatrice thought (or what David thought; he would have a response all his own, and it wouldn't be a friendly one), because I liked my novel; I thought it was a good story and I wanted to publish it.

So when I had finally drafted a message and addressed it to David with the subject line "manuscript attached," it was not with righteous conviction that I dispatched my novel to its first two readers. My fingers hovered over the keyboard for many moments. I pulled back, repaired to the kitchen, refreshed the eternal cup of tea, returned, read the message again, added a comma, sipped the tea, went through the hovering exercise again for several tedious moments. At last I said, "Oh, what the hell," and bringing my index finger down firmly, I pressed Send.

Two weeks passed without a response. They were reading, I concluded. They were talking.

Then I received David's response in an email. No subject line, no greeting.

I'm not sure I understand why you felt the need to send my mother this disagreeable manuscript, but I assume you are trying to protect yourself in some way. I read only enough of it to be offended, but my mother insisted on finishing it and it made her very unhappy. I never liked the idea that you had set up at the villa in search of stories to steal and that you were spying on my family, as writers are always doing, spying on other people's lives because their own lives are so empty, but my mother appeared to enjoy your company and trust you, so I didn't protest.

I'm certain there's nothing we can do to keep you from publishing this scandalous take on my family's personal affairs, so there's nothing I can say, but I will remind you that in doing so you have proved yourself no friend to my mother or to me. Please don't try to communicate with my mother in future. I will not pass on any messages you attempt to send her through me. You've done enough damage.

No complimentary close. No signature.

Oh, right, I thought. David is wounded. He imagines I came to Villa Chiara just to spy on his family. Writers are spies who have no lives of their own. I should be ashamed of myself.

It just isn't true. I am always on the lookout for stories, but I don't steal plots from other people. I write fiction; I make stuff up. That's what I do. I wrote two books that had nothing to do with David's family while he was cleverly managing to lose his rightful inheritance because he couldn't bring himself to show some small interest and courtesy to his poor old aunt. How hard would that have been?

I hadn't gone to Villa Chiara with the intention of writing about his family's history. It hadn't even crossed my mind until years later, when I rediscovered the notebooks and spent a long afternoon reading the daily accounts of conversations, events, sundry details about the war and the family. Beatrice's stories sparked my imagination; they possessed the essentially revelatory quality of narrative we imply when we say "Truth is stranger than fiction." *I really should get some of this down,* I thought. I began to visualize the scenes she'd drawn with such sure, quick strokes during our various conversations over the years. Beatrice's manner is dismissive, but she has a sharp eye for detail and a fine sense of irony. The stories put down roots, the characters began to sprout and grow and unfold their leaves in my imagination.

It was a generational saga, I knew that, and telling it would require research. And so I undertook that; I bothered myself. I'd wager David doesn't even know the name of the hospital where his poor uncle spent forty years in captivity, but I do. I know who the director was, and how the treatment methods changed over the years, and how it became an overcrowded dumping ground for political prisoners during the war, how it was eventually emptied and abandoned.

What nerve David had to tell me I'd done damage to his mother, when it was he who treated her like a servant, who stole her furniture, abused her when she attempted to raise enough money to repair the villa, kept her always dancing on a string for his approval and occasional indulgence. Now that he had revealed his long-standing antagonism toward me, could I believe a word of what he told me? I began to fret about Beatrice's safety. Should I go to Germany and rescue my friend from her overbearing son?

A week later I received a square envelope with an attractive array of German stamps but no return address. I recognized Beatrice's handwriting and opened the envelope at once. Inside I found a thick cream-colored card with a crest on the outer flap, very like the one she'd sent me years before. The message inside was short and began pleasantly enough.

Dear Jan,

It has been many years and many changes for me since last I heard from you. You can imagine my pleasure when David told me you'd sent the manuscript of your new novel for me to read. Of course, I knew from the first lines that the story was set at Villa Chiara—anyone who has been there would recognize it.

I'm sorry to say that my pleasure soon turned to shock and dismay. I can't say I recognize myself in these pages. This character you call Beatrice is a shallow cartoon at best. Though some of the story follows events in my life, much of it is clearly fantastical and cruelly so. You make my family out to be decadent and heedless fascists—you have even accused my uncle, a man you know nothing about, of fratricide, a monstrous offense, even in wartime. For myself, I strongly protest two assertions; first that I was indifferent to the criminal theft of my patrimony, and second that I ever offered you the right to make a mockery of my life.

I'm very disappointed in you, Jan. I feel as if my life has been stolen by someone I trusted as a friend. David tells me we have no legal grounds to stop the publication, as our names are not used. Even if we did, I no longer have the energy to undertake legal adventures.

These last years have been difficult for me. My health is very poor and reading has become one of the few activities I can still enjoy. How ungrateful of you to make even this simple pleasure one more trial I must patiently bear.

And then, with no complimentary close, Beatrice signed her real name.

I read this message once, then again. My desk chair has wheels, and I felt my feet, of their own accord, pushing me away from the card, which fluttered to the floor. When I banked on the carpet, I leaped up and rushed down the stairs, through the kitchen, out the back door, and across the lawn to the edge of the small wood that borders my property. There I stood while the birds chirped and a warm breeze ruffled the leaves overhead, my brain ablaze and frantic, scouring every cell for the material of my self-defense.

It was too much. David called me a spy, and now Beatrice calls me a thief. She tells me that she doesn't see herself in my novel, that I have it all wrong, that she never offered it to me, that I've stolen her life.

Beatrice, for God's sake: these are contradictory assertions. If I got it all wrong, I've done you no harm. It's fiction. And if I got it right, why can't you see yourself as I do, as the honorable, brave survivor of a complex plot? I always admired you. I was genuinely interested in you. If I've offended you, I regret that, but I was always your friend. I am still your friend. Beatrice, you must see that and you must forgive me.

For God's sake, Beatrice, forgive me.

Acknowledgments

I would like to thank the Bogliasco Foundation for a residency fellowship at the beautiful Bogliasco Study Center in Liguria, during which I completed the first draft of this novel.

Thanks are also due to my agent, Molly Friedrich, a tireless advocate, trusted reader, and true friend to all my literary endeavors. I'd also like to thank Heather Carr and Lucy Carson, the early readers of the manuscript at the Friedrich Agency.

At Serpent's Tail, my editor Rebecca Gray's notes on an early reading of this novel resulted in a much-needed reappraisal and revision.

Thanks are also due to Dan Meyer and Carolyn Williams, my readers at the Nan A. Talese imprint, and to my scrupulously attentive copy editor, Liz Duvall.

My appreciation for the enthusiasm and commitment of my editor, publisher, and friend, the indomitable Nan A. Talese, cannot be overstated.

As always I am grateful for the unwavering support and love I continually enjoy from my partner, John Cullen, and from my daughter, Adrienne Martin.

A NOTE ABOUT THE AUTHOR

Valerie Martin is the author of ten novels, including *The Ghost of the Mary Celeste, The Confessions of Edward Day, Trespass, Mary Reilly, Italian Fever,* and *Property;* three collections of short fiction; and a biography of Saint Francis of Assisi, titled *Salvation.* She has been awarded grants from the National Endowment for the Arts and the John Simon Guggenheim Fellowship, as well as the Kafka Prize (for *Mary Reilly*) and Britain's Women's Prize (for *Property*).

A NOTE ON THE TYPE

This book was set in a version of the well-known Monotype face Bembo. This letter was cut for the celebrated Venetian printer Aldus Manutius by Francesco Griffo, and first used in Pietro Cardinal Bembo's *De Aetna* of 1495. The companion italic is an adaptation of the chancery script type designed by the calligrapher and printer Lodovico degli Arrighi.